Axe Me No Questions

Books by Paula Charles
HAMMERS AND HOMICIDE

Books written as Janna Rollins
AN ESCAPE GOAT
GOATS JUST WANNA HAVE FUN (Feb. 2025)

ASK ME NO QUESTIONS

A Hometown Hardware Mystery
Book Two

Paula Charles

ISBN (paperback): 979-8-9913828-0-9 / ISBN (ebook): 979-8-9913828-1-6

Edited by Brittany Sumpter

Book Cover by Melissa Bourbon of WriterSpark

First edition: January 2025

To Dad ~ Who has always smelled like sawdust and coffee.

And

In Memory of Dawn Dowdle, agent extraordinaire, without whom this series would never have found its wings. You are missed more than your Blue Ridge Literary family can say.

Chapter One

"I have no doubt you're going to kill your competition this year." I grinned and handed the big lumberjack his change before tucking his purchases into a brown paper bag with my store's logo and name stamped on the front in bold navy blue lettering—Carpenter's Corner Hardware and Building Supply.

Shaking hair out of his eyes, Scotty Trimmer stroked one hand down his short, red beard, hazel eyes twinkling. "I plan on it. Nate's going to wish he'd stayed home this year when I get done with him." Scotty was a giant of a man in his mid-thirties, soft-spoken and powerful, with gingery red hair and crinkle lines framing laughing eyes.

"Well, you know the whole town is behind you. You can count on the Carpenter women to be there tomorrow, cheering you on like always."

"I appreciate your support, Dawna." Scotty tipped his chin, tucked his change into the front pocket of his blue flannel shirt, and lifted a hand in farewell. A swirl of dust kicked up and danced in a patch of sunlight on the rustic wooden wide plank floor as he left the store.

Scotty had dropped by my hardware store to purchase a new sharpening file and a tub of axe wax ahead of Pine Bluff's annual Timber Festival that would be kicking off bright and early the following morning. While the Timber Festival showcased all things wood and paid homage to our town's sawmill and logging history, the weekend-long lumberjack competition was the main event. And Scotty was the local axe-throwing champion—our town's pride and joy. A modern-day lumberjack, he'd worked in the Oregon woods for Erickson Brother's Logging Company for a decade before purchasing a logging truck and striking out on his own. Two years in, he now employed a handful of loggers and his small fleet of shiny, metallic green logging trucks were a common sight on our country roads.

Pine Bluff sat in a picturesque valley in the heart of Oregon's Blue Mountains, with the Elk River flowing around the eastern edge of town. The proximity to the river and wilderness provided easy access for fishing, hiking, and a rich abundance of other outdoor activities. With our fairly remote mountain location, Pine Bluff's population had hovered under twelve hundred people for decades, and we liked it that way, thank you very much. My parents had moved our family to town when I was nine and I'd been here ever since. My high school sweetheart and I had married shortly after graduation, then started a family and a business. Even though we'd enjoyed traveling when we'd had the chance, in all those years we'd never once thought about picking up and moving anywhere else. Bob's death hadn't changed that for me one bit. If anything, it had made me set my feet even more firmly into my hometown soil. This was my town and I was as proud of it as if I'd created it myself.

As I snapped the cash register drawer closed after completing Scotty's transaction, the store phone rang. I lifted the receiver, glancing at the caller ID as I picked it up. Elkins National Bank. For crying in the buttermilk. *How many times do I have to tell them that stupid loan isn't mine?* I let the call go to voicemail.

In late August, I'd received a certified letter stating a twenty-five-thousand-dollar loan with Elkins National was delinquent and I had six months to bring it current before they started foreclosure proceedings on my hardware store. I'd talked to the lender and let them know they had made a grave error in their documentation since I'd never taken out a loan with them. For the first couple weeks after the initial conversation the bank had called once a week, but now six weeks had passed and the intrusive phone calls were amping up to at least once a day. Somehow, they'd even gotten ahold of my cell phone number. It was starting to feel more and more like harassment. So far, I hadn't figured out a way to convince the bank the loan wasn't mine and make them stop calling. Maybe it was time to talk to an attorney.

With fists propped on my hips, I turned my gaze to the plate-glass window facing Main Street and raised my face to soak in the October sun streaming through the window. The warmth immediately eased my mind and calmed me down. Autumn had always been my favorite time of year in my small mountain town. The cool, crisp days and vibrant colors sent my heart soaring. The cooler weather allowed me to wear cozy sweaters and boots, eat everything pumpkin, feel the leaves crunching under my feet, and watch my favorite not-so-spooky Halloween movies. I was a chicken at heart so chose *Hocus Pocus* or *Practical Magic* over Freddy Krueger every time. Most people complained about the loss of light with it getting dark earlier and earlier each evening this time of year, but the shorter days fed my inner couch potato. When it was dark outside, there was zero guilt about putting on my flannel pajamas and fuzzy socks by six in the evening. It was too dark to putter around with outside chores anyway so a person might as well get comfortable.

In my humble and unbiased opinion, our town was at its finest in the autumn. Everyone in Pine Bluff threw themselves into preparations for the Timber Festival. The festival itself took place at Steam Engine Park, but the entire town overflowed with delightful things to take pictures of, delicious things to eat, and fun things to do. Cornstalks, scarecrows, and piles of cheerful orange pumpkins adorned every corner of Main Street. Banners sporting cute images of ghosts, goblins, and witches hung from each lamppost lining the downtown streets. A hot apple cider and decadent caramel corn stand had popped up in the parking lot at Literally, the charming and cozy bookstore a few blocks from my store. A large plywood cutout of pumpkins and another of scarecrows, with holes to stick your head through for photo ops, stood proudly beside the cider booth. Every store and business in the downtown area offered platters full of various delicious fall treats for their shoppers. For the entire month of October, I had a standing order at Cookie Crumbles Bakery for two dozen doughnuts—plain cake, powdered sugar, cinnamon twists, pumpkin, and apple fritters—that I picked up on my way to work each morning. Along with the doughnuts, I kept a pot of my traditionally bad coffee going for any souls brave enough to give it a try.

"Hey, Mama, come out here and tell me if this works. I need your opinion." My thirty-four-year-old daughter, April, stuck her head around the open doorframe. Her hair glinted the color of red-hot coals in the golden-hued fall sunshine.

The sight of April caused a grin to spread across my face. After years away, she'd moved back to Pine Bluff six months ago and I was tickled to death to have her back in town. As the youngest of my three kids, I was more than suspicious April had drawn the short straw among her siblings when the three of them decided someone needed to come back to Pine Bluff to keep an eye on their crackpot of a mother. I was well-aware they had been worried about me, completely unfounded of course, ever since my husband of forty-plus years had died suddenly three years ago. I'd only mentioned once or twice how I thought their dad's spirit was still hanging around the house and I'd been having full-blown, albeit one-sided, conversations with him. You'd think I'd said I thought aliens were invading. Suddenly the kids were all bent out of shape and concerned about my mental health. I snorted. They acted like I hadn't always been a little bonkers. *All of the best people are, aren't they?* Anyway, whatever the reason, April was here to stay and seemed to have settled back into small town life without a hitch.

I stepped outside to see what magic she had created for our October display.

"Ta da." April spread her arms wide to show off her handiwork. "What'd you think?"

Until she had mentioned it, I'd never utilized the large front window of the store, except to stare out of and hang random sale flyers on now and again. With April's eye for detail, she'd begun creating displays of her beautifully refinished furniture in the window, comingling with products I carried in the store. It shocked me how quickly the pieces she displayed sold, and how many people came into Carpenter's Corner because they fell in love with something they saw in the window. Ultimately, they'd leave with something else they'd been meaning to pick up—a package of lightbulbs or a roll of duct tape. I could kick myself for ignoring the great marketing tool I'd had right in front of my face all this time. Better late than never, I suppose.

"This is perfect. I love everything about it. The table is gorgeous. I hope you have something else in the works, because it's going to sell in a heartbeat."

The window showcased a sofa table the color of morning fog. April had discovered it at an estate sale where it had been lounging in someone's barn covered in chicken poop only a few weeks ago. Now it was a stunning piece of furniture. She'd stripped it down to bare wood, sanded it to a smooth finish, painted it a gorgeous foggy gray, and given it a durable semi-glossy topcoat before displaying the table in the window. If I was a betting woman, I'd wager it would be snapped up within the week.

"Have you seen my stash of furniture stuffed in the corner of your warehouse?" April snorted. "Believe me, I won't have any problem choosing my next project."

I laughed. "True enough. Good thing I don't have a big lumber order coming in this week. There wouldn't be enough room for it," I teased.

April had recently moved her furniture restoration business, Carriage House Designs, into a section of my warehouse. It worked well for both of us. She could fill in at the hardware store when I needed an extra hand, and I kept the rent for her space reasonable.

I turned back to the window to study the rest of the display. A large ceramic burgundy mixing bowl from the sparkly new kitchen nook I'd recently added to the store sat on top of the table, along with an antique tin orchard bucket overflowing with miniature pumpkins and colorful Indian corn. April had leaned three brooms upright against the wall and placed a tall black witch's hat on top of each one. A hand painted sign stating "The Witch Is In" hung crookedly off the back of a dark-blue wooden distressed chair placed at an angle beside the sofa table. I chuckled. The entire display was silly and whimsical; exactly what I craved in my life.

"Boy, do those flowers ever pop against the gray stone building. Using the rusty old wheelbarrow as a plant stand was brilliant." I sat on the weathered wooden bench to soak in all the fall loveliness.

April had filled the patinaed vintage wheelbarrow with burgundy and yellow fall mums in terra-cotta pots, then had tucked a mixture of orange and white pumpkins between the flowers with two black plastic crows perched on the flowerpots.

"So, are you happy with it, then?" April asked.

"No." I wrinkled my nose. "I'm not happy with it. I love it!"

April grinned and pointed to the entryway. "On the far side of the bench, I'm thinking about adding a bale of straw and piling more pumpkins on top."

I raised my eyebrows. "We have more pumpkins?" I eyeballed the five in the wheelbarrow with the flowers and the two enormous pumpkins flanking the bench.

"There's six more in the back of your Jeep, along with the bale of straw. It's entirely possible I bought out the pumpkin patch."

"Then I say do it," I answered. "Orange twinkle lights and fall-colored leaf garlands would look great strung around the front window and door too."

"I like the way you're thinking. I'll pop down to Country Roads and see what they have left for fall décor and lights."

Darlene Lovelace stepped out of her boutique, Lipstick and Lace, next door. She wore a mid-thigh brown floral dress with pops of persimmon, chocolate-colored tights, and a long faux fur vest in shades of brown and cream. At least I thought it was faux. You could never be sure with Darlene. Taupe western ankle boots completed the outfit.

I cringed, waiting for whatever snarky remark she had for me this time. The woman didn't disappoint.

"This is so much better. Good job, April." With arms crossed over her chest, Darlene flung her long dark hair over her shoulder while she studied our display. "Normally, your mom sets out a pumpkin or two and calls it good. It's embarrassing to be in the same building with her."

April leveled Darlene with a look smacking of warning. "Gee thanks. We're both glad you approve, your highness."

"Feel free to find yourself another store to rent, if it's so embarrassing to have your boutique in *my* building." I stared at Darlene over the top of my glasses. "I won't hold you to your contract."

I owned the building both of our shops were in. Darlene had initially signed a three-year contract but now, at year four, I was only signing year-to-year leases with her. Main Street storefronts were limited in Pine Bluff, so if she decided to move her western clothing boutique, I wouldn't have a problem finding another tenant for the space.

Lipstick and Lace was only about a quarter of the size of my hardware store, so Darlene's front window was much narrower than mine. Her window display looked great, but after her snide remark, I kept any praise to myself. She'd placed two dress forms in the window and clothed them both in rich fall colors. A strapless, olive-green maxi-dress with a thick, beaded western belt and a long silver pendant was draped over one dress form while the other wore a pair of acid-faded denim jeans with rhinestones lining the front pockets, topped with a rust-orange wool blazer. Darlene had paired the outfit with a necklace featuring leather fringe and silver and turquoise medallions. A vintage wooden crate displayed a pair of wine-red women's cowboy boots. Strings of colorful fall leaves hung from the top of the window frame and two terra-cotta pots with fake boxwood shrubs rounded out the look.

Without replying to either one of our snarky responses, Darlene whirled around, her long fur vest whipping out behind her, and flounced back into her store. The windows of the old building rattled as she slammed the door. Darlene had been a few years ahead of April in school. Where April had been athletic and a tomboy, Darlene had been the captain of the dance team. There'd never been any love lost between the two of them.

"What a twit." April brushed her hands off on her jeans and stepped back to take a final look at her display. "By the way, Scotty mentioned a bunch of people are going to Timber Creek later. It sounds like most of the lumberjack contestants will be there. Do you want to go over and get something to eat after work? We could mingle a bit and wish them all luck for the competition."

Timber Creek Saloon was one of three bars in Pine Bluff. Located on Evergreen Avenue a few blocks east of my store, it was the favorite gathering place for the local loggers. I imagined the bar would be filled to the rafters with friendly banter between the contestants before the competition started in earnest, bright and early in the morning.

"Sounds fun. I'm in. Besides, it's been a dog's age since I've been in Timber Creek."

"Good. There's something I've been meaning to talk to you about anyway. It'll be a good time to get it done."

Uh-oh. No matter the context or person, a knot of dread always formed in the pit of my stomach when someone said, "we need to talk."

"Talk about wha..."

The roar of a motorcycle drowned out anything else I was going to say as sixteen-year-old Westen Lund backed his red-and-black Honda Rebel up to the curb and cut the engine. He pulled off his helmet and ran a hand through his unruly curls before greeting me and April with a wide smile.

Westen, a high school sophomore, was the oldest son of a local logging family. He'd be competing in the junior division of the lumberjack contest over the weekend. This afternoon, however, he'd be working for me at Carpenter's Corner. I'd hired Westen two months before for three after school shifts a week, and a six-hour shift on most Saturdays. He'd been an excellent choice. The kid was a hard worker; always eager to learn. His happy-go-lucky personality was an added bonus.

Choosing not to question April any more, we got back to work and the afternoon flew by. I balanced my ledger and took an afternoon walk to the bank and post office while Westen manned the cash register and April worked on a furniture project in the warehouse. Once I returned from running my errands, Westen restocked shelves and swept the floor while keeping up a constant chatter about this weekend's upcoming lumberjack contest.

"Who do you think is going to win?" Westen leaned on the broom he'd been sweeping the entryway with. "Is Scotty going to walk away with the trophy again? I hear the competition's going to be tough this year. I mean, we all know Nate was right on Scotty's heels last year, but Coach was saying there's a couple guys who haven't entered before who'll be throwing this year. He said these new guys are younger and stronger than Scotty." He shook his head. "Hard to believe. I sure hope he takes champion. I want to see him compete at State."

This weekend's contest was the last in the district for the year. The winner would get the opportunity to move on to the state finals held in Albany later in the month.

I shrugged. "You never know what might happen. Scotty's been reigning champion for what, five years? Some fresh blood in the competition will be interesting. Just think, Westen, in a few years, you'll be throwing in the adult division."

Westen's blue eyes sparkled. "I plan on taking first place in the junior division this year. At least in axe-throwing. I'm pretty sure I'll end up making a big splash in the log rolling contest. My balance has never been the best."

"It's a good thing the weather's supposed to be fairly nice this weekend, then. You shouldn't get too much of a chill when you fall into the pond," I answered in a dead-pan tone.

Westen laughed before pulling his cell phone out of his pocket and thumbing it on. "It's six already. Is there anything else you want me to do before I head out, Dawna?" He brushed light brown bangs out of his eyes and leaned against the counter.

I glanced at the clock on the wall. "Good night! Where'd the time go? No, there's nothing else. Get out of here, Wes, and get some rest tonight so you're ready to go tomorrow."

He grinned. "Will do."

I locked the door behind him and flipped the sign to "Closed." As I turned back to the interior of the store, a shadow crossed in my peripheral vision and I jumped a foot off the ground, pressing a hand to my racing heart. If I didn't know better, I would've thought my husband had walked in from the lumber yard behind the store.

Bob had died of a sudden heart attack over three years ago, and I'd been practically insane with grief for the first year. Since then, I'd carried on the best I could, though I'd give anything for a single word from him. There'd been a dozen times or more in the last couple of months where I'd sworn the man was in the room with me. Sometimes the smell of Bob—sawdust and coffee—came out of nowhere and knocked the wind out of my lungs. Other times, a shadow danced across the room, or a light touch brushed my cheek when no one was anywhere near. Much to my kids' dismay, I swore he was still around, watching over me. Though a couple of months before, April had finally admitted maybe I wasn't quite as crazy as a bedbug. She'd felt her dad's presence in the family home more than once and thought she'd caught a glimpse of him as well. We didn't talk about it much, but it was nice to know I wasn't the only one.

Sometimes I thought if I could concentrate hard enough, maybe I'd actually be able to see Bob for more than a fleeting second. I propped my elbows on the counter, steepled my hands, and leaned my forehead into my thumbs, closing my eyes for a minute to calm my thoughts, and attempted to conjure my husband.

"Hey, Mom, are you ready to head over to Timber Creek?" April called as she strode out of the hardware store's warehouse, effectively ending my ghost charming meditation.

"Boy, am I." I'd never been much of a drinker, but an ice cold beer sounded spectacular this evening.

Chapter Two

The heavy wooden door to Timber Creek Saloon stood propped open with a bale of fragrant yellow straw. A scarecrow sprawled on top of the bale, his loose limbs looking suspiciously like a man who'd imbibed a bit too much of the ale the saloon kept on tap. They'd tucked a brown jug under the scarecrow's stuffed arm and tilted his head down. A straw cowboy hat covered his painted-on face.

"Now, that's cute," April said, "but I think this guy should've been cut off a while ago." She tapped the brim of the scarecrow's hat as we passed.

Stepping inside the bar, I spied an empty table halfway into the room and made a beeline for it. The table was a small two-top pushed up against the wall and out of the way. Perfect for the two of us.

"Looks like we arrived in the nick of time." I pulled off my pine-green wool cape and draped it over the back of the wooden captain's chair before I took a seat.

The bar hadn't completely filled up yet, but a steady stream of people flowed through the open doorway. Timber Creek Saloon was housed in one of the oldest buildings in town, and even though the building had gone through a dozen different owners over the years, it had remained a bar in every single one of its reincarnations. The current version mixed country rustic with a fancier era of western décor. A copper bar ran the length of the front room with a wide variety of bottles of liquors ready and waiting on the glass shelves lining an enormous gilt-framed mirror. Wooden swivel stools with leather seats lined the bar with a polished brass rail near the floor to prop tired feet on. Vintage tin tiles, original to the building, still clung to the high ceilings.

A server navigated the crowd, making her way to our table. "What can I get you ladies this evening?" she asked once she arrived tableside.

"I'll take a pint of the hefeweizen you have on tap," April replied.

"Make it two," I added, holding up two fingers. "And then we're going to share a basket of steak strips and fried mushrooms, please."

"You got it. Do you want ranch or blue cheese for dipping?"

"Both, please," April and I answered together.

When the server left to put our order in, April threw her head back and scanned the ceiling. "Ah, it's still there." She pointed to a dime-size hole in one of the tin ceiling tiles.

"Sure is. I can't imagine anyone will ever plug up that bullet hole. It's too good of a story."

As the story went, a squabble had broken out over a hand of poker and one old cowpoke had fired his pistol into the ceiling as a warning that tempers better settle down or else. A hundred years had passed since the infamous poker game, and I wasn't sure how the game had turned out, but the bullet hole was still clearly visible to this day.

"I'm going to use the restroom before our dinner comes," I said.

Timber Creek's his and hers restrooms were tucked in a corner of the back half of the bar. Two steps led to the slightly sunken room where a stage took up the back corner of the large room. The bar was already loud with so many people milling around, so I was glad to see there wasn't a band setting up on the stage tonight. The pool table and dart boards were already bustling with lively games.

When I came out of the restroom, Scotty stood at the end of the bar, laughing with his best friend and biggest lumberjack rival, Nate Durand. I said a quick hello, marveling at the size of the two boys, then chuckled at myself for thinking of thirtysomething men as boys. Nate towered as tall as Scotty, but instead of being big and bulky, he was lean and whip strong. Nate was as dark complected as Scotty was light. They'd always reminded me of the yin and yang symbol—two sides of a whole. From the time they'd started school, wherever one of them was, you could bet your last dollar the other was nearby. Both boys were born and raised in Pine Bluff, but Nate lived thirty miles down the road now, in a little town called Lost Canyon where his great-grandfather had settled a hundred years ago. At the hardware store earlier, Scotty had told me he didn't care if he won the championship title; his only goal was beating Nate. He'd said it with a mischievous grin.

Like his best friend, Nate worked in the woods. He'd started his own logging business several years ago and was a one-man operation, taking smaller jobs from people who needed their land cleared for one reason or another.

"I've heard good things about Nate's business. Glad it's going well for him," I told April once I made my way back to our table. I pointed out the two men with a nod of my head. "Apparently, he's built a small sawmill on his place and is cutting lumber now."

"Interesting. Do you think it's going to affect your lumber sales at the store much?"

I flapped a hand at her. "Gosh, no. Not a bit. Nate's producing specialized lumber, locally sourced and milled. Completely different from what Carpenter's Corner offers. Bill said Nate already has a huge waiting list for his live edge planks. People are wanting to use them for fireplace mantels and bar tops. Apparently he's been taking jobs farther from home now so he can get his hands on more hardwood than what grows in this area."

Bill Wilder, the source of my information, was a long-time friend of my family. He and Bob had been partners in their construction business, but Bill bought me out and took over when Bob died. He kept me up to date on anything new going on in the construction world and was the first person I called to consult with when a customer in the hardware store asked questions I didn't know how to answer.

"I'm going to have to check out what Nate's been doing. Maybe I can make a live edge table or two for clients." April rubbed her hands together. "They'd be a great addition to Carriage House Designs."

The server arrived with our mugs of cold, frothy beer and steaming plates of fried food. She slid them in front of us and I thanked her, reaching for a slice of lemon to squeeze into my beer. A loud yell near the front of the bar startled me, causing me to knock my hand into the mug and slosh golden brew all over the table. I grabbed the stack of napkins the server had left and mopped up the spill while still attempting to look over my shoulder to find out what the shouting was about.

A man and a woman stood silhouetted in the open doorway. Because of the backlight, I couldn't make out who they were.

"Nate Durand, I have a bone to pick with you," the man yelled.

The couple stepped farther into the bar, and I recognized the guy as a local chainsaw artist named Tommy Keifer. Tommy shook his fist Nate's way as his wife tugged on his arm and whispered something I couldn't make out. From the look on her face, she wasn't happy Tommy was kicking up a fuss.

I widened my eyes and turned back to April. "Crickey. What's that all about?"

April jammed a breaded mushroom into her mouth and shrugged. "How should I know?" It sounded more like, "Ow ew I oh?" but thankfully I was fluent in interpreting full mouth speech.

"Obviously it was a rhetorical question." I stuck my tongue out at her.

April frowned and nodded her head toward the couple. "If we listen instead of yakking, we might find out."

She had a point. I dipped a steak strip into creamy blue cheese dressing and took a bite while glancing around the bar. Nate had stepped forward with Scotty right beside him. A group of lumberjack competitors congregated behind the two men. They all remained silent, their faces as still as stone as they stared at the newcomers.

"Yikes. Whatever it is, looks like it could get ugly fast." April took a sip of her beer and scooted her chair as close to the wall as she could get. I swiveled mine sideways so my back was against the wall and I wouldn't have to crane my neck so hard to watch the commotion.

Tommy strode forward, his wife trying to pull him back the whole time. He twisted out of her grip. "Mandy, let go of me. It's time Nate and I settled this once and for all."

Hands planted on his thin hips, Tommy brushed Mandy off when she reached for his arm again. He stepped forward a few paces and stopped a foot from our table, facing off with the group of lumberjacks. I pressed up against the wall to avoid getting whacked in the head by the man's jutting elbows. If fists were about to fly, I wanted to make myself as small as possible.

"I told you to stay off my property," Tommy spit out.

Nate broke away from the other lumberjack contestants and stepped up to the chainsaw artist with a calm stride. He towered over Tommy, his height even more frightening than the fire in his eyes. Scotty stepped up beside his friend, arms crossed over a massive chest. Together, the two giant woodsmen created a solid and intimidating wall.

Nate cleared his throat. "And I've told you, I have every right to be on your property. I own the timber rights to that tract of land. It says so in your title work and right on your deed. If you didn't want that to happen, you should've addressed it before you bought the property." His voice remained steady and calm.

"Nobody explained timber rights to me. The whole thing was underhanded, and you know it!" Tommy's face turned red with rage. He darted up to Nate, dancing around the lumber-jack like a banty rooster looking for a fight. Even though Tommy wasn't a tiny man, Nate's towering strength made him appear small.

Nate sighed and lowered his voice a notch. "I'm sorry you didn't understand how timber rights work, man. How about I buy the property back from you for what you paid for it and we call it even? No more hard feelings."

"You know we've already started construction on the house and workshop. I don't want to sell it back to you. What I want is for you to stay off my place."

"Once I get those two acres logged, I promise you I'll stay off your land for the next twenty years. I'll even sell you those timber rights if you want them. In the meantime, you're going to have to deal with it."

Tommy raised his fist. By the look in his eye, it was loud and clear he wanted to pop Nate squarely in the nose.

Nate narrowed his eyes and dipped his chin while looking Tommy straight in the eye. "Look, I've tried to make this right, but now it seems like you're asking for a fight. Are you sure you want to do this?" He tilted his head slightly to indicate the group of lumberjacks standing behind him and Scotty. Nate raised his eyebrows, giving Tommy a chance to size up the woodsmen he'd be taking on.

I leaned in and whispered to April. "Yikes. Doesn't seem like a fair fight. Eight giants against one normal-size guy."

April shook her head. "I'm sure they're just trying to intimidate him. Nate won't let things get out of hand."

A slap of metal on wood rang out as the owner of the bar flipped up the hinged pass-through and whipped around the bar like a madman. While Kevin Owens was friendly and welcoming, he didn't take guff from anyone, drunk or sober. Showing no fear, Kevin strode around the loggers and up to Tommy until they were nose-to-nose. He thrust out an arm, pointing to the door. "Out. Unless you can all act like civilized human beings, you don't belong here. Nobody's fighting in my bar tonight."

It appeared to be the out Tommy was looking for. His wife heaved a sigh of relief as they turned to leave, but Tommy wasn't quite done yet. He puffed up his lean chest one last time. "You haven't heard the last of me." He pointed a skinny finger at Nate's chest. "Watch your back, you...you...doorknob."

Nate laughed. "Doorknob? That's the worst thing you could come up with?"

Tommy shot him with a glare as Mandy dragged her angry husband out of Timber Creek Saloon. Everyone in the room took a collective and relieved breath.

"That was exciting. Reminded me of David and Goliath. It's a good thing Nate controls his temper so well, or the other guy would've been squished like an ant." April bit into another breaded mushroom. "At least Kevin didn't have to resort to firing a bullet into the ceiling to get everyone's attention."

"True enough." I took a deep swallow of my beer, then wiped my mouth with a napkin. "I feel kind of bad for Tommy, not understanding Nate would retain the timber rights. Can you imagine buying land to build your dream home and raise your family on, only to wake up one morning to the previous owner cutting down your trees?"

April shook her head. "It would be pretty terrible, if I'm being honest."

"Land disputes are notorious for getting violent. Wars and long-running feuds have been started over property rights."

"Hopefully we didn't witness the start of a land war playing out in front of us."

"Agreed."

With the Keifers out of the bar, Nate turned to the bar owner. "Sorry about the ruckus, Kevin."

"Not your fault, man. Thanks for keeping it calm." Kevin shook Nate's hand. "I appreciate it."

"No worries." Nate sighed. "Lesson learned. If I ever sell off any more acreage, I'll make sure the buyer knows what retained timber rights means. I wasn't trying to pull the wool over his eyes. You guys know me. I like to be honest and upfront with all my business dealings."

"Really?" A local logger, Matt Forester, swiveled around on the stool where he was sitting at the bar. "Strange. Must be a new leaf the great Nate Durand is turning over." He glanced around at the other loggers. "Or maybe it's only me you treat like dirt?" Matt sneered and turned back to the bar. He took a swig out of the bottle of beer in his fist.

Nate grimaced at the man then rubbed his forehead and joined the rest of the lumberjacks without replying.

I dipped another steak strip into the blue cheese dressing and took a bite, contemplating the man at the bar. "I wonder what Matt's going on about?"

April swiveled her head to look at him, then clucked her tongue. "Who knows? Matt's always been an oddball. Probably thinks Nate did him wrong at some point. With Matt, nothing's ever his own fault."

Matt was a logger who, like Nate, worked independently. He'd recently purchased a rusty rattletrap of a logging truck and sold the timber he cut to the local sawmill. I was pretty certain his logging truck spent more time broken down then it did actually hauling timber. It was common knowledge Matt had to go into business for himself because he couldn't seem to get along with anyone he worked with. Word was, he'd burnt all his bridges with the logging companies in the area and there wasn't anyone left who'd hire him. Matt was only in his mid-thirties but held himself like a skinny ancient man bent into the shape of a crescent moon. He had a foul mouth and an attitude to match. Even in the crowded bar, the barstools on either side of him sat empty while people milled around, choosing to stand rather than sit next to the guy.

"It's kind of sad. Imagine the type of life Matt must live. It's got to be lonely," I said.

We both turned to look at the man in question. Matt picked that moment to raise his voice as Kevin set a fresh beer in front of him. He was addressing the bartender, but apparently didn't care who else heard the conversation. "I'm looking for a good woman who isn't afraid of a little hard work, and who's not dragging a bunch of baggage around with her. The last thing I want is to have to try and fix her. Not my job. I need a woman who can chop a load of wood, cook me a tasty dinner, and clean the dishes. Is it really too much to ask?" When Kevin only grimaced and turned to pull a beer for another customer, Matt supplied the answer himself. "I'm starting to think it is these days. Nobody wants to work." He sighed and took a swig of his beer.

April shook her head in disgust. "I can't decide if he's looking for a girlfriend or a handyman. What a jerk."

My daughter had a valid point.

Cheers and laughter rang out from the lumberjack contestants who were gathered around a cluster of tables they'd pushed together. It was fun to see them all enjoying each other's company before the competition heated up in the morning. The men raised icy dripping mugs in toasts as they let loose with racy jokes and bits of song.

With the excitement and drama over, I asked April what it was she had wanted to talk to me about.

She took a swig of her beer, I assumed to add more steel to her backbone, then set the bottle back onto the table with a sigh. "Ever since we went to Astoria back in August, Becky has been after me to get you to consider selling the house and downsizing."

"What? Why?"

"She thinks you don't need that much space, and she's not exactly wrong." April shrugged. "It's a lot to keep up for one little woman..."

"Hey. Watch it," I growled through clenched teeth.

"In a smaller house, your power bills would be a lot less, the maintenance would be much more manageable, and it would free up a lot of your time."

I pursed my lips and quietly waited for her to continue.

"Mom? Say something." When I didn't answer, April also threw her brother under the bus. "Patrick thinks so too. The house was great when Dad was alive and all of us kids were at home, but now you're the only one rattling around in all those empty rooms."

"Oh, Patrick thinks so too, huh?" I said as little as possible so as not to explode and punch my own bullet hole in the ceiling. Good thing I didn't have a gun in my purse.

Becky was my oldest child. She had a sweet family of her own and lived on the Oregon coast where she owned a bookstore and her husband fished the waters of the Pacific Ocean. Patrick, my only son, was two years older than April. He'd gotten an animal husbandry degree and now owned and operated a dairy farm in Kansas with his wife and their young son. I loved my family, but they were overstepping their boundaries as far as I was concerned.

April gulped. "Yeah, Patrick thinks so too."

I tilted my head, leaned closer to my youngest child, and kept my voice low. It sounded menacing even to my own ears. Let her tremble in her boots. I didn't care a hoot. "The three of you have been discussing how your old crackpot of a mother isn't smart enough or capable enough to take care of herself anymore, is that it? You do all realize, do you not, that I am only sixty-two years old, not eighty-two? Sure, maybe in twenty years I can see you all sitting me down for this conversation, but as of now," I narrowed my eyes, "I suggest you back off."

April threw her hands in the air. "Fine. They've been hounding me to death about it, but I told them you would take it this way. It's not that we don't think you're capable, Mom, we just think it would make life easier for you."

"Oh, would it? Would it make my life easier? Would it lessen how badly I miss your father? To have to go through forty-some years of accumulations and decide which memories to toss out and which were worthy enough to carry into my new, smaller, life? Would it be better for me to sell the beautiful house your dad and I raised our family in? And," I was on a roll now, "have any of you considered where our family get-togethers would take place, or are they simply a thing of the past now, as well? What about the big family Christmas we've been planning? Is Christmas off the table now, too?"

April had shrunk down in her chair at my backlash. "Well, no. Patrick thought we could still have Christmas this year, then you could start looking for your new place after the first of the year."

I nodded and attempted to bring my voice back into my normal range. "I see. One last hurrah, then the house goes on the market."

"Yes, that's the thinking."

I leaned back in. "Read. My. Lips. Not going to happen."

April sighed and took another steak strip. "Fine. Let's table it for now and enjoy the last of our meal."

I forced a fake smile and took a sip of my beer. *We're tabling it forever, Missy.*

April tried to lighten the mood by regaling me with stories of the pranks the high school soccer girls played on the coaches on their latest overnight trip. As the assistant coach, April bore the brunt of a few of the jokes. Not one to typically hold a grudge, I let her coax a few laughs from me until I'd let go of my mad. By the time we'd finished our snacks and beer, I'd forgiven my kids' interfering, and was ready to call it a day. April and I wandered over to wish the lumberjacks good luck before we headed out.

"You guys do know there's a lumberjill competition during the Timber Festival, don't you?" April asked, looking around as if confused. "Where are the Jills? I thought they'd be here celebrating with you."

"We invited them, but they all said they were resting up for tomorrow and saving their partying until after the competition." Scotty's eyes twinkled as he chugged the rest of his beer and reached for the pitcher in the middle of the table. "Silly women."

The comment burned in my craw. Maybe I hadn't fully let go of my mad yet.

"I scoff at that," Nate yelled, raising his glass in another cheer. The server squeezed her way in, thumping two more sweating pitchers down on each end of the table.

"Let the women rest," another contestant bellowed, then laughed while reaching for one of the fresh pitchers. "More beer for us!"

Glancing around the table, I recognized most of the contestants. A few faces were new to me, but since competitors had to live in the region to compete in our local competition, they were simply neighbors I hadn't met yet. Whoever they were, it was clear they were having a good time. A young man wearing round Harry Potter-ish glasses reached for the pitcher and knocked his neighbor's beer over with his elbow in the process. Thankfully, there'd only been about an inch of liquid in the glass. Instead of anyone getting mad about it, the entire group laughed. The man who'd knocked over the beer leaned down and sucked it off the table.

Coming up for air, he looked around the table where all eyes were on him. "What? No sense in wasting good brew, is there?"

I shook my head at the absurdity of it all while the rest of the lumberjacks guffawed.

Once things quieted down a bit, I broke into their revelry. "April and I are headed out but we wanted to stop by and wish you all the best of luck tomorrow." I eyed the pints and pitchers of beer emptying at an alarming rate. "Though you might want to think about slowing down. I'd think you'd want to be at your best for tomorrow's competition." I indicated the drinks with a nod. "You know, like how the *smart* lumberjills are resting and making sure they're in top form. Just a thought."

"Mother!" April made a disgusted sound in her throat and rolled her eyes. "Sorry, you guys. Sometimes my mom can't seem to stop herself from handing out unsolicited advice."

My daughter grabbed me by the elbow and frog-marched me out of the saloon.

Chapter Three

Saturday morning, I was up before the sun. Of course, it wasn't much of a brag since in October the sky didn't start getting light until almost seven. Two months ago, I'd started taking yoga classes and was already addicted, though it sure wasn't the case in the beginning. Halfway through the first class, I'd been certain I'd rather die than ever go back. My muscles had felt like Jell-O, my joints had popped and cracked in protest, and my body had screamed from the wacky poses the instructor had been trying to force my unwilling body into. Before that class, I'd considered myself fairly flexible. I could still stand on my head at sixty-two and not many people can boast that particular skill. Yoga was going to be a cake walk. Boy, was I ever wrong. After forcing myself to go to a few more sessions, my body decided to not be such a drama queen and had started to loosen up. I'd been hooked ever since.

With my sky blue yoga mat tucked in a tote bag slung over my shoulder, I headed outside, pulling the door of my big brick house shut behind me. There was a welcome chill in the early fall air, so I zipped up my lightweight jacket even though walking to class would have me toasty in no time. I'd discovered walking was a great way to warm up my muscles ahead of the yoga session. Not only did I get a good portion of my daily step count in, it gave me a chance to cruise through Pine Bluff while the town was still quiet with sleep. I took a deep breath of the crisp fall air. The slow whistle of an early freight train trilled through the dark from somewhere in the distance. A hint of wood smoke lingered from last night's fireplaces, taking me right back to evenings spent with Bob and the kids in front of our own crackling fireplace.

I was trotting along, lost in nostalgia and happily minding my own business, when an enormous white dog charged toward me from behind a picket fence, barking loud enough to wake the dead. I yelped and pressed a hand to my galloping heart. "Good night!" I held my fingers out for the Great Pyrenees to smell. "Hello, Gus. You remember me, don't you? Good boy."

As soon as I spoke to him in a calm voice, Gus stopped barking and stood tall with his front paws on the top of the fence. His tail beat a furious tempo. Not wanting to be late for yoga, I gave the dog a quick pat on the head. He rewarded me with a slobbery lick in return, and I kept walking.

Two blocks later, I stopped on the sidewalk under a street-light and looked both ways before crossing Douglas Avenue. A beefy two-tone blue and silver Chevy pickup rumbled by. As the streetlight streamed into the cab, it illuminated the driver. I recognized the chainsaw artist, Tommy Keifer, behind the wheel. After the truck passed, I stepped out onto the empty street and continued on my way.

To shave off a couple of minutes, I cut through the football field at the combined elementary and junior high schools instead of walking the two blocks around the buildings. The sports field butted up against Pine Bluff's community center where the yoga classes took place. The sun was barely peeking over the ridge, casting buttery golden rays into the sky. The first sweet dee-dee-dee of chickadees greeted the morning light. It looked like it was shaping up to be the perfect autumn day. When I was halfway across the field, I noticed the sun glinting off something in the bushes surrounding the community center. For a split-second, the object shot a blinding ray of light straight into my eyes.

"What the heck?" I muttered to myself, squinting to see better. What appeared to be a tennis shoe protruded from underneath the foliage. Was someone lying in the bushes? I picked up my pace. My heart stuttered and the palms of my hands began to sweat.

A silver and black ten-speed bicycle sprawled in the bark chips with the back tire wedged under one of the hawthorn bushes near the shoe. I leaned down and peered under the foliage. A pair of round eyeglasses over closed eyelids and sallow skin glinted back at me. I gasped and jerked back. A thorn from the bush penetrated my skin and left a raised and red scratch on the back of my hand as I dropped the foliage back in place. Spinning around, I spied a jogger coming down the hill on the opposite side of the street.

"Help!" I jumped up and down, waving my hands in the air. "I need help!"

The runner changed course and sprinted my way. As she got closer, I was relieved to see the jogger was Samantha Everett, a Pine Bluff police officer. Sam ran through our quiet streets every morning, changing up her routes every day. It was fortuitous she'd chosen this side of town for her run this morning.

"What's wrong? Are you okay?" Sam's long raven-black ponytail swayed as she came to a stop next to me.

I gestured frantically to the man lying under the hawthorn bush. "I think he might be dead. Maybe a car hit him and he made it here before he collapsed, or...I don't know. I was on my way to yoga when I saw him lying there." My hands shook as I pointed at the unresponsive man.

Sam squatted beside the bike and gently lifted the branches of the prickly bush. She leaned forward for a better look, then quickly jerked back as I had done. Sam blinked her eyes and swished a hand in front of her nose as if to clear out an unpleasant odor. "He's dead all right. Dead drunk."

"What? Seriously?" Pent up tension drained from my shoulders.

"Yep. See for yourself."

I crept closer and bent down. Sure enough, as I stared at him, the man's mouth dropped open and a thunderous snore roared out. The reverberating snore was apparently loud enough to penetrate his drunken stupor, because his eyes opened with a jerk and he immediately tried to sit up. All he managed to do was get himself more entangled in the prickly bushes.

"Thank goodness. I truly thought he was dead." I peered closer at the man, unafraid once Sam had verified he was alive and well. "Wait a minute. I recognize this guy. He was at Timber Creek last night with the lumberjack competitors. At one point, he slurped spilled beer off the table. I think he's one of the contestants, but I don't know his name. They were all drinking pretty heavily. I warned them to take it easy, but I guess he didn't listen."

Sam helped the guy shimmy out from under the thorn bush and got him to a sitting position. A leafy barbed branch was twisted into his hair.

Sam glanced at me. "Thanks for your help, Dawna. I'll take it from here. Don't want you to be late for yoga." Sam winked, effectively dismissing me.

Inside the community room, the colorful and eccentric seventy-year-old Beth Byrd was already leading the class in a series of gentle stretches. This morning she was wearing leggings with bold geometric designs in shades of bright orange, navy blue, and fuchsia topped with a peachy tank top. A rainbow striped headscarf was wrapped around her tousled short hair.

Slipping off my tennis shoes and trying my best not to be disruptive, I tiptoed to an empty spot beside my best friend and Pine Bluff city manager, Evonne Ford, and unrolled my mat. My heartbeat was beginning to settle back to normal after the scare of thinking I'd found a dead body. Some morning zen in the form of relaxing yoga was exactly what the doctor ordered.

"Morning, friend." I whispered to Evonne. "How're you this lovely day?"

Evonne bunched her eyebrows together in a good-natured frown. "How do you think? It's still dark outside." Evonne stood a good six inches taller than me. She sported a salt-and-pepper no-nonsense pixie cut and was dressed in a dark blue scoop neck tee over black yoga pants and bare feet.

"Nope. The sun just came up. Look for yourself." I pointed to the window.

"Maybe so, but it doesn't change the fact that I still haven't had my first cup of coffee. I don't know why I let you talk me into this nonsense all the time."

"Because you know yoga makes you feel better and gets your muscles loose and ready for the day."

She frowned at me. "It's not like I'm a circus performer."

Ignoring her sarcasm, I dropped my chin to my chest and slowly rotated my head over my left shoulder along with the rest of the class. As I brought my head back to center and opened my eyes, our instructor was staring straight at me, a finger held to her lips to shush me. It wasn't the first time I'd been reprimanded for talking in class. And I'd bet a dill pickle it wouldn't be the last.

Forty-five minutes later, the yoga session ended, and all my bottled-up tension was gone along with it. It was a much more grounded and stable me who rolled up my mat and put my shoes back on.

"Don't forget tomorrow morning at sunrise we'll be having a session at Steam Engine Park as part of the Timber Festival. It will be a great experience to feel the ground under your bare feet and draw on your connection to Mother Earth," Beth announced. "See you all there."

"Fat chance," Evonne whispered for my ears only.

"You never know. It might be fun. I plan on going."

She glowered at me.

I chuckled. "Do you want to grab some breakfast?"

She shook her head. "No time. I'm manning the booth at the Timber Festival for the first couple of hours this morning." Evonne paused while she shoved her yoga mat into her bag. "I'm starting to run low on cookbooks, though. How many do you have left?"

Evonne was the president of our Women's Service Club, and we were knee-deep in fundraisers earmarked for the purchase of the town's historic Emery Theater. We'd gathered recipes from everyone in the area who wanted to share one with us, then had six hundred cookbooks printed. People loved them and a lot of people purchased multiple copies to give as gifts to friends and family who no longer lived in the area. The cookbooks had been one of our top money makers for the project so far.

"I still have a couple of cases. Do you want me to bring a box to you at the booth?"

"Would you mind? That'd be great, if you have enough time to drop them off before you head to work."

"No problem. I'm not opening Carpenter's Corner until noon today. April and I don't want to miss the axe-throwing this morning. If somebody has an urgent need for a box of nails, they can always call my cell."

"Perfect. I'll see you in a bit, then." Evonne leaned in for a quick hug before she hurried out the door.

An hour later, I was showered, fed, and had managed to gulp down a cup of coffee before pulling on a bulky, goldenrod handknit sweater layered over a sage green T-shirt in case the nip in the air burned off. I finished off my look with a pair of comfortable jeans and some tan leather ankle boots, then topped it all with a pumpkin-colored canvas jacket I'd purchased at Lipstick and Lace on a whim a couple of weeks before. I was finally ready to head for the park.

Muttering to myself, I smacked the steering wheel of my candy apple red Jeep as I pulled into the parking lot at Steam Engine Park. Even though I'd hurried, I hadn't managed to beat the crowd. Every parking space was full. I circled the lot one more time, hoping someone would back out and let me in. No such luck. I was going to have to lug the heavy box of cookbooks farther than I'd anticipated. I accelerated out of the lot and kept my eyes peeled for an empty spot. Cars lined the curb on both sides of the street for the entire length of the park. *Son of a biscuit eater*. I whacked on my blinker and turned right, making a giant circle around Steam Engine Park. My speedometer may have read a hair over the legal speed limit.

Back where I'd started, I passed the pull-in leading to the main parking lot and kept going. Halfway down the block, a car pulled away from the curb. I sped up to claim the spot before anyone else could weasel in, then jimmied into place between a giant SUV and an oversized diesel pickup. It took three tries before I finagled my Jeep between the two larger vehicles. Parallel parking had never been my strong suit, but I was bound and determined to get into this spot. With my back passenger side wheel wedged against the curb, I called it good. So what if my parking was a little cattywampus? It wouldn't kill anyone. I cut the engine, got out of the Jeep, and slammed the door as hard as I could.

One deep breath and the smell of sourdough pancakes and savory bacon from the Lions Club's annual Paul Bunyan Flapjack Breakfast went straight to my brain. It was all it took to settle me down. I looked around, hoping nobody had seen my little temper tantrum over not being able to find a parking spot. I glanced into the vehicles I'd wedged my car between to make sure nobody was sitting inside. Nope, they were both empty. Thank goodness for small miracles.

From where I stood at the edge of the park, the only parts of the vendor's booths visible were the tops of the colorful tents standing over the tables. A stack of logs ready to be used for the various events in the logging show hindered my line of sight. I planted my fists on my hips, studying the park for the quickest route to the Women's Service Club table. If I took the sidewalk, I'd be lugging the heavy box of books the equivalent of trotting around a full city block. I huffed, pushed my glasses up my nose, and wrestled the box out of the back seat of my Jeep. "Since I'm not a pack mule, I guess I'll be cutting through the park."

It was a little more than two-hundred yards as the crow flies, but dew had been heavy in the night. Even though we hadn't had any rain in over a week, the grass was sopping wet, littered with fallen leaves, and the ground felt soggy under my feet. I was glad I'd worn leather boots, even if they were only ankle high. A hundred or so yards later my arms ached, and I'd only made it halfway.

"I should've brought a wagon to haul these darn things in," I grumbled to no one in particular, regretting my choice of fall attire since I was hot and sweaty with the exertion.

With my next step, the toe of my boot sank into the soft grass. I stumbled but managed to remain upright while the box of books wobbled in my grasp. Steadying my load, I gave myself a much-needed pep talk. "You've got this, Dawna. The booth is right on the other side of the logs. You're almost there." With the smell of pancakes and bacon urging me on, I convinced myself I deserved a second breakfast after my hard work. The thought of a plate of steaming sourdough pancakes and sweet maple syrup made me pick up my pace. "Treat yourself" was my favorite motto. I summoned my strength and kept moving.

As I sailed around the end of the ten-foot-high stack of logs, a flash of red and black disappeared around the corner of the pile just as my foot caught underneath something hard. I tripped again, but this time I couldn't rescue myself and went down hard. The box of books flew out of my arms. Cookbooks scattered across the ground like falling leaves. I landed with a splat, sprawled in the wet grass with the wind knocked out of my lungs. For a full minute, I lay where I'd landed, gasping for breath. Once my lungs filled back up, I blinked several times. The whole world was blurry and soft around the edges. My glasses had flown off my nose when I'd hit the ground and I was as blind as a bat without them. I patted the ground within reach. *Oh, come on. Where are you? Please don't be broken.*

I pushed myself up to my knees and peered around, feeling like Mr. Magoo as I searched for the wayward glasses and whatever had made me trip. A long, blurry object lay on the ground. A log must have rolled off the stack and I hadn't seen it over the box I'd been carrying. To my right, the sun glinted off something shiny. My glasses! I reached for them and attempted to dry off the wet lenses with my sweater, which wasn't much drier. I only managed to smear them more, but stuck them back on my face anyway. They were a bit wonky and smudged, but not broken thank goodness. I'd have to make a trip into Greenwood to get them adjusted since we didn't have an optometrist in Pine Bluff.

With my glasses settled back on my face, the world came into sharper focus despite the streaks on the glass. I turned my attention to the log I'd tripped over, then frowned. *Since when do logs wear boots?* It took my muddled brain a minute to register that the log wasn't a log at all. I'd tripped over a pair of lace-up work boots which stuck out from behind the log pile, toes pointed to the sky.

"Oh, good night! Not another drunk lumberjack."

I crawled forward on my hands and knees, following the boots up to a pair of black denim jeans on long, muscular legs. My gaze traveled to the buffalo plaid red-and-black flannel shirt tucked into those jeans. A blood-curdling scream ripped through the air when my eyes glommed onto the double-bladed throwing axe sticking out of the man's wide chest.

Nate Durand sprawled in front of me, and this time the lumberjack I'd found wasn't dead drunk. He was really truly dead. A dark stain spread over the upper half of his shirt and ran off of his side, forming a pool under his body. Nate's brown eyes were wide open in an expression of surprise. It took me a second to realize the scream ringing through the air was coming from my own throat.

I scrambled to my feet and exchanged my scream of fright for a plea for assistance. Waving my arms over my head to get the attention of anyone near the vendor booths, I yelled for help.

Chapter Four

Squatting next to Nate's lifeless body, I stretched out my hand and checked for a pulse. I was fairly certain I wouldn't find one, but then again I didn't have any background as a medical professional and I didn't want to stand there doing nothing if there was a chance to save his life. I was concentrating hard when something touched my shoulder, causing me to recoil and let out a screech.

Matt Forester, the logger who had been looking for a hard-working woman when we'd seen him at Timber Creek Saloon the evening before, had come up beside me and placed a hand on my shoulder. He shook his head. "He's gone," he said, confirming my suspicions.

Matt had a cell phone pressed to his ear with his free hand. Queasy and light-headed, I squirmed out from under his hand and sat down hard on my behind, not caring a fig about the wet seeping through the seat of my pants. Sprawling on the ground after tripping over Nate's boot had already soaked me to the skin anyway; a little more wet couldn't possibly hurt.

My head was foggy and I shivered with cold. I glanced up at the stack of logs. Everything seemed surreal. Nate was dead and someone had clearly murdered him. *This can't be happening.*

Matt ended his call and crouched beside me, tucking his cell phone into the chest pocket of the green flannel shirt he wore. "The police are on their way." He stared at me instead of the body in front of us. "Did you see who killed him?" Matt leaned in close. Too close.

I edged away and tried not to gag at the rancid fumes the logger breathed into my face. *Would it be bad manners to offer him a piece of mint gum?* Probably. Instead, I shook my head. "No, I didn't see a thing until I tripped over his feet."

Unblinking, Matt continued staring at me until a second scream tore through the air surrounding us. This time, it wasn't me screaming. I twisted around in time to watch a small woman dressed in a copper-colored down jacket and figure-hugging black jeans break from a crowd of people forming twenty feet behind us. Shayna Granberg, Nate's long-time girlfriend and one of the lumberjills competing in the logging show, ran forward and dropped to her knees beside me, staring at Nate. Her screams turned to gut-wrenching whimpers of pain.

"No, no, no, no." Sobs racked Shayna's body as she ran her hands over Nate's face. She lowered her forehead onto his, her body shaking as grief overtook her.

Wanting to provide some comfort, I reached over and rubbed Shayna's back. My own breath still came shallow and fast, but with the attempt at comforting someone else, my heart rate began a slow descent back to normal. "I'm so sorry, Shayna." The words felt trite and useless as they left my mouth. I pulled myself to my feet, then reached out to tug Shayna up and away from Nate's body.

A tall woman with sandy blonde hair pulled into a classic French braid strode around from the backside of the log stack. She paused to take in the scene, then broke into a jog to reach us. The woman tugged the sobbing Shayna out of my arms and wrapped her in a hug.

"Katelynn, he's gone. Nate's gone," Shayna sobbed. "It's all over."

"Shh now, I know. I know. Everything's going to be okay." Katelynn stroked Shayna's long, chestnut brown hair. Over her friend's head, the blonde woman nodded at me. "Thank you for your help. I've got her now."

Two minutes later, the crowd parted to let Pine Bluff Chief of Police J. T. Dallas through. He wore the standard navy-blue police issue uniform, but in a concession to his own style he'd paired it with scuffed brown leather cowboy boots and a mocha-colored wool Stetson hat pulled low over his dark hair. Officer Sam Everett, who'd helped me at the crack of dawn with the drunk lumberjack, and the young, fresh-faced Officer Pete Bowman flanked Chief Dallas. I'd known J. T. his entire life. His parents had been some of Bob and mine's best friends and we'd practically raised our kids together. J. T. had grown up to be a highly capable and respected force in Pine Bluff. My shoulders slumped with relief as I stepped away from the body and let him take charge. The officers worked together to push us back and secure the area as an ambulance crew and other first responders arrived. Within minutes, yellow crime scene tape fluttered in the morning breeze.

I mindlessly stared at the flurry of police activity and heard the low murmurs of the other onlookers but, lost in the foggy landscape of my own brain, I didn't pick up any actual words. Shaking my head, I tried to clear the clouds, but the only thing rattling around in my head was that I was forgetting to do something. What was it? *Shoot.* The clouds parted and I remembered Evonne was waiting for my box of cookbooks, which lay scattered pell-mell over the wet grass where they'd landed when I took the nosedive onto the ground. I headed for them, but Matt must've read my mind and beat me there. He helped me pick up and wipe off the books the best we could before placing them back in the box. As I picked up the cookbooks, I gasped as a sharp pain shot through my left wrist and up to my elbow. Wincing, I pulled the arm to my chest and finished picking up the mess using only my right hand.

As I plucked the last book off the ground, I noticed a round metal button, about two inches in diameter, laying on the ground. Scotty Trimmer's bright smile greeted me from the face of the black button. The words "Axe Kicker," printed in white letters, circled Scotty's photo. A sharp metal pin on the back allowed the button to be attached to clothing or bags. What a cute idea. Scotty must've had them made up for his fans. I slipped the button into my jacket pocket and placed the cookbook into the box with the others. With all the books collected, Matt closed the flaps on the cardboard box, wiped his wet hands on his faded blue jeans, and hefted the box into his arms.

"Where were you headed with these?" Matt asked. "I'm happy to carry them for you, if you'd like."

"Yes, please. I'd appreciate your help more than I can say," I replied. "They need to go to the Women's Service Club booth. I'll walk with you."

We'd made it all of approximately two feet when Chief Dallas bellowed my name. "Dawna! Where do you think you two are going?"

I placed a hand on Matt's arm, stopping him in his tracks, and swiveled around. "Matt's helping me deliver these cookbooks to Evonne," I answered.

J. T. scrunched his dark eyebrows together. "Fine. Take them to her but get right back here once they're delivered. We'll need to talk to both of you soon."

"You have my word."

As Matt and I walked in silence, I couldn't help but notice how nice and helpful he was being, a far cry from the image I'd always had of the guy. Maybe I'd had Matt pegged wrong all along.

We made it to the Women's Service Club booth where Evonne was tucking money from the sale of a cookbook into the army-green metal box the club used as our cash register.

Matt set the heavy box down on the table. "There you go," he said without making eye contact with either one of us. "I'm gonna head back now."

"Thanks. I really appreciate your help," I called after him. No response.

Well, maybe he hadn't heard me. I'd make a point to thank him again later.

"Hell must've frozen over." Evonne frowned and raised an eyebrow. "Matt Forester helping you out? I don't think I've ever seen the man raise a finger to assist anyone before today. It's a day for miracles. And what's with all the commotion going on over there?" She jerked her head toward the log stack and the place of Nate's untimely demise while she studied me with a frown. "Why are you soaking wet, and what happened to your glasses? Did you fall down?"

"You sure ask a lot of questions."

"Well, answer them." Evonne crossed her arms over her chest and impatiently tapped her foot.

With a sigh, I plopped down onto one of the empty folding chairs behind the table and told my best friend about not being able to find a close parking spot, subsequently having to carry the books much farther than anticipated, then tripping and falling, scattering the books across the wet grass, losing my glasses, finding them again, and discovering Nate dead with an axe buried deep in his chest.

Evonne's head whipped around to the activity surrounding the log stack. "Nate's dead? Are you sure?"

"I'm positive." A shiver racked my body at the thought of Nate's lifeless eyes staring up at the sky.

"Oh, my gosh. His poor family." Evonne stroked a hand down her throat and then let it rest against her collarbone. Her lower lip quivered and her voice shook. "Nate's mother, Lisa, worked at city hall with me for quite a few years. You couldn't find a nicer person. I can't even imagine what they're going to go through once they get word about Nate's death."

We sat in silence for a few minutes, then I finished my story with Matt calling the police and helping me pick up the scattered books and deliver them to the booth. "He's been incredibly helpful. And nice," I added, hardly able to believe those words were coming out of my mouth in conjunction with Matt's name. "I feel bad about always thinking he was such a turd."

Evonne snorted. "Don't feel too bad. He generally is. You must've caught him on a good day."

"People can change. I'm going to give Matt the benefit of the doubt from here on out." *Even though he'd been a real nincompoop at Timber Creek Saloon last night.*

Evonne wobbled her head, not in full agreement with me. She reached into the box I'd brought and spread a few more cookbooks out on the table after wiping them off with a paper towel. A couple of them had blades of grass sticking out from between the pages. Evonne held up a couple with the edges stained green. "Looks like we'll need to discount these ones." She stacked them in a separate pile.

She'd set the Women's Service Club booth up with two long tables in an L-shape, then covered the tables in linen tablecloths with a colorful fall leaf pattern. White wooden crates sat on their sides, their openings facing out with cookbooks displayed both inside them and on top. Some books were standing up, spines out, with others stacked in neat piles. A garland of orange and yellow fabric leaves surrounded each crate and small decorative pumpkins dotted the tables. Pamphlets about the Women's Service Club's mission and some various projects we'd been involved with were displayed in a clear plastic holder, along with a membership envelope for the ease of anyone interested in joining our group.

"You did a fabulous job with the booth, Evonne. It looks incredible. I'm sorry I can't stay and help, but I need to get back over there. J. T. wants to interview me in a few minutes." I got to my feet and brushed more strands of wet grass off my jeans.

Evonne leaned in for a hug. "No worries. Are you still going to be up to taking tickets with me at the play tomorrow evening, do you think? If not, we'll need to find someone to fill in."

"Don't you dare. We've worked too hard for this. I wouldn't miss it for the world. I'll see you there."

Paul Bunyan—A Tall Tale, was being performed on stage at the historic Emery Theater as part of the Timber Festival weekend. One of our club members had miraculously finagled a respected traveling children's troupe to perform the play as a fundraiser for our purchase of the theater. We had big dreams of the profits filling our coffers so had been promoting it nonstop.

The event had been the talk of the town for weeks now and I wasn't about to miss it.

Last summer, we'd nearly lost out on purchasing the Emery Theater to a smarmy land developer. It was fortuitous for us, though not for the land developer, when he met a premature death. We hadn't wasted a minute redoubling our efforts to raise the funds. As president of the club, Evonne reached out to the owner who'd been unaware our group was interested in buying the theater to gift to the city of Pine Bluff. Delighted the Emery, which her several times great-grandfather had built, would no longer be sitting empty and would be used for its intended purpose, the owner granted us a lease for one whole dollar a year. She had also agreed to sell our group the theater for only half of what it was worth. We'd already gotten a quarter of the way to our goal and expected when the evening's profits were tallied, we'd push close to the final amount needed. Fingers crossed.

Back at the crime scene, I edged my way around the growing crowd to find a place to stand by myself. Finding Nate dead had been a tremendous shock and I didn't want to have to field any questions, except from the police. Turning my back on the sight of law enforcement personnel scurrying around the body, I studied the blues and greens of the mountains surrounding our valley and tried to soak in the earthy, calming scents the pine trees released into the air. Beautiful fall colors of yellow aspen and golden birch leaves dotted the surrounding foothills. My meditation was rudely interrupted when the ground shook as if a thundering herd of buffalo were about to run me down. I spun around and jumped out of the way before I got trampled. One death in Pine Bluff was plenty for the day.

"Thor! Stop!" April yelled as she charged toward me, pulled along in the wake of an eighty-pound Black Labrador Retriever. She needn't have worried because the dog came to a screeching halt at my feet, his entire body wiggling with pleasure. April had adopted the dog recently when his previous owner left town and needed to rehome him. He'd quickly adopted both of us as his forever people. Thor and April were meant to be together and, even though I loved the dog, I was thankful April had a place of her own.

Wearing his new bright red collar and matching harness, the dog looked happy and stylish. Five-year-old Thor hadn't been mistreated by his previous owner one single bit, but he hadn't gotten much in the way of training either. The dog had never even been on a leash until he went to live with April. The harness she purchased for him was supposed to help Thor learn to walk calmly and not strain at the leash. So far, it didn't seem to be having the desired effect.

I started to reach out to pet the massive dog's head then decided to go all in instead and bent down to throw my arms around his thick neck in a comforting dog hug. "How's my buddy today? What a good boy. Yes, you are." His tail slapped me in the face, effectively getting dog hair in my open mouth. "Yuck." I straightened and brushed at my tongue, laughing when Thor thunked himself down on his haunches and smiled at me, his tongue lolling out of his open mouth.

"Holy Toledo. What's going on? I thought all the commotion was prep for the logging competition, but that doesn't seem to be the case." April craned her neck, trying to see around the crime scene tape and the police officers blocking her view. "What's on the ground over there?"

I swallowed hard, trying not to cry. Despite my best efforts, my voice came out shaky. "It's Nate Durand laying on the ground. Somebody killed him. And I was the one who found his body when I tripped and fell over his feet."

"Nate?" April's free hand shot up to cover her mouth. Her green eyes swiveled from the crime scene to me. "What do you mean somebody killed him? That can't be right. Nate's one of the nicest guys around."

"Someone hit him in the chest with..." My throat swelled with tears so I couldn't get any more words out.

"Hit him with what, Mom?" she prodded.

I swallowed hard. "An axe. They killed him with an axe."

April gasped. "We have an axe murderer in Pine Bluff?"

We stood in silence for a few minutes as both April and I tried to process Nate's death.

"I can't believe this is happening." April turned to me and looked me up and down, noticing the disheveled state of my clothes for the first time. "Did you hurt yourself when you fell? Your glasses are all wonky and you're covered in mud."

"My wrist hurts a bit but I'm okay." I hugged the offending arm to my chest. "My glasses are fine. They're going to need an adjustment one of these days. Soon, I guess."

"Let me see your wrist." I held out my left arm and let April run a light finger over my sore wrist. "It looks a little swollen. Did you catch yourself with your hands when you fell?"

I clucked my tongue and shrugged. "Maybe, I don't know. I fell hard with a big splat. I suppose I could have caught myself with my hands, but I don't think my wrist is broken."

April sighed. "Let's keep an eye on it, anyway. I'll drive you to get it checked out if you end up needing to go in."

"Alright, but I don't think I'll need to." When April cocked an eyebrow at me, I conceded, but not much. "I'll keep an eyeball on it, promise. Sheesh."

J. T. approached as April dropped my arm. "Morning, ladies. Good to see you. It's been too long." He sounded like he was addressing both of us, but the police chief only had eyes for my daughter.

April tried to hide the instant flush of her cheeks by patting her dog's head as a distraction. "Don't be silly. We saw each other last night."

Last night? April must be confused. J. T. hadn't been at Timber Creek Saloon while we were there. She must've been thinking about another time. They both tittered and I wanted to unpack what that meant right then and there, but April tended to get testy when my interfering mom personality showed up.

Not to mention I had a dead body on my mind we needed to deal with first and foremost.

I waved my hand in front of the chief's face. "Sorry to interrupt whatever this is, but remember me? I'm the one who fell over Nate's feet."

J. T. cleared his throat. "Oh, Dawna. Yeah, sorry. I need to ask you a few questions if you don't mind." He sent an apologetic glance to April. "It'll only take a few minutes, then you can have your mother back."

"And if I do mind?" I asked.

"Tough." J. T. transitioned from flirting suitor to capable and hard-nosed police chief in about two point five seconds. The police chief side gave me a pointed, sideways glance before taking a few steps away from the gathered crowd and jerking his head for me to follow. I obeyed. He fished a small notebook out of his shirt pocket and flipped it open. "How much can you tell me about what happened here this morning? I understand you found the body. Again."

"What do you mean again? The other guy this morning wasn't dead, just drunk."

"What guy this morning? I don't know what you're talking about." J. T. gawked at me.

"The guy I found passed out under a bush at the community center. Officer Everett was there and took care of him. She must not have told you."

"No, I haven't had a chance to speak to her yet this morning about anything other than Nate's murder. By finding the body again, I was referring to Warren Highcastle. Remember him?"

"Oh." I opened my eyes wide in understanding. Warren had been killed inside my hardware store a few months before and had been the first murder in Pine Bluff in recent memory. "Of course I remember him. Don't be ridiculous. I obviously thought you were talking about the guy this morning."

J. T. pinched the bridge of his nose like I was giving him a headache. "Glad we got that cleared up. Now, back to my original question, if you don't mind. Did you see what happened to Nate this morning?"

I shook my head. "No, I didn't see anything. I was taking a box of cookbooks to Evonne for our Women's Service Club fundraiser." Nervously, I wrung my hands, sending a spark of pain through my injured wrist. "The box was big and heavy. I couldn't see over it to watch where I was going, so I tripped on something and fell. My glasses flew off and I didn't even see Nate lying on the ground until after I found my glasses again. It was his feet I'd tripped over. At first, I thought he was drunk and passed out, you know, like the first guy this morning? I figured Nate must've had too much to drink last night, too. They were all having a good time when April and I left Timber Creek Saloon."

J. T. scribbled down some notes. "Did you happen to see anyone around the log stack before you fell? Is there anything at all you can remember noticing while you were walking?"

I grimaced, trying to remember. "No, I don't thi...well, wait a minute." I squeezed my eyes shut, concentrating harder. "There *was* somebody around. I saw a flash of a red-and-black checkered shirt disappear around the corner of the log pile right before I fell. I'd forgotten all about it." I glanced back at Nate's body and frowned. "Well, like the shirt he's wearing, come to think of it. Maybe I saw Nate fall and didn't realize it." My stomach clenched with the thought.

"Or maybe you saw the killer," J. T. added. His piercing blue eyes roamed over the crowd where the contestants for the weekend's lumberjack contest were gathered a few feet away from us.

I shifted my stance to follow the chief's gaze. "Oh, my stars."

All of the contestants who would be competing in the logging show were dressed in identical black jeans and red-and-black buffalo check flannel shirts. The same collar was visible under Shayna's zippered jacket. "Any of them could have done it," I whispered. "Do you know how long he's been dead?"

J. T. shook his head. "Not yet, and you know I shouldn't talk about the investigation with you, but my best guess is his murder happened within the last hour. Let's just say, if you didn't see Nate being murdered, you must've barely missed the whole thing."

I pressed a shaky hand to my heart, once again struggling to catch my breath.

"Now, you mentioned you and April were at the bar last night. And Nate was there as well?"

"Yes." I nodded affirmation. "Most of the lumberjack contestants were there. The men, anyway. Scotty had been in Carpenter's Corner earlier in the afternoon and told us they were getting together at Timber Creek last night. He mentioned we should come by, so we went in for a quick dinner and wished them all good luck for the weekend competition."

"Did anything out of the ordinary happen while you were there? Anything strange you may have noticed?"

"Not between any of the contestants." I pushed my glasses up my nose.

"But? I hear hesitation. What happened?"

"There was an argument between Nate and...the chainsaw artist guy. I'm trying to think of his name." I paused before snapping my fingers. "Tommy Keifer. Do you know him?"

J. T. nodded. "Yeah, I've seen his work. Nice stuff. You're saying Nate and Tommy got into a squabble last night?"

"Yes. Tommy and his wife, Mandy, came into Timber Creek last night. Apparently, the Keifers recently bought some land from Nate but didn't realize Nate had held back the timber rights. From the sounds of things, Nate's been logging on the property the Keifers purchased, and Tommy isn't happy about it one bit. He thinks Nate pulled a fast one on him by not explaining timber rights to him before they bought the property."

J. T. tipped his head in agreement. "He's probably not entirely wrong, except my hunch is Tommy's real estate agent is the person who should've made sure he understood timber rights." He sighed. "How did it end? Were any punches thrown?"

"No, just some yelling. Kevin threw Tommy out before it got physical, but Tommy told Nate he hadn't seen the last of him and warned Nate to watch his back."

"Good information, Dawna. Thank you." J. T. jotted notes in the small red field notebook, flipped it closed, and tucked it back in his shirt pocket. He nodded at me in dismissal, then stepped in front of the gathered crowd, raising his arms in the air to get their attention. When all was quiet, the police chief addressed the crowd. "As you all have seen, Nate Durand has died. Sometime within the last couple of hours, he was murdered with his own throwing axe."

I gasped. "His own axe? How can you be sure it was his?" The questions flew out of my mouth before they'd even fully formed in my mind. Standing beside me, April gave me a sharp nudge in the ribs with her elbow. "Ow." I rubbed my side.

J. T. swiveled his head and leveled me with a glare of his steely blue eyes. "Yes, Dawna, I'm sure. Nate's name is engraved on the handle. There's no doubt the axe belonged to him." A muscle jumped in his cheek. "May I continue?"

With a sweep of my hand and a small nod, I replied, "My apologies. Please go on."

The chief turned his attention back to the crowd. "If any of you know anything about what happened here this morning, please see me or one of my officers as soon as possible. Rack your brains. Is there anyone you can think of who had a beef with Nate? Someone holding a grudge or maybe even someone who had a reason they wouldn't have wanted him to compete this weekend? Tell us everything, no matter how small you might think it is." J. T. informed the group the county coroner was on the way and a thorough sweep of the park would be conducted, including interviews with all the lumberjack contestants and anyone who'd been in the park this morning. With a pointed look thrown my way, he asked if anyone had any more questions.

Chad Sawyer, the Timber Festival's organizer, stepped forward. "I feel terrible about Nate, and horrible for Shayna." He nodded to the distraught woman. "I don't want to sound callous, but are we going to be allowed to continue with today's planned activities? Pine Bluff has a lot of money sunk into this festival. It'd be a shame to see it canceled."

"You're unbelievable." Scotty emerged from the crowd, striding up to Chad, his face as red as a ripe apple with anger and grief marring his features. "Someone murdered my best friend this morning and your only concern is for the festival? The games must go on at any cost. Isn't that right, Chad?"

"Hang on." J. T. stepped between the two men. "At this point, I don't see any need to cancel the festival." When Scotty opened his mouth to protest, J. T. raised an open palm. "Now hear me out. We'll be interviewing all of you, like I said. It would make our jobs a whole lot easier if you'd all stay here at the park until we can get those interviews done. As far as the competition goes, I suggest you all sit down and hash it out. Make a decision as a group whether or not you think Nate would want you to carry on." He paused while the competitors mumbled their agreement. "That being said, I want to attend your meeting. Give me half an hour, alright?"

Both Scotty and Chad reluctantly agreed.

"If I'm not there," J. T. said, "do not start without me."

Chapter Five

Despite the promising morning sun, gunmetal gray clouds had moved in, resembling pads of steel wool. No rain fell from the churning sky yet, but I shivered anyway. I was cold and wet and wanted nothing more than a comforting cup of hot coffee and a slice of pie. Maybe a hot bath, but a long soak would have to wait. "Do you want to get something to eat?" I asked April.

"You bet. Let's go find a table first so you can sit with Thor while I get the food. Do you already know what you want?"

"Well, I'd planned on getting a flapjack breakfast from the Lion's Club booth, but it's getting kind of late for breakfast." I pulled my cell phone out of my pocket to check the time. "It's almost eleven." The air was full of fragrant scents from the myriad of food booths scattered throughout the venue. As we walked toward an empty picnic table, I inhaled the varied aromas, from the tangy scent of onions sizzling on a grill to the sweet, heady aroma of almonds, pecans, and cashews being caramelized in butter and cinnamon. A spicy, savory scent tickled my taste buds and rumbled my stomach. "Chili. Yum. Doesn't it smell incredible? A bowl of chili should warm me up nicely. With cheese but no onions, please. And a wedge of pumpkin pie."

"Got it." April chuckled and deftly wrapped Thor's leash around the leg of the picnic table. "Do you want something to drink?"

"Definitely. Coffee, please. I think Lily Anne's here with a coffee stand." I sat on the bench and swiveled to swing my legs under the table. "Are you sure you don't mind grabbing it all?"

April waved a dismissive hand. "Of course not, Mom. Sit and rest for a minute. I'm going to grab the coffee first, then go back for the food. Be right back."

I pushed the crooked glasses up the bridge of my nose and let out a breath so heavy my bangs fluttered off my forehead. What a day, and it wasn't even noon yet. My wrist throbbed and my knees ached. I hunched over the table, ready to indulge in a good old session of feeling sorry for myself, but when I closed my eyes, an image of Nate's prone body hammered its way behind my eyelids.

I flinched and every muscle in my body tightened. My eyes flew open as a shiver rattled my bones. Thor stared at me, whining with concern. *The dog's right, Dawna. Knock it off. What do you have to complain about?* Unlike Nate, I was sitting upright, somewhat at least, at a picnic table, about to have hot coffee and a delicious meal delivered to me. I swiped a finger under my glasses to wipe away a tear. I didn't have any right to feel sorry for myself when Nate's morning had been a million times rougher than mine.

My thoughts had swung to Shayna and Scotty and what they must be going through emotionally, when a dark thought struck me like a lightning bolt. It'd been a red-and-black buffalo checked shirt I'd seen slipping away from the murder scene, which meant there were at least sixteen people, including Chad, the logging show MC, who could've done the dirty deed. Narrowing it down to only one of them was going to be next to impossible. I hated to think my interview with J. T. might have thrown both Shayna and Scotty into the suspect lineup simply because of their lumberjack attire. I didn't know much about Shayna, but I'd known Scotty since he was a mischievous little tyke and I couldn't imagine a situation that would push him to kill his best friend.

Deep in thought, I propped my chin on my injured left hand. "Oooh," I groaned, cradling the sore wrist against my chest. Thor whined again and shoved his gigantic head under my elbow, resting his jaw on my thigh and looking up at me through worried brown eyes. I smiled and stroked his silky black head. The warmth radiating from his hairy body was comforting, like I had my own portable heater. "Don't worry, buddy. Everything's okay. You're such a good boy. Yes, you are."

As I looked down at the dog with his head in my lap, something shiny under the picnic table caught my eye. I gently pushed Thor's head away and stretched my leg out far enough to nudge the object with the toe of my boot, then slowly worked it closer until it was within reach. Bending under the picnic table, I scooped it up. Scotty grinned up at me from another Axe Kicker button. I tossed the button onto the picnic table.

"Here you go, Mama." April plunked a large, white paper coffee cup stamped with the Rocking M Coffee Company brand down in front of me. She picked up the button. "Too funny. Where'd you get this?"

"It was on the ground under the table."

April rubbed the button clean on her jeans, then pinned it to her shirt. "It's mine then. Finders keepers."

"You can have it. I have another one in my pocket I found earlier." I wrapped my hands around the steaming cup of coffee. "Thanks for my coffee. What flavor did I get?"

"Toasted coconut and caramel latte made with hemp milk."

"Yum. It sounds delicious." I lifted the cup to take a sip but stopped short. "Is that a piece of hay?" I eyeballed the yellow strand of hay sticking up from the cup's straw hole.

"It's a straw," April replied, excitement in her voice. "Lily Anne said it's her new thing. An attempt at helping the environment by not serving plastic straws in her to-go cups anymore. Isn't it cool?"

"It's certainly interesting, anyway." I took a sip and closed my eyes, savoring the sweetness and letting the caffeine go straight to my foggy head while the warmth spread through my chilled body. "Alright, I'm on board. The straw seems to work fine, and it doesn't taste like the barn. What did you get?" I eyed April's drink.

"The same. It sounded too good to pass up." She took a sip before setting her cup on the table. "I'll be back with sustenance in a snap. The lines aren't too long yet. Do you still want the chili?"

"You bet I do."

With April off fetching food, I sipped my coffee and mindfully tried to relax my shoulders. It wasn't working. The longer I sat on the hard bench, the stiffer my neck and back were getting. I twisted my back, trying to get the muscles to release. As I swiveled, Tommy, Mandy, and a teenage boy were coming down the sidewalk. Each of them pulled a flatbed cart loaded with carved woodland creatures. The Keifer family pulled their rattling carts up to two large white tents standing side by side at the end of a row of vendor booths. Mandy and the boy unloaded their wares into the first tent and sat up a table while Tommy loaded the second tent with supplies for his chainsaw carving demonstrations.

Dressed the same as he'd been at Timber Creek Saloon last night—black jeans, a red hooded sweatshirt, and a black baseball cap over his walnut curls—Tommy's attire gave me pause. The colors were the same as the lumberjacks and jills wore, except Tommy's sweatshirt was solid red instead of sporting the red and black checkerboard pattern. Could I have seen Tommy running away from the scene and mistaken the blur of colors for a buffalo plaid shirt? I scratched my head, trying to conjure up the memory. Everything had happened so fast and swirled around in a messy jumble inside my head. It was entirely possible I'd been mistaken about the buffalo plaid when all I could picture in my mind was simply a flash of colors. Maybe the murderer was nonchalantly setting up his booth right in front of me.

Unwinding Thor's leash from around the leg of the table, I stood, leaving the coffee on the table to claim our territory. The carving booth was only a few feet away and I didn't plan on being gone for more than a minute anyway. I tugged on Thor's leash. "Come on, big guy. Let's go find out exactly what these fine folks are selling."

Thor and I marched straight over to the artist's booth where Mandy stood on a stepladder hanging a long white vinyl banner that read "Keifer's Carvings" in pine green lettering. They'd filled the booth with a menagerie of woodland creatures, but carved bears were the most prominent offering. There were giant bears taller than me, petite little guys only a foot high, and every size of bear in between. I laughed out loud at four small brown bears holding sticks of wooden marshmallows and sitting around a carved campfire. There were four-foot-tall blocks of wood carved into stacks of books with wise owls perched on top, wooden benches with bald eagles gazing regally from each end, and spirited wolves with their heads thrown back, caught in mid-howl. But of all the whimsical creatures in the tent, I couldn't take my eyes off the bookstack owls.

Tommy started his chainsaw in the demonstration tent, and a handful of people gathered to watch. I tore my gaze away from the enchanting owls and sidled over to join the throng of spectators.

Letting the chainsaw idle, Tommy smiled at the gathering crowd. He nodded at the block of wood he'd placed on a riser. "Howdy folks. Thanks for coming by. From this chunk of wood, I'll be carving one of the smaller bears you see over there." He pointed the bears out in the other booth. "If you have any questions, I'll be happy to answer them when I'm finished, or you can ask my lovely bride for more details." Tommy flipped blue safety goggles from the top of his head down to cover his eyes and revved the chainsaw.

In seconds, sawdust was flying and chunks of wood were falling at the carver's feet. The skill it took to create pieces of art with such a large and dangerous tool fascinated me. In no time, an adorable bear had emerged from what had been a chunk of raw wood only moments earlier. It was pure magic. Tommy cut the power on the saw, grabbed a sandpaper block, and gave the bear's rough edges a quick smoothing over. With a battery-operated drill, he carved out eye sockets, inserted marble eyes, then aimed a blowtorch in all the right places to highlight the bear's ears, nose, and fur. The entire time he worked, Tommy talked to the crowd about his process. He was way more charismatic than I would have given him credit for.

Finished with the bear, Tommy cut the chainsaw and held out his arms like a magician. "There you have it, folks! Yogi the Bear, and this one won't eat your picnic."

I glanced at my watch, amazed. From start to finish, the adorable carved bear had taken the chainsaw artist less than ten minutes. Impressive. "What an incredible skill. How did you learn to carve in such detail using a chainsaw?" I asked.

"Me and a buddy were out cutting firewood one day and started messing around. Our first attempts were terrible, but it was fun. I wanted to learn different techniques and hone my skill, so I started watching videos on YouTube and kept working on it until I got it right. It's taken time and lots of practice, but I've finally found my own style."

"Well, you have quite the talent. Do you only sell your work at shows like this?"

Tommy nodded. "For now. There are six major shows I'm a regular at every year. Most of the time I get enough special orders from those shows to keep me busy carving all year."

"You said for now. Do you have plans to add more shows to your calendar?"

"Not more shows, necessarily. No, we're building a house and a workshop out Lost Canyon way. I hope to sell products out of my workshop by this time next year."

Aha. "I see. That sounds perfect, though I hope you'll still do our Timber Festival show."

"Yes, ma'am." Tommy smiled and nodded at me. "Are you in charge? I'm sorry we got a late start today. We had a bit of a rough morning."

"Oh? What happened?" *It couldn't have been a rough morning because you were killing Nate, could it?*

"We're staying at a motel in Greenwood while the house is under construction, and my truck wouldn't start this morning."

"Vehicle trouble's the worst, isn't it?" I shook my head, commiserating with him. "No worries from me though. I'm not the one in charge here. Did you get your truck fixed?"

"Eventually. It was my own stupid fault. I managed to leave the interior light on overnight and it drained the battery. None of the staff at The Stardust Inn had battery cables with them, so we called around and finally found a mechanic to come by and give us a jump start. Thank goodness. My son, Storm, is in the junior lumberjack competition this afternoon. He'd have been one unhappy kid if he'd missed it." Tommy waved an arm toward his son, who was helping Mandy with a customer. Storm grinned and waved.

"Things happen all the time, despite our best efforts." *And you are a liar, good sir*, I thought, remembering seeing Tommy driving through town early this morning. In my peripheral vision, I noticed April on her way back to our table. Perfect timing. "Oops, there's my lunch. Gotta run, but I'll be back later to get one of those adorable owls!"

Back at the picnic table, I broke up the saltine crackers inside the plastic wrapper they came in, then tore them open and dumped them into my bowl of steaming chili. With the first spoonful, a string of melted cheese swung off the spoon and slapped me on the chin. Wiping cheddar cheese away, I groaned with pleasure, then eyeballed the Polish sausage in April's hand. "This chili is delicious, but your sausage smells amazing, too."

"It totally is," April agreed. "Everything looked so good, it was hard to decide, but Polish sausages get me every time. And the brown mustard adds the right amount of kick." She took a big bite, juice from the roasted sausage squirting into the air. April wiped her face with a brown paper napkin. "Now that you have some food in your belly, tell me what you were talking to the chainsaw guy about."

"His carvings, of course. You've got to go watch one of his demonstrations. It's incredible!" I turned and pointed to the Keifer's Carvings booth. "And check out the carved owls. I'm going to go back and get myself one before the weekend is over."

April cocked an eyebrow. "Where're you going to put it?"

"Probably on the front porch."

"It'll look great there." April nodded in agreement. "Did he recognize you from Timber Creek last night? I think Tommy's a prime suspect for Nate's murder, don't you?"

"Oh." I raised both eyebrows. "Are we talking suspects already?"

"I'm just saying."

"And I'm agreeing with you. To answer your first question, no, I don't think he recognized me. Tommy was too busy yelling at Nate last night to notice who was watching his theatrics. I did tell J. T. about the altercation between the two of them when he interviewed me this morning." I scooped up another bite of chili. "Tommy lied to me a few minutes ago, though."

April cocked her head. "Lied to you about what?"

"When I was chatting with him about his carvings, he thought I was in charge of the vendor booths and made an excuse about why they were late getting their booth set up. He said his truck wouldn't start this morning. In Greenwood."

"Okay?" She shrugged. "Why do you think he wasn't telling the truth?"

"Because on my way to yoga this morning, a few minutes before seven, I had to wait to cross Douglas Avenue because a pickup was going by. I'd swear on your dad's grave it was Tommy."

April's green eyes narrowed. "First of all, please don't swear on Dad's grave, and second of all, weird. Why would Tommy lie about having car problems? Unless he's trying to make it seem like he wasn't in Pine Bluff at the time Nate was killed."

I touched my nose. "Bingo. That was my first thought as well..." My voice trailed off.

"Except?"

"Except Nate was killed with his own throwing axe. How would Tommy have gotten ahold of it? I can't imagine him overpowering Nate, unless he took him completely by surprise. Maybe Nate had put his axe down and Tommy grabbed it." I turned to study the carver. "Tommy seemed so nice and friendly when I talked to him a few minutes ago, but he certainly showed another side of himself at the bar last night. I wonder if the battle over those timber rights could have led him to violence?"

"Mom, I don't like the crazy look in your eye. Don't even think about sticking your nose into this investigation. Leave it to the police please." April narrowed her eyes and glared at me.

"You're the one who brought up the subject of suspects, missy. It won't hurt to keep my eyes and ears open."

"Oh, you don't think so, do you?" April waved an index finger around in the air. "May I remind you…"

"No, you may not," I interrupted. Standing, I grabbed the piece of pumpkin pie still covered in plastic wrap. "You won't mind cleaning the rest of this up, will you? I need to get the store opened. Thanks for lunch, daughter. See you soon."

Chapter Six

The lumberjack contestants, seven men and eight women, milled around under the biggest of the two covered picnic shelters in Steam Engine Park. When I spied them on my way to my Jeep, I stopped in my tracks. *I wonder what they're going to decide to do about the competition.* Would they scrap it all, or would the logging show still take place this year? It took me all of two seconds to decide to listen in on their meeting.

Trotting behind the tall stack of hay near the shelter that had been set up for kids to climb on, I slid my backside onto a bale of hay. From my vantage point I should be able to hear what was said but remain hidden from the contestants. A dart of guilt for eavesdropping pinched my chest but I pushed it away. After all, I was the one who'd found Nate's body and I deserved to know if the competition would continue or not. Not to mention that if it was one of the lumberjacks who'd murdered Nate, they might say something incriminating. I glanced at the time on my phone. There were still a few minutes to spare. Nobody would perish if Carpenter's Corner stayed closed an extra half hour.

Having justified my snooping, I leaned back against the haystack only to have my lower back catch with the movement.

The sharp and sudden pain straightened me up fast. The last thing I needed was for my back to seize up and leave me stranded on a bale of hay while I was trying to be snoopy. Hunching my shoulders, I twisted my back slowly until I felt the tension-releasing pop. The jolt I'd taken from hitting the ground so hard was rearing its ugly head in the form of a thousand different aches and pains. My entire body could use a good long rest. I massaged my throbbing wrist. *Please don't be broken.* The swelling was getting worse but I hadn't bothered to mention that minor fact to April. Once I got to the store, I'd get some ice on it and it'd be right as rain in no time.

Five minutes passed, but the meeting still hadn't started. Shoot. If they didn't get underway soon, I was going to have to give up my post and get to the hardware store. I had decided I'd give it two more minutes when Chad Sawyer and Chief Dallas finally strode into the pavilion. Yes! I scooted farther back behind the hay bales where, if I leaned forward, I could barely peek around the corner. J. T. shouldn't be able to spot me from here and tell me to leave. By no stretch of my imagination did I think he'd want me poking around in his investigation.

Chad cleared his throat. "After this morning's tragedy, we have some hard decisions to make. I've thought about it and agree with Chief Dallas. The decision whether or not we continue with this year's competition should be up to all of you. First, I'd like to hear from Shayna, then Scotty, before we put it to a vote. Does that seem reasonable to the rest of you?"

In his mid-fifties, Chad was tall and still powerfully built. He sported a shiny bald head and a neatly trimmed salt and pepper mustache, though his short beard was as gray as morning fog. Back in his prime, Chad had taken the state champion lumberjack title more than once. After his fifth win, he'd stepped back from active competition but kept his passion for the sport fueled by throwing himself into training up-and-coming competitors, as well as spearheading Pine Bluff's annual Timber Festival. His booming voice and larger-than-life presence made Chad the perfect choice to act as master of ceremonies during the logging competition.

After a murmur of agreement from the other contestants, Shayna stepped forward. Swallowing hard, she fought back tears before speaking. "Everyone who knew Nate will agree he loved this competition. There's no doubt in my mind he'd want us to continue. Every day after work, he'd head out to the backyard to spend the last bit of daylight left to practice for this event. Honestly, the amount of time Nate spent focused on perfecting his throw caused more than a few arguments between us." Shayna's voice shook slightly as she spoke, but I was in awe of her composure.

When I'd lost Bob, I'd been a complete wreck for weeks, but Shayna stood with shoulders square and her back straight as an arrow, even though her eyes were red and her face swollen from crying. She'd pulled some inner strength from somewhere. My guess was the shock of Nate's loss hadn't fully settled in yet.

Shayna wiped tears from her cheeks. "Beating Scotty this year is all Nate talked about for months. He's had total tunnel vision, and I'm sure if the shoe was on the other foot, he would vote for the competition to go on, so that's my vote as well." She stepped back and was immediately scooped into a hug from Katelynn, the same friend who'd come to her aid at the crime scene.

Scotty stepped forward, his head hanging and his chin resting on his chest. His usual glow had been replaced with sallow skin and disheveled hair. Scotty clasped his hands to the back of his head and paced in front of the other contestants.

After composing himself, he addressed the group. "Nate has been my best friend since the day we started kindergarten. We thought of each other as brothers. He was one of the best people I've ever known. There'll never be anyone else like him. I'm completely broken over his death. My only focus right now is finding out who killed Nate." Scotty paused as he unsuccessfully attempted to hold back a sob. He clenched his fists and took a deep breath. "Personally, I don't want to continue. I think we should pack it up and go home. How are any of us supposed to compete knowing Nate isn't here but his killer is walking around free?" He focused his gaze on Shayna's face. "However, the last thing I want to do is fight about this, and we need to take Shayna's feelings and wishes into account. If we're going to continue, I propose we honor Nate and name the axe throwing portion of the competition after him. The Nate Durand Memorial Throw. Not only this year, but for every year from here on out. Thanks for hearing me out." Scotty stepped aside.

Chad took his place and called for a vote. "All in favor of continuing with this year's competition, raise your hand." Ten hands shot into the air. Five were opposed. "By a majority vote, the logging show will continue. As Scotty suggested, we will dedicate the axe throwing portion to Nate."

The lumberjack with the thick round glasses, who I'd found passed out under the Hawthorne bush earlier in the morning, spoke up. "I hate to bring this up, but without Nate, we're a man short. The Jack and Jill team events will be out of balance. What's your plan there?"

"Good question," Chad said. He flipped open a black binder he carried, thumbing through the pages before looking up with a frown. "Matt Forester is the first name on the backup list. Has anyone seen him around today?"

The week before the competition, would-be contestants participated in timed qualifying trials Chad held at the training course on his property. During the trials, the lumberjacks who cut the fastest, threw the most accurate, and walked the logs the quickest rose to the top of the pile. Eight men and eight women advanced to the Pine Bluff Logging Show competition. From the sounds of it, Matt must've come in ninth place in the men's qualifying trials and was in line to take Nate's place.

"I spoke to him a few minutes ago." Chief Dallas jerked a thumb over his shoulder. "Matt's the one who called in the report of Nate's death this morning." J. T. turned to scan the park before pointing to the man in question. "There he is now."

I swiveled my head and leaned forward. Matt was walking up the path about twenty yards from the pavilion.

"Matt," Chad hollered. "Got a minute? Come on over."

Matt broke into a jog. "Yeah, you need something from me, Chad?"

Chad looked Matt up and down, then frowned. "Well, it seems with Nate's death, you've made the competitors list. All contestants are required to wear black jeans and a red-and-black buffalo plaid shirt. Going to be a problem for you?"

Matt glanced down at the faded blue jeans and scruffy green flannel shirt he wore. "Nah, got all my gear in my truck. I can be ready to roll in ten minutes."

"You got your throwing axe and chainsaw? All your supplies?"

"Yep, I got it all. Came prepared and planned on sticking around in case anyone got disqualified and I was called up."

"Great, you're in then. You'll be paired with Shayna Granberg in all the Jack and Jill events, naturally."

Shayna flinched and swallowed hard, staring at the ground. To her credit, she didn't voice an objection to being teamed up with Matt. I couldn't imagine what the woman must be thinking. Not only was there no comparison between Nate and Matt's personalities, but they were a million miles apart in their lumberjack skills, from what I understood. It seemed to me insult was being heaped upon injury for poor Shayna.

Chad glanced at his wristwatch and sighed. "On second thought, I'm going to propose one more change of plans."

"Which is?" J. T. asked.

"The competition was supposed to have started this morning, with the adults taking the afternoon off for the juniors to take over the course. I propose we don't change the junior's schedule. Let's let them compete as planned. We'll push the events which were scheduled to take place this morning to tomorrow. It might end up being a long day, but we should still be able to fit it all in. The delay should give you all time to wrap your head around Nate's death and come back in the morning ready to compete."

Not one voice objected.

As the lumberjack contestants left the picnic shelter, I ducked back behind the haystack. I sat back and closed my eyes, willing my screaming back to relax. The sun had peeked out for a few minutes, but a cloud suddenly passed over, causing me to sigh at the loss of the warmth on my achy bones. I was late getting the doors open at Carpenter's Corner anyway, so I figured I'd better get a move on.

Jerking my eyes open, I shrieked. J. T. peered down at me. He was the cloud stealing my warmth.

"What are you doing here?" J. T. rubbed his chin while he stared at me. "Please tell me you're simply soaking up the sun."

"Of course, until you blocked it." I struggled stiffly to my feet, avoiding his all-knowing gaze. "What else would I possibly be doing?"

He shook a finger at me. "Don't meddle, Dawna. I mean it."

Chapter Seven

The brass bell over the door tinkled as I unlocked and pushed open the front door at Carpenter's Corner, announcing my arrival to the empty store. I stowed my purse under the counter and retrieved the cash drawer out of the safe. With the Timber Festival in full swing, I expected a slow afternoon, but I couldn't justify being closed for the entire day. Any bit of revenue the store could bring in during the limited hours I planned to be open would help the bottom line. Not to mention being alone in the quiet of the hardware store gave me a chance to lick my wounds. I glanced at my arm. Ugh. The definition where my wrist should have been was gone, and a tinge of purple was beginning to spread up my forearm. I grabbed a plastic shopping bag with the Carpenter's Corner Hardware logo printed in blue ink on the front, pried the lid off the to-go cup of ice I'd picked up at Hungry Bear Drive-In, and dumped the ice into the bag. I tied the handles into a knot, then pressed the cold ice to my wrist. *Ah. Relief.*

It was the first time I could ever remember being glad there weren't any customers in the store. I eased myself into the chair at my desk behind the check-out counter and wrangled the plastic wrap off my slice of pumpkin pie. Not an easy task, as it turned out, with only one working hand. The longer the day went on, the more my body screamed at me about the fall I'd taken. I stretched my neck from side to side in an unsuccessful attempt to work out some of the kinks. "A good long soak in the bathtub would be nice," I said to myself.

After finishing off the delicious slice of pie, I flipped the daily ledger open on my desk and pulled yesterday's receipts out of the desk drawer. Trying to keep from using my left wrist so the ice bag would stay in place, I picked up a receipt with my right hand, studied it, set it back down, picked up my pencil and filled in the appropriate tiny column in the ledger. After only a handful of receipts, I sat back and sighed. The process was bulky and time consuming. Maybe April was right and it was time to think about giving up my paper ledger. She'd called my system a dinosaur and told me I needed to get with the twenty-first century. April had gone as far as researching various point-of-sale computer systems, and while I found the price tag less staggering than I'd expected it to be for my small business, I had yet to bite the bullet and have the system installed. When the bell over the door jingled, I gladly pushed away the thought of a new sales system and looked up to greet the lone customer.

"It's about time you showed up." Darlene tapped lavender manicured fingernails on my counter to make sure I was aware of her impatience. She wore a royal-purple cable knit sweater dress over black leggings and high-heeled black leather ankle boots. Her thick, dark hair was pulled back in a loose, low bun at the nape of her neck with a strand of wavy hair framing each side of her face. Silver earrings with amethyst gemstones sparkled in the light, and a matching long necklace twinkled against the deep purple dress. If there's one thing I could count on, it was Darlene being the sparkliest object in town. She glittered like a diamond chandelier.

It wasn't like I was jealous of her sense of style or the way the darn woman never seemed to have even one hair out of place. Not one tiny bit. But I did wonder if she had that gorgeous dress in stock at Lipstick and Lace in my size. I glanced down at my jeans and chipped a bit of dried mud off my thigh. Okay. Maybe I was a hair jealous, but only a tiny bit, I swear. I sighed. "Is there something you need, Darlene?"

"Yes, I'm hanging a few new pictures in the boutique and need some of those itty-bitty nails. The white ones."

"Right over there." I pointed to the aisle where small boxes of pre-packaged nails and screws hung from display hooks on the pegboard shelving. "I'm surprised the boutique is open today. I thought you'd be at the park watching the lumberjack contest and enjoying the festivities with everyone else."

She trotted to the nail display and selected the box she wanted, addressing my comment over her shoulder. "Why would I? Those lumberjacks are little more than cavemen. Not my type." She shuddered at the thought. "I'm taking advantage of the slow day to give my shop a refresh and get new product out. It wouldn't hurt this dusty old place for you to follow my lead."

Typical Darlene, looking down her tanned nose at everyone. Why she stayed in Pine Bluff was beyond me, since she made it clear ninety percent of the townspeople weren't up to her lofty standards.

Instead of pointing out the freshly painted walls and the fact I'd completely reorganized the hardware store over the last two months, I decided to change the subject. "How about the play tomorrow evening? Are you attending, or is local theater below you as well?" I went into every conversation with Darlene intending to be nice, but no matter how hard I tried, I couldn't manage to hold in my disdain. I'd feel guilty about my snarkiness when it played on repeat in my brain while I was in bed trying to sleep later.

Darlene batted her long, thick synthetic eyelashes. "Now *that*, I wouldn't miss. But Paul Bunyan was the best you could come up with? I don't know why you all couldn't have chosen a play with a little more class. Phantom of the Opera would've been nice, but I suppose a show about some uncouth logger and his cow will have to do. It's not often this one-horse town gives me a reason to dress up. Even if there aren't any eligible men around to appreciate my efforts."

Thinking about Matt's comments at Timber Creek Saloon the evening before, I nearly snickered out loud wondering how skilled Darlene was at chopping wood and whipping up a tasty dinner.

Unaware of my inner comedian, she eyed me from top to bottom, dragging a judging finger along with her eye movement. "I sincerely hope you're planning on putting a little effort into your attire tomorrow night. And what is up with those glasses?" Darlene tilted her head and frowned. "They make you look like your face is on crooked."

Behind my wonky glasses, I rolled my eyes. "Obviously they need to be adjusted. They got mangled when I tripped and fell over Nate's feet. I'm thankful the lenses didn't break." I blew my silver bangs out of my face. "Poor Nate wasn't so lucky. I still can't believe he's dead."

Darlene jerked back in surprise. "Excuse me, what did you just say? Nate's dead? What are you talking about?"

"Oh gosh, that was callous of me. I figured you would've already heard, the way news usually travels in this town."

She shook her head, chocolate brown eyes wide. "Nobody has been in Lipstick and Lace all day. I haven't heard a thing. What happened to Nate?"

"He was murdered in the park this morning. Someone killed him with his own competition axe."

"It wasn't Shayna, was it?" Darlene held a manicured hand over her open mouth.

"Shayna? No, I don't think so. Why would you think she killed him?"

Darlene leaned across the counter, her svelte eyebrows pulled together in concern belied the glitter of glee sparkling from her eyes at the chance to gossip. "Last night I heard she broke up with Nate recently but she hadn't been able to afford to move out yet. Apparently, he spent so much time working and on business trips, Shayna thinks he had a little something-something on the side, if you get my drift. It wouldn't be the first time a spurned lover killed in a fit of rage, now would it?"

"Good gracious. Are you sure about this?"

Darlene shrugged, fiddling with something at the counter. "I mean, it was just a rumor but I'm sure it had some teeth behind it. Shayna's best friend, Katelynn Norris, is the one who told me all about the breakup." She tossed a five dollar bill on the counter to cover the purchase of the nails and held up the object she'd been rolling between her fingers. "I'm going to take this with me."

The object in Darlene's hand was another Axe Kicker button. *Now how did that get there?* I patted my jacket pockets, but the button I'd found earlier was right where I'd left it. My thoughts were torn away from the button when I suddenly remembered who Darlene said had told her about Shayna and Nate's breakup. Katelynn

Chapter Eight

After dropping her juicy tidbit of gossip, Darlene made herself scarce. I was still sitting at my desk chewing on the news of Nate and Shayna's alleged breakup when April stopped by Carpenter's Corner.

"Hey, Mama. Thought you might like an update on this afternoon's junior competition." April dropped Thor's leash and let him wander around the store to sniff all the smells he could collect in the time he was allocated.

"Great! I've been wondering how it was all going. How'd Westen do?"

"Fantastic! It was so fun to watch. He took first in the timed axe throw and log climbing. The kid scurried up the pole like a squirrel. I wish you could've been there. Here I took a video for you."

She pulled her phone out of her jacket pocket and brought up the video. There was Westen with the harness and rope around his waist at the base of the pole. As soon as the whistle blew, he threw the rope higher on the pole and climbed, repeating the motion over and over until he was close enough to reach out and ring the bell hanging twenty feet off the ground.

"Wow. Westen's incredibly fast, though I'm not surprised. He must be tickled. I'll shoot him a text to congratulate him." I winced as I attempted a one-handed text.

"Doesn't look like your wrist's doing so hot. Let me see." April reached for my arm.

I pulled away from her, grimacing when a sudden pain shot from my wrist to my elbow. "Honestly, I feel like I've been drug through a knothole backwards. I'm stiff and sore, and yes, my darn wrist hurts." Giving in, I held out the offending arm, which had progressed from a tinge of lavender to a nasty shade of purple within the last hour.

"That does it. I'm driving you to the urgent care clinic in Greenwood. Right now." April studied my wrist. "It looks broken to me. I should've insisted you go in earlier."

"Shoulda, woulda, coulda. I didn't want to go earlier." I huffed. "Guess I'm ready now. It's starting to throb pretty good. Business has been slow this afternoon anyway. No surprise there. I guess it won't hurt a thing to close a couple hours early." Year end was quickly rolling up on me and I needed to start organizing and prepping the store for inventory, but it was going to have to wait for another day.

I opened the register to take out the cash drawer and put it into the store's safe, but April gently pushed me aside. "Let me take care of the register. Do you want me to count the drawer down for you, or just put it away?"

"Not much there to count. I'll do it Monday morning."

I'd made the executive decision to keep the store closed the next day so I could enjoy the festivities along with everyone else. The Paul Bunyan play would be performed on the stage of the Emery Theater at six in the evening. Originally, the lumberjack competition should have wrapped up by noon, but with everything pushed back due to Nate's death, I was a little worried the audience for the play would be smaller than we'd anticipated. Fortunately for our fundraiser, a good portion of the tickets had been sold ahead of time, so even if folks chose to stay at the park to watch the lumberjack finals, we'd already made enough on ticket sales to cover the cost of the play and add a few hundred dollars to our coffers.

Before we left, I opened the app on the tablet I used for my new security system and started the backup. It would run and finish on its own without any more help from me. After a scary incident in my store in August, I'd ponied up the cash and invested in a basic system. It wasn't top of the line, but neither was it the cheapest on the market. Carpenter's Corner now sported outside cameras at both the front door and the warehouse entrance, as well as four cameras mounted in strategic locations inside the store. My favorite part about the system I'd chosen was how quick and easy it had been to set up. April and I were able to install everything ourselves in one afternoon. And the app was simple to access. I even had it loaded on my phone in case I needed to check on the store remotely. For less than a thousand dollars, the security cameras provided me with peace of mind. It was something Bob and I should have done years ago. Thankfully, the only suspicious activity the cameras had picked up so far was a dog lifting his leg on the warehouse door late one night and a teenage couple stealing a kiss under my front awning one evening. With any luck, that was the level of excitement we'd maintain around here for a long time to come.

I reached for my purse. "Alright, I guess I'm ready."

April swung by her rented cottage to drop Thor off before we headed to the medical clinic. Her baby blue VW Beetle was a bit small for two grown women and a massive dog to be able to ride in comfort.

Using the sleeve of my sweater, I wiped dried dog drool and nose prints off the inside of the passenger-side window. "Good grief. What a mess."

"What did you expect? Thor can't help it if he's a slobber monster."

"I know he can't, but you have to admit it's kind of funny. Until Thor came along, you kept this car in pristine condition. It's gone from having the new car smell to reeking of wet dog." I chuckled and plucked a strand of black dog hair off my jeans, then rolled down the window to release it to the wild.

"It's true. My poor little Beetle Smurf." April patted the dashboard in affection. She'd named the Volkswagen after her favorite childhood cartoon.

"I have a great idea." I slid a glance at my daughter to judge her reaction. "Since we're going right by and all, let's swing into the Stardust Inn really quick." We were less than a mile from the motel.

April scrunched her nose. "What in the world for?"

"Hear me out before you go getting all blustery on me. When I was talking to Tommy earlier, he said he and his family are staying at the Stardust while their house is being built. Remember I told you he said they'd gotten to their booth late because his truck wouldn't start, yet I saw him driving through town at o-dark-thirty this morning?"

"Yeah...and your point is?"

"I don't think it'd hurt to drop in and ask some questions. Are they even honestly staying there? And did they have a problem with their truck this morning? Which I already know they didn't, but it'd be nice to verify it."

April sighed heavily. "Here we go again. You can't help yourself, can you?"

I shrugged. "Nope. I keep thinking about poor Nate and the way Tommy threatened him last night. Tommy seems like a nice guy when you talk to him face-to-face, but the fact is, he told Nate to watch his back less than twenty-four hours before Nate wound up dead. Do you really think it's a coincidence?"

April arched her neck and blew out a breath. "Maybe not, and I suppose it's easier to go along with you once you sink your teeth into something than to fight you on it." She flipped on her blinker and wheeled the car into the parking lot of the Stardust Inn.

"Excellent. I'll be quick." I swung open the passenger door and eased my way out of the low-riding car, every one of my mistreated muscles screaming in the process.

The Stardust Inn was old and more than a bit run down. Single story rooms for rent spread out in a horseshoe shape with one parking spot in front of each door. Only a handful of cars occupied the lot. A grassy area in the middle of the horseshoe held a rusty swing set with a slide, and one lone green garbage can in a black metal cage. A discarded McDonalds cup lay on the ground near the trash can. The litterer must not have been able to reach the extra six inches to deposit the cup into the can. On one end of the motel, next to the road, a neon "Open" sign flashed in the window. "Motel Office" was painted on the door in faded gold lettering.

Inside, I approached the young woman behind the counter who was smacking on a piece of bright blue gum. The girl huffed and reluctantly looked up from the cell phone screen she'd been scrolling through. "Need a room?" she asked in a gruff and uninterested tone.

"No, I'm looking for some friends who're staying here. The Keifers? Tommy said his truck wouldn't start this morning, so I wanted to offer them a ride if they need one," I lied, knowing full well the Keifer family was selling carved bears in Pine Bluff.

The clerk squinched up her nose, blew a ginormous blue bubble, and snapped it before answering. "Car trouble? I don't think so." She half rose and craned her neck to see out the front window. "But their truck's not here, so if they did, they must've gotten it figured out."

"Oh good. Glad to hear it. What makes you think they didn't have any car trouble?"

"I mean, I guess they could've, but I came on at eight this morning. Got here about a quarter till. The Keifer's truck wasn't here then. I always notice because their truck and trailers take up several parking spots. Both of the trailers were still here, but not the truck. Anyway, Mandy came down for coffee," the clerk indicated the metal coffee pot and white Styrofoam cups with a nod of her head. "She said she was waiting for Tommy to get back and pick her and the boy up. She was irritated he'd run off to take care of something and was going to make them late for whatever show they were supposed to be at this morning." She shook her head, a green lock of hair falling over one eye.

I frowned. "Do you remember when Tommy got back?"

"Sure. He was gone for a couple of hours. Didn't get back until about ten, I think. He pulled in and hitched up their trailer right away, then they took off. Could've been ten-thirty, I guess; I didn't check the time."

"Hmm, okay. I must've misunderstood about the trouble with his truck." I slapped a hand on the counter. "Good. Everything's fine then. Thanks for your help."

The young woman shrugged. "No worries. Do you want to leave a message for them?" She pushed a small pad of paper with Stardust Inn printed across the top in gold foil letters across the counter, along with an ink pen. "I'm off in a few minutes but I can leave the note for the night clerk to give to the Keifers when they get back."

I raised a palm to decline. "Nah. I'll shoot Tommy a text. Thanks again for your help. Have a good rest of your day."

As I turned to leave, the clerk pointed out the front window. "You're in luck. They're pulling in now."

My heart jumped to my throat as I jerked the door open and scurried out. Head down, I hurried across the parking lot and slid into the passenger seat of April's car, scrunching down as far as I could. "Go. Get out of here," I hissed.

I chanced a peek over the dashboard as the two-tone blue and silver pickup pulled into an empty spot. It was most definitely the same truck I'd seen early this morning. Mandy slid out of the driver's seat and jogged over to a utility trailer parked under a tree. Maybe they'd sold out and she'd come back for more bears.

Gravel sprayed out from underneath our tires as we left the parking lot of the Stardust Inn. As soon as we were a block away, April started to giggle. "That was fun. I never thought I'd have a chance to be the getaway driver." She glanced at me. "What did you find out before the object of your curiosity showed up?"

"That Tommy lied, of course, like I suspected." I glanced behind us. No Chevy pickup followed us to demand why I'd been snooping. "They didn't have any problem with his truck this morning. Not at the motel, at any rate. The clerk said Tommy was gone early this morning but came back sometime between ten and ten-thirty to get his wife and son for the show. I told you I thought it was him I saw driving through Pine Bluff before dawn, and now I'm certain of it. It's awfully suspicious that he felt the need to lie about whatever it was he was doing." I let out a long breath. "I guess I'm going to have to ask him."

"Oh, no you're not," April replied adamantly. "It sounds like Tommy had plenty of time to kill Nate and get back to pick up Mandy and Storm. You need to tell J. T. what you've found out. He's perfectly capable of doing his job."

"You're right. I'll take off my sleuthing cap right now." I rolled down the window and pantomimed taking off a hat and tossing it out the window. "Happy?"

Chapter Nine

"**Y**ou have a distal radius fracture. A broken wrist, in laymen's terms," the doctor stated after studying the black and white x-ray films. "Unfortunately, fractures like this are not uncommon for someone your age who has taken a fall. You're lucky you didn't injure yourself worse. Women your age can easily break a hip in a fall like you described."

"Good gravy. How old do you think I am?" *It's not like you're a spring chicken*, I thought to myself, eyeballing the doctor's blatantly dyed charcoal black hair. Even his eyebrows appeared to be at least three shades too dark for his skin tone. Sure, I was creeping up on my sixty-third birthday, but who did this guy think he was, pointing out my age? Not once, but twice in as many sentences. The good old doctor's bedside manner could use a serious overhaul. The more he talked, the less I liked him. I sat up straighter on the exam table, putting a little more iron in my backbone.

The doctor scratched his temple, then pointed at the chart in his hand. "Sixty-two. You filled it out yourself. Is this information wrong? Did you take a blow to the head when you fell?"

I sighed and let my shoulders sag. "No and no." And apparently he didn't recognize sarcasm when he heard it, either.

"Remove your glasses for a moment, please."

I sighed and took my glasses off.

The doctor looked deep into my eyes for an uncomfortable length of time. He extracted what I thought was a pen from the chest pocket of his white lab coat, clicked the button on the end of the pen, and flashed a spotlight into my eyes without warning. I blinked and jerked away.

"Your eyes appear to be sensitive to light. Given that you're also confused about your age, I'm concerned you might have a concussion."

"For crying in the buttermilk!" I wanted to jump off the exam table and leave right then and there, but giving in to my anger wouldn't do my throbbing wrist any good. "I am not confused about my age, and, like I said before, I did not hit my head. My eyes are fine, you just didn't warn me you were going to shine a death ray into them. It was a knee jerk reaction. Now can we talk about my wrist, please?"

The doctor muttered to himself as he made a notation on my chart. "Patient shows clear signs of head trauma—confusion, light sensitivity, and crankiness—but refuses any treatment not pertaining to arm injury."

You think this is cranky, buddy? I'm about to show you how cranky this old broad can get.

One more look into my eyes and he must've noticed I was about to blow a gasket because the good doctor finally began to explain how he was going to reset the broken bone. By the time he was done, my wrist would be outfitted with a trio of wrap, splint, and sling.

"You'll need to see your primary physician in two weeks for another x-ray to make sure the swelling has gone down and the healing process is under way. There's a possibility you'll need surgery, but if your wrist is mending well, he'll probably put you in a cast and allow you to stop wearing the sling at that time."

"She," I corrected him.

One raised eyebrow. "Come again?"

"She. My primary physician is a woman."

The doctor wisely chose not to respond.

Back at home with my arm in both a soft wrap and a sling, I tried to get some sleep, but tossed and turned in bed instead. No matter what I did, I couldn't get comfortable. All the poking, prodding, and twisting at the clinic had made my arm ache worse than it had before. The doctor had offered me a prescription for the pain, and even though I generally don't like to take pain meds, I had accepted and picked them up at the pharmacy when we'd gotten back to town. I'd taken one, but so far the darn thing hadn't kicked in.

I rearranged my pillows, propping three against the headboard and attempting to recline against them. Nope. I slid them down and tried to lay on my right side. No success. As a last resort, I kicked the pillows onto the floor, then lay flat on my back with my throbbing arm squeezed to my chest, but that didn't work either. I gave up and stomped out to the living room, mad at myself for getting hurt, and mad at the world for, well, everything.

Sliding into Bob's comfortable recliner, I kicked the chair back and pulled his favorite blue knitted afghan over myself, missing him so much I couldn't breathe. Between the chair and the blanket, it felt like sinking into the warmth of home; the next best thing to Bob actually being there. I sighed and closed my eyes only to find the prone body of Nate superimposed on the inside of my eyelids once again. Flipping my eyes back open, I did a double take. The image of a wavering and semitransparent Bob kneeled beside my chair. I froze in surprise while my husband reached over and gently laid his hand on my injured arm. The pain receded. I blinked and he was gone. Golden globes of light floated across my vision. I shook my head, trying to clear my mind and make sense of what I'd just experienced. Had Bob really been there? Or was the irksome doctor right? Did I have a concussion? No, I was one hundred percent sure I hadn't whacked my head when I fell.

"Holy buckets, those pain pills are stronger than I thought." I tried to convince myself the meds had finally kicked in, but my heart insisted Bob's touch had done the trick and taken the pain out of my arm. Too bad he hadn't stuck around for a bit.

In the last year or so, well-meaning friends, and even some family members, had been nagging me about moving on. They had my best interest at heart, but every time the subject came up it stung. How did a person simply move on after the death of the love of their life? And move on to what exactly? Bob had been my everything. My heart and mind were still full of him, and I never wanted those feelings to fade. After forty plus years of a marriage filled with love, respect, and a whole lot of laughter, I had absolutely no desire to try again. And who was the all-knowing being who decided three years was long enough to grieve anyway? Maybe I was kidding myself, but in my humble opinion I was doing perfectly fine on my own, thank you very much.

With a heavy sigh, I grabbed for the remote control and turned on the television before my thoughts either turned more melancholy or ran off on a tangent to wrestle with Nate's murder. I flipped around until I found a station running nonstop episodes of *Reba*, a comedy sitcom I'd seen every episode of more than once. I turned the volume down so it was more background noise than anything and settled in to watch, hoping the silly show would distract me enough to keep my mind from racing. With any luck, it would put me to sleep and allow me to get some much-needed winks. As I stared at the screen and finally started to slip into oblivion, my fluffy white cat, Lilac, jumped onto my lap with a soft, squeaky meow and gazed at me through sweet lavender eyes. With my good hand, I stroked the little cat as I fell into a deeper sleep. The warmth of her small body on my lap and the quiet rumble of her purr was the therapy I'd needed. The only problem was, Lilac had been dead for years.

Before I knew it, sunlight splashed across my face. I blinked and stared at the TV. *Reba* had been replaced by a morning talk show. I clicked the red power button on the remote and blessed silence filled the house. Stretching my one free arm, I felt somewhat rested, if not exactly refreshed. I glanced around the room. *Where did that cat get off to?* It took me a minute to realize both Lilac and Bob were most likely figments of my active imagination, though I fully believed in ghosts. Lilac had been visiting me quite often the last few months and I was happy to have her around, but I'd give anything for a nice haunting from my dearly departed husband.

There'd been skads of times in my life I'd felt spirits around me. My parents and siblings had thought I was crazy, but even as an adult woman, I swore my imaginary childhood friend hadn't been imaginary at all. Just because I was the only one who could see and talk to Karen didn't mean she didn't exist.

April and I had gotten ourselves into a bind a few months before, and I swore Bob had come to our rescue. Even April admitted she'd seen something she couldn't quite explain and had felt her dad's presence in the house. Maybe her mother wasn't as crazy as she'd originally thought.

I sighed and wiggled the fingers on my injured arm, testing the level of pain. A dull ache radiated from my elbow to my fingertips. "Yep, still broken. I'll give it a five." The pain was much more manageable than it had been the night before. Hoisting myself out of the recliner, I readjusted the sling. The strap had been digging into my neck while I'd slept, and I was stiff and sore in places I didn't even know existed. "Apparently, falling isn't the best idea for an old lady like me." Despite my best efforts,

I'd let the doctor's callous comments about my age get under my skin.

I shuffled to the kitchen to start a pot of coffee. Setting the glass coffee carafe inside the white cast-iron sink, I turned the water on and held the pot under the stream of water to fill it. Even though my left wrist was injured, and I was right-handed, it surprised me how only having one working arm complicated the simplest of tasks. As the carafe filled, my right wrist wobbled without my left hand to balance the weight. Shakily, I tried to set the pot back in the sink so I could turn off the water, but my wrist wobbled again and smashed the carafe against the side of the sink. The thin glass shattered into a thousand pieces. With more force than necessary, I threw the black plastic handle I still held back into the sink on top of all the shards of broken glass.

"Son of a biscuit eater!"

I sagged against the counter, lamenting my bad luck, when the kitchen door swung open and April hurried through. As soon as I saw her worried face, I burst into tears.

"Mama, what's wrong?" April asked, concern showing on her face. "I thought I heard breaking glass from outside."

Normally I'm not a crier, so I was sure my emotions were catching her off guard.

"You heard right." I sniffed, swiped at another tear threatening to spill down my face, and pointed to the mess in the sink. "And everything is wrong. I fell over a dead body, broke my wrist, and can't even manage to make a pot of coffee without creating another disaster." My chin wobbled. "And, that dumb doctor said I'm old," I howled.

"The guy needs to learn some manners," April said.

I noticed right away she didn't dispute his claim, however.

April surveyed the shattered glass in the sink. "Yesterday was pretty stressful, wasn't it?" She sounded like she was trying to placate a toddler.

Indulging in my little pity party, I slouched over to the breakfast table and collapsed bonelessly onto the bench. "To say the least."

"Tell you what, Mom. Why don't you go get comfortable and relax, read a book or something, while I clean this mess up and make a coffee run. I'll whip up some breakfast when I get back. Sound good?"

"Perfect. April to the rescue, once again."

"We also need to do something about those wonky glasses of yours. Don't you have a backup pair somewhere in case of emergency?"

Sighing, I turned to head toward my bedroom. "Yeah, I do. They're just so stinking ugly, but I guess they'll do in a pinch." *Jeez. When did I get so whiny?*

"It's only until you can get these ones fixed." April took my shoulders and swiveled me around. "Go sit. I'll grab the glasses. Where are they?"

"In my nightstand drawer." Instead of arguing about how I could take care of myself, I swiveled around and shuffled my way right back to the recliner where I'd spent the night. I'd let my daughter coddle me for a minute, but after this short intermission I vowed to stop feeling sorry for myself.

Mayhem in Circulation by Leah Dobrinska lay on the side table where I'd left it after my last reading session. April came back and handed over the pair of backup glasses I'd had since the early 1980s. Thin, gold-toned metal frames sported large, square eye pieces. They made me resemble John Denver when I wore them. *But vintage is back in style, right?* Everything comes back around at some point. I replaced my wonky glasses with the aviator frames and cracked the spine of the book. Diving into the cozy mystery at chapter seven where I'd left off, I was soon lost in an entirely different world.

I was completely enjoying my fictional time in Larkspur, Wisconsin with Greta and her gang of library friends when April cleared her throat, causing me to startle and drop the book into my lap. My daughter stood in front of me, holding out a white paper coffee cup.

"Back already? I didn't even hear you leave." I fumbled with the book to find my place and inserted a bookmark, then reached for the warm and life-giving brew.

April chuckled. "Must be a good book."

"It is. I'll let you borrow it when I'm finished. But I want this one back."

"Good deal. Scrambled eggs and toast sound okay?"

"Sounds great. Whatever you want to make. Beggars can't be choosers."

April huffed. "If you'd rather have something else, all you have to do is say so."

"No, eggs and toast sound great. I didn't mean anything by that comment. Sheesh."

"Fine."

With her living close now and the two of us working out of the same space, it was inevitable for April to get fed up with me once in a while. The road went both ways; she got on my last nerve from time to time as well. I was lucky to have my daughter living in Pine Bluff, and equally thankful we weren't roommates. April went to the kitchen and I dove back into my murder mystery.

Ten minutes later, I had another chapter under my belt and breakfast was on the table. I sat down and made a show of breathing in the delicious scents and gushing over the first bite. "You're a master in the kitchen." She'd added diced green chilis to the scrambled eggs and my praise wasn't unfounded.

"Knock it off." April grinned. "Now that you've got some caffeine and food in your belly, how're you feeling today?"

I closed my eyes and tilted my head back, searching for the answer. After a moment, I replied, "Kind of like I've been run over by a bus. Every single muscle aches, but I guess I did hit the ground pretty hard. The doctor was right when he said it was lucky I wasn't hurt worse, however I still didn't appreciate his cracks about my age. Pretty darn rude, if you ask me."

April raised her eyebrows. "Welp, whatchya gonna do?" Wisely, she changed the subject. "How long did he say you'd be in a cast?"

"Anywhere from six to twelve weeks. I'll make an appointment with Dr. Coates for about two weeks from now and see how it goes from there. In the meantime, I'll figure out how to function one-handed." I sighed. "Good thing I got in a case of replacement coffee carafes for the new kitchen nook in Carpenter's Corner the other day."

Recently I'd looked around the dusty hardware store and realized I'd gotten complacent and hadn't changed anything in years. I'd thrown a clearance sale, getting rid of outdated items that had been on the shelves before dinosaurs went extinct. I chucked out shiny gold faucets, fluorescent light fixtures, dark paneling, and had even unearthed four rolls of vibrant orange and avocado green wallpaper that had to have been around since the seventies. What didn't sell during the clearance sale, I'd donated to charity. Next, I gave all the walls a fresh coat of creamy white paint, brought in some new shelving and created my kitchen nook. Carpenter's Corner now carried everything from the latest must-have kitchen gadget to cute towels and sponges.

"True story." April laughed. "Not to bring up a sore subject, but this whole thing is one more reason why you need to think about finding a smaller house."

My blood pressure immediately rose about a thousand percent. The look I sent my daughter was hot enough to set her red hair on fire. "Don't you dare say another word."

She took my advice.

After a deathly quiet finish to our breakfast, April broached the subject of the Timber Festival. "What do you think about today? Are you going to be up to watching the lumberjack contest? It starts in a little over an hour."

"You bet I'm going. It'd be easy to curl up on the couch to rest and recuperate all day, but I don't want to miss out on the festivities. Maybe there'll be news about Nate's murder."

"Good deal. I think we should bring lawn chairs and a thick blanket for you. You'd be more comfortable than sitting on those hard bleachers."

"Great idea."

"I usually have them," April replied with a wink.

As long as the subject of selling my beloved house didn't come up again, we'd called a truce.

Chapter Ten

Unlike the day before, the sky was back to the brilliant blue of early October. Puffy white cumulus clouds floated lazily through the sky as if they were kites dancing in a soft breeze. The oak trees in the park stretched their branches high, their rusty orange leaves a stark contrast against the azure sky. Between the beautiful day and the morbid curiosity about the previous day's murder, the crowd of spectators for the lumberjack contest was larger than normal. The bleachers were filling up fast. April set up our chairs close to the arena, but with so many people milling around about the only thing we could see from our ground level vantage point were the rear ends of people walking back and forth in front of us.

"This isn't going to work. We need to find a place in the bleachers," I said after the umpteenth group of people stopped directly in front of us.

"Agreed," April answered. "Why don't you head up and score us seats while I stow our chairs under the bleachers."

Shielding my eyes from the bright sun, I spotted a couple of empty seats about three-quarters of the way up the stands. The dazzling sunlight made me miss the transitional lenses on my broken glasses. I wished I'd thought of bringing a pair of clip-on sunglasses. *Nothing I can do about it now.*

Mapping out a path, I headed up the bleachers, apologizing left and right as I stepped between, and occasionally on, people already seated. As I slowly worked my way toward the empty seats, I noticed Scotty's beaming face shining from Axe Kicker buttons pinned to the shirts and jackets of a good portion of the spectators. I was about halfway up the bleachers when someone grabbed me by the elbow. I teetered backward but somehow managed to keep my balance. Glancing behind me, I found April gripping my elbow in an attempt to keep me steady. Her efforts had the opposite effect. Irritated, I swatted at her hand.

"Mom, I'm only trying to help. We don't need you falling again."

"I know you're trying to help, but it's not working. You're going to *make* me fall," I groused. "I'm not an invalid, for crying out loud. It's only a broken wrist." I stopped and took a breath, knowing I was acting unreasonably grumpy but not able to stop myself from sniping.

Once we'd made it to the empty seats and squeezed in, I turned to April. "Sorry I snapped at you, but I hate feeling helpless."

"Oh, I'm well aware." April took her own deep breath and faced forward, her green eyes scanning the arena. "You're right about one thing, though."

"Only one thing? Do tell."

She held up one finger. "It is way easier to see from up here."

Before I could answer, Chad stepped up to the microphone and began to announce the schedule of the day's events. Red and black buffalo checkered flannel-clad lumberjacks and lumberjills lined up behind the master of ceremonies, who wore a matching shirt.

"As most of you are aware, yesterday we tragically lost one of our top contestants, Nate Durand." Chad's deep voice broke. He paused a moment before continuing. "Our hearts are heavy today, but after much debate the contestants have chosen to continue with the Pine Bluff Logging Competition. We believe it's what Nate would have wanted. The axe throwing portion of the competition will be our First Annual Nate Durand Memorial Throw. With the help of our generous donors, the winner in both the men's and the women's divisions this weekend will walk away with a cash prize of five thousand dollars, as well as advance to the state competition. The first event of the day will be timed axe throwing. But before we get underway, we'd like to take a moment of silence to honor and remember Nate."

With a sweep of his hand, Chad indicated the contestants behind him. Each stood with feet planted wide, arms extended long and clasped at the wrist, and heads lowered in respect for Nate. All except Matt. He had the same wide stance, but his arms were crossed against his thin chest, and his head was up, a big grin splitting his face. Whispers and pointing fingers from the spectators around us indicated I wasn't the only one who'd noticed Matt's inappropriate demeanor.

Chad once again spoke. "A moment of silence please."

The whispers from the crowd died down.

Three minutes passed before the first strains of "America the Beautiful" spilled out of the loudspeakers.

April leaned over and whispered in my ear. "From where I'm sitting, it sure looks like Matt doesn't give a rat's patootie about Nate being killed."

I acknowledged her statement with a nod.

Once the song finished, Chad made one more announcement. "Because of Nate's death, there's been a change to the roster. Matt Forester was the first runner up after the time trials, so he will be the lumberjack stepping up to fill the gaping hole Nate has left behind." Chad turned to Matt. "Good luck, man. You have big shoes to fill."

April nodded. "Oh, okay. Maybe Matt's so happy to be competing he can't keep the grin off his face."

I scowled. "Maybe, but no matter his reason, it's still wildly inappropriate."

"Agreed, but I'm not sure Matt's ever been known for showing the best judgement."

"True." I chewed on my lower lip. "You went to school with him. Do you think he's capable of murder? The chance to win five-thousand dollars doesn't seem like a large enough amount of money to be a significant motive, does it?"

April squinted as she stared at the logger. "I mean...not for most people, unless they were desperate. It might feel like a windfall to Matt. Are you thinking he may have killed Nate to get a spot in the lumberjack contest?"

I shrugged. "It's a possibility. I wonder what the jackpot is for the state competition?"

"Not sure," April said, "but the state champions will qualify to compete at the world championships, and I've heard the prize package is upward of fifty thousand."

"Good night, that's a bucketload of money. But obviously, he would have to win this competition first, then the state contest to even qualify for world, so the money isn't a given."

"No, not by any stretch of the imagination," April replied.

"Where are the world championships held? Norway or Sweden?"

April laughed. "Wisconsin."

The competition area was marked off with temporary orange webbed fencing to keep the spectators out and safe. As the various events took place, we'd most likely have to move around the park in order to watch everything. Timed axe throwing was the first event, and four large log rounds were set up behind the podium. Our seats in the bleachers were ideal.

Red, white, and blue targets had been painted on each of the log rounds. In the timed axe throwing, the lumberjacks and jills would throw one at a time. The contestant would throw an axe at each of the four targets in a total time of one minute or less.

"Scotty Trimmer is last year's reigning Bull of the Woods," Chad announced, "and will be the first thrower in the timed event. Scotty, set up your axes."

Scotty placed an axe at the throw line of each target, then stationed himself in front of the first one, scraping his feet in the sawdust as he looked for the perfect stance.

A man wearing a red and black checkered shirt similar to the lumberjacks paced back and forth in front of the retaining fence while Scotty was setting up his axes. The guy was heavy-set, wore a black ball cap, and was shaking a power fist in the air. "You got this, Scotty. Focus. Focus. Don't let them get in your head," he yelled.

I pointed the guy out to April. "It looks like Scotty has himself a coach, whether he wanted one or not."

Chad raised a hand over his head, dropping it at the same moment he blew a whistle to signal the start of the round. Scotty reached for the first axe, eyeballed the target, brought the axe up over his head, and let it fly. It hit the bullseye with a hollow thunk, but as the crowd started to whoop it fell to the ground. Without a second's hesitation, Scotty raced to the second target and tried again. This time, the axe sunk deep into the target, the handle reverberating with the stopped motion as it dangled in the air. Target three and a stuck axe, but too low to be a bullseye. Scotty's final throw yielded up a hit a hairsbreadth to the left of the bullseye. The crowd whooped and hollered.

"Scotty Trimmer, twelve points," announced Chad.

Scotty's unofficial coach clapped and yelled along with the rest of us. When the guy turned away from the competition, I recognized him as Zach Moyer, a local public accountant. The ball cap he wore matched the swag button I'd found earlier with

Scotty's shining face front and center. Zach had several of the Axe Kicker buttons pinned to his flannel shirt. From the looks of things, he was Scotty's biggest fan, and that was saying a lot here in Pine Bluff.

"Not the best throwing I've ever seen Scotty do, but I'm not surprised he's a little off his game," I said to April. Not being able to clap using my broken wrist, I put two fingers in my mouth and let out a loud wolf whistle. The man next to me stuck his finger in his ear, blinking and shaking his head. "Sorry," I said with a grimace, embarrassed to not have considered the people around me before letting the whistle fly.

He smiled. "No worries, but you could warn a guy next time."

"I promise to keep my whistles to a minimum from here on out."

At the podium, Chad announced the next lumberjack. "Up next, Harris O'Neill."

When a bespectacled lumberjack stepped up to place his axes in front of the targets, I elbowed April and pointed at him with my chin. "That's the guy I found under the bush yesterday morning."

"The guy you thought was dead?"

"Yep. One and the same."

Other than a large scratch down Harris' cheek, he appeared to be in better condition than he had the day before when Officer Everett had pulled him out from underneath the scratchy bush.

Harris' round was over before I could blink, and the next contestant stepped up. The timed axe throwing was a fast-paced and exciting event with each contestant racing to sink their axe and move on to the next target in record time. Each time I glanced at Zach, who'd moved off to the side of the bleachers once Scotty's round was over, he was standing with arms crossed over his chest and a scowl on his face as the competition progressed. Once all sixteen contestants had thrown, Chad announced the winners of both the men's and women's divisions.

"Harris O'Neill, a newcomer to the scene, takes the men's timed axe throwing with an impressive total of twenty-one points." Chad paused to let the crowd clap. "Not to be outdone, Shayna Granberg couldn't be beat. She threw four bullseyes for a grand total of a perfect twenty-four points."

The crowd erupted in cheers. All except Zach, who booed and hissed in true bad loser fashion. I motioned to the man sitting next to me to let him know I was about to let loose with another wolf whistle. He nodded and covered his ears with the palms of his hands. "Go ahead."

I did.

April thumbed on her cell phone. "Thor's been alone now for a couple of hours. I'm going to run home and take him for a walk by the river before I come back to watch more of the competition. Do you want to come along?"

"Tempting, but I think I'll stay put. The distance throwing starts in fifteen minutes and I don't want to miss it."

Chapter Eleven

By the time I spotted April coming back with the giant black dog by her side, the distance throw had wrapped up with both Harris and Shayna maintaining the top slots in their divisions. The Jack and Jill crosscut saw event had gotten underway, so I'd moved off the bleachers and stood with the other spectators watching the competitors race to saw off the ends of logs in record time. April and Thor joined me as the second Jack and Jill team got started.

Four teams screamed through their cuts before Shayna and Matt were up. Within seconds it became clear the two of them didn't work together well. The crosscut saw was a two-person tool that took a smooth push and pull between the team members to utilize the strength of each person. If the team's speed and rhythm was off, the long saw blade would bend and the teeth would snag on the wood. On Matt's pull, I noticed how he angled the saw down so instead of pulling it back at shoulder-height, it came back closer to his waist, making it nearly impossible for Shayna to pull the blade back through the log. When Matt tried to push it back, his end of the saw jumped out of the ditch they'd managed to create.

"Pull. Pull," Matt yelled at Shayna, as if it were her fault their timing was off.

The whole thing was almost painful to watch. When the end of their log finally fell to the ground and the stopwatch clicked, Matt and Shayna's time was triple the time of any other team who'd already taken their turn. Matt threw his hardhat and safety glasses onto the ground and stalked off in a huff. Shayna glared daggers at his retreating back.

I turned to April. "On that note, I'm ready for a mid-morning snack. What say you?"

"I say yes. Snack is my love language, in case you've forgotten."

"How could I forget? You inherited that particular trait from me." I chuckled and looked at my daughter fully for the first time since she and Thor had gotten back to the park. Her faded blue jeans were soaking wet up to the knees and her black converse sneakers were covered in mud. "What happened to you? Did you fall in the river?"

April gestured to the dog, who grinned at me with his tongue hanging out. "Thor happened to me. I didn't so much fall in as get dragged in." She sent Thor a playful glare. "At least I managed to stay on my feet. Thank goodness the river's still low."

The Elk River ran around the edge of town and bordered Steam Engine Park on the far side. Since our normal heavy fall rains hadn't started yet, the water level was still low from the hot, dry summer our region had experienced.

With my good hand, I rubbed Thor's head and crooned to him. "You're a menace, aren't you boy? Yes, you are." The big dog smiled and whacked me with his tail.

Once April and I had steaming lattes and matching slices of bourbon pecan pie topped with mounds of whipped cream, we settled at the end of a picnic table lit by golden rays of sun angling through the trees. A cluster of orange and red leaves danced in the light breeze, with one landing between us on the table.

I picked up the leaf by the stem and twirled it between my fingers. "Which part of the river did you and Thor go to for your walk?" I asked.

She pointed over her shoulder in the general direction of the river. "The trail from the park. I figured it was the easiest way since I was coming back here anyway. Too bad I didn't know I'd need a change of clothes." She playfully frowned at Thor.

"Wouldn't hurt to carry extra clothes with you. You never know what's going to happen with this big lug around," I said. "Why'd he take off? Was he after a duck or something?"

"No, there was somebody messing around up on the bend of the river. The guy threw something in the river. It made a big splash, then he turned and left. I figured he was throwing rocks, but when Thor and I got to the spot where he'd been, the big dummy charged into the water and the rest is history." April pulled a tool out of her jacket pocket, depositing it on the table between us.

I frowned. "Why do you have a pipe cutter in your pocket?"

"It's what Thor went into the river after, and what I assume the guy threw into the water. I think it's a bit odd to toss away a perfectly good tool, don't you? There doesn't seem to be anything wrong with it."

"Indeed." I took a bite of pie while I stared at the pipe cutter. "The only reason I can think of is someone was trying to get rid of it. But why throw a pipe cutter in the river? Could it have something to do with Nate's death? You don't know who the guy was, do you?"

April shook her head. "He was too far away to be sure, but it had to be one of the lumberjacks."

"Why do you think that?"

"He was wearing one of the buffalo check shirts."

Those shirts kept coming up. They were everywhere. I sighed. "Which doesn't narrow it down much. Even Zach had one on today, in solidarity with his hero."

"True, and honestly I don't see how the pipe cutters could be connected anyway. We all know Nate was killed with his own axe. What does one thing have to do with the other?"

I pressed a hand to my quivering belly. "I don't know, but my gut tells me they're connected somehow."

"You might be right. I'll mention it to J.T. next time I see him," April replied. She took a bite of her pie and changed the subject. "Tell me how the distance throw went. Who won?"

I filled her in on the event she'd missed while she'd been out walking Thor. When I was finished, April frowned. "Shayna won both of the axe throwing events, huh? She's got quite an incredible arm on her, doesn't she?" April tapped her chin with her fork, absently leaving a smudge of whipped cream.

I leaned across the table and wiped my daughter's face with a napkin. "What are you thinking?"

"Well, Shayna and Nate were a couple. Tradition dictates the spouse is almost always a person of interest in any murder investigation. As far as I know, there wasn't any trouble between the two of them, but Shayna certainly demonstrated she has the skill to have been able to throw an axe with deadly force. And she would've had plenty of access to Nate's axe."

I shoved my John Denver glasses up higher on the bridge of my nose and leaned in. "You're right, but I think I forgot to tell you what I learned from Darlene yesterday afternoon."

April eyed me. "From Darlene? Nope. You didn't mention anything. What did the Wicked Witch of the West have to say?"

I opened my mouth to speak, but a tractor pulling a long line of barrel cars painted like Babe the Big Blue Ox beeped its horn behind me and wove its way around the picnic tables where we sat. The tractor was a small green John Deere, not much bigger than a riding lawnmower. The adorable attached cars were made from metal barrels placed on their sides with a cut out for a seat. Axels and tires were affixed to each barrel, and they were all hooked together like a passenger train. Most of the riders in the cars were children, but a few adults were squeezed into cars, their knees nearly folded up to their ears and young children perched happily on their laps. The passengers hooted and hollered as they drove by. The Blue Ox Train was a

Pine Bluff Timber Festival staple all the kids in the area looked forward to with glee. The ticket cost for a train ride was one dollar, and the route wove all around and through Steam Engine Park. If enthusiasm for the ride was the same as when my own kids were young a gazillion years ago, the line to ride the Blue Ox Train would be long the entire day. April and I waved and grinned at the riders as they passed.

Once the chaos had moved on, April focused her green eyes on me. "Spill it. What did Darlene tell you?"

"She said Shayna's best friend, Katelynn something-or-other, told her Shayna and Nate broke up a few days ago."

April's eyes widened. "What? Seriously? They seemed like the perfect couple. I never would've guessed they'd split up. Did she say what happened?"

"Only that Shayna was the one who broke up with Nate because she thought he was cheating on her."

"No way!"

"Yes way. And from what Darlene said, the breakup happened so recently, Shayna hasn't even moved out of the house yet." I took a sip of my coffee. "Interesting, don't you think? When Shayna was advocating to keep the logging competition going, she didn't say a thing about her and Nate not being together. She did mention he spent so much time practicing, it'd caused a few arguments between them."

April squinched up her face. "When Shayna was advocating to keep the competition going? How did you hear that? Don't tell me you eavesdropped on their meeting."

I smiled slightly and shrugged. "Fine. I won't tell you."

"Mother!"

"What can I say? If you want to learn something, you have to take advantage when the opportunity presents itself. They met in one of the picnic shelters and this park is a public place the last time I checked."

"True, but I don't have to remind you how people who go looking for trouble almost always tend to find it."

"I've stared trouble in the eye more than once in my lifetime. Where do you think I got all this gray hair?"

"From me. Isn't that what you've always told me? And since when is your hair gray? You've been pretty darn adamant the color is silver."

"It's gray when it suits my narrative." I fluffed my silver hair with my good hand. "Do you know this Katelynn woman? I wouldn't mind having a conversation with her."

April closed her eyes and sighed. "Here we go again." But when she popped her eyes back open, there was an adventurous sparkle in them. "No, I don't know Katelynn except by sight. Her last name is Norris. She's one of the lumberjill contestants, though. It shouldn't be too hard to catch her for a quick chat when she's between events."

I leaned across the table again. "Here's the thing that's been bugging me about Katelynn. Right after I found Nate's body, Shayna ran over and was a sobbing mess. I was trying to soothe her but then Katelynn came and took over."

"So what?" April replied. "They're best friends. It makes perfect sense to me."

I paused to remember those few minutes. "Except all the other contestants were gathered in a group behind us."

"I'm hearing a but."

"Exactly. All of them *but* Katelynn. She came out from behind the log stack before she jogged over to where Shayna and I were standing."

April lowered her voice. "The same log stack someone disappeared behind seconds before you tripped over Nate's feet?"

I nodded emphatically. "The only log stack in the park. And that's what has been troubling me. Why was Katelynn behind the stack and not gathered with the other contestants?"

"I'm assuming she was dressed in the red-and-black buffalo check flannel, right?"

"Yep. They all were." My pie was gone. I was ready to get back and start snooping. "Are you done?" I nodded at April's paper plate, which still held a bite or two of pie.

She shielded her plate from me. "Back off, lady." One last large forkful and the pie was gone. "Come on, let's get back over there. I think the pole climb should be coming up and I love watching them scramble up the pole. It looks like so much fun."

Back at the competition arena, Chad was announcing the winners of the chainsaw run. In that event, the log was placed in a brace on a fairly steep incline. The lumberjacks had to run up the log carrying a chainsaw. Once at the top, they would fire up the saw and slice off a log disc, shut off the saw, turn around, and run back down the log. The fastest lumberjack to complete the task without falling off the log was the winner. Matt had taken top honors in the men's division and Katelynn had won the women's portion. Chad announced a twenty-minute break before the pole climbing event was scheduled to start.

"Scotty hasn't won a single event yet," April noted.

"Yeah, he's completely off his game. Not surprising, considering his best friend was murdered yesterday."

I glanced around at the crowd. Zach paced up and down in front of the orange fencing around the logging competition area. With each announcement of the winners in various events, the accountant's pacing had increased and his scowl had deepened into furrows between his eyes. "Scotty!" he yelled. "Get your head in the game, man. What're you doing? We need to win!"

We need to win? What in the world did Zach have to do with Scotty winning? Sure, Scotty was the Pine Bluff favorite and we'd all like to see him win, but Zach was taking his overzealous fan role a bit too far.

A compelling need to say something took over, and since I'm not known for holding my tongue, I marched up to Zach. "What's wrong with you? Give Scotty a break. Don't you know the man's grieving. Show some respect."

Zach's glare almost made me back off. "He'll have plenty of time to grieve when this competition is over," he spit out, pointing to a banner hanging on the temporary fence. The name of his business, Moyer Accounting Solutions, was printed in large black block letters against a white background. "I'm the biggest sponsor of this competition and my lumberjack better win or this lousy logging show won't be getting another dime from me."

My irritation at his attitude clicked up a notch. Or seven. "*Your* lumberjack? I wasn't aware you owned Scotty."

"Yes, mine. I sponsored him. Bought new gear for the guy and wasted money on this crap." He angrily tapped one of the Axe Kicker buttons pinned to his shirt then ripped off his matching ball cap and stomped it into the dirt. "His pathetic attitude is messing with my reputation. Scotty should be glad Nate's gone. Now he doesn't have to worry about the guy taking his title. But no, instead he's acting like some kind of sad sack and letting the new guy win." Zach gestured violently toward Harris.

I gasped. It was fairly unusual for me to not have anything to say, but Zach's tirade left me speechless. Had he killed Nate to remove him from the competition? Remembering the swag button I'd found near Nate's body, I changed tactics. "Do you know where a person could get one of Scotty's Axe Kicker buttons?"

Zach scowled at me. "Like I said, I ordered these specifically and handed them out to my clients. I don't recall you ever setting foot inside Moyer Accounting Solutions, so you don't meet the requirements to receive one. What do you think, I'm going to give them away for free? Not likely."

Well, then. I guess he told me. Too bad for Zach I wasn't easily offended. "Do you mind my asking how many of them you had made up?"

"Not sure why it's any of your business, but two hundred. It was the minimum order, and I have a tremendous number of clients, so only my top account holders were lucky enough to receive one." Zach glared Scotty's way. "With Scotty's showing so far, lucky isn't the word I'd use at this point. The idiot is making a fool out of me." Zach clenched his fists and kicked at the orange webbed fencing.

I hated to be the one to let him in on the secret that it wasn't Scotty who was making a fool out of him.

If two hundred people were wearing Scotty's face on Axe Kicker buttons, which one of them lost their button on the ground near the murder scene? Even more Axe Kicker buttons were floating around the Timber Festival than buffalo plaid shirts. I stepped aside and studied the angry accountant. It was beginning to feel more feasible that Zach may have killed Nate to rid the lumberjack competition of Scotty's biggest competition in an attempt to save his own reputation. I didn't think for a second Scotty winning or losing reflected on Zach and his accounting company in the slightest, but apparently Zach thought so. What if, by sponsoring Scotty, Zach was owed a portion of his winnings, all the way up through the world championships? Could money be the reason Zach was so focused on needing Scotty to win our local logging show? His attitude added another person to my growing list of suspects.

Along with every single person who'd been handed an Axe Kicker button.

Chapter Twelve

For the pole climbing competition, two forty-foot poles were set up, side by side. Contestants carried a handsaw in a sling on their backs, wore spiked shoes, and had a loose rope tied around their waist and the pole. They used the rope to assist themselves in scrambling up the pole as fast as they could go. At the top, the contestant would saw off a disc from the top of the pole, then do a combination of a slide and a scramble back down to the bottom. The Jack and Jill with the fastest times would take top honors in the event. It harkened back to a time when woodsmen would need to climb trees to take off limbs and lop off the top of the tree before they fell it. It wasn't a practice used in the woods much anymore, but pole climbing sure made for an exciting sporting event.

The women were up first. One lumberjill took up her position at the bottom of each pole. When the whistle blew, they scrambled neck and neck to the top. When the first two women were finished, the next two took their turns. Shayna's friend, Katelynn, had been one of the first to go, and had won her round. April and I watched as Katelynn threw off her gear and strode out of the arena.

I nudged April. "We should follow her. Might be as good a time as any to find out what she knows about Shayna and Nate's alleged breakup and get a feel for if she might've been the one who killed him."

April made a disgusted sound in her throat. "Dang it. This is my favorite event. I really wanted to watch."

"Suit yourself. I'm pretty sure I can handle having a conversation by myself."

April's expression told me she was torn between going with me and watching the rest of the pole climbing. "But if Katelynn killed Nate, the conversation could get dangerous real quick."

"Not with all these people around. Seriously, you stay here. Watch the climbing and keep your eye out for anything else suspicious. I'll be fine and will be back in two shakes."

"Are you sure?"

"Yep. If I'm not back in five minutes, ten at the most, come looking for me." If I didn't hurry up, I was going to miss my chance.

My daughter had already turned back to the competition before I was done speaking. I caught a glimpse of Katelynn's blonde French braid bobbing along above her red-and-black buffalo plaid shirt and jogged to catch up with her. She disappeared into the women's side of the public restroom, so I ducked in after her. Hovering near the sinks, I waited until I heard the toilet flush, then turned on the faucet and awkwardly began to wash my hand that wasn't strapped to my chest in the sling. When Katelynn stepped up beside me to wash her own hands, I glanced at her, feigning surprise.

"Katelynn, is it?" I asked, as I pulled a paper towel from the dispenser. At her nod, I continued. "I just watched your pole climb. You make it look so easy. I hope your first place status holds. You deserve it."

"Thank you." Katelynn's cheeks blushed pink. "I appreciate your kind words. It's a lot of fun, but climbing those poles takes a ton of training and core strength."

"I bet it does. I can tell you work hard at conditioning for competition." I finished drying my hands, or rather, hand. "You're Shayna's friend, aren't you? I'm not sure if you remember me, but I was the one who found Nate."

Katelynn nodded. "Yes, of course I remember you. Thank you for helping Shayna until I could get there." She pushed a wayward strand of long blonde hair out of her face.

I waved away her appreciation. "It was the least I could do. How is the poor woman holding up? It's got to be hard. Such a horrible thing to have happened. I feel awful for her."

"Shayna's doing surprisingly well," Katelynn replied. "The logging competition has given her something to focus on besides Nate's murder. I'm sure when it's over, it'll hit her harder and she'll need all the support she can get. Shayna's a strong woman, though, both mentally and physically. In the long run, I'm sure she'll be fine."

Katelynn's word choice, "it's over," reminded me how Shayna had said the same thing when she'd been sobbing on her friend's shoulder. Two entirely different scenarios but it made me wonder what Shayna had meant. Could the two of them have been in on Nate's murder together and Shayna had meant the deed was done? I shook my head, sure I was reading too much into the innocent comment.

"She'll definitely need all the support and understanding she can get from her friends." I sucked on my bottom lip and shoved my glasses up my nose. My next question was going to sound heartless and rude, but I didn't know a gentler way to go about it, so plunged in. "I hate to ask you this, but there's a rumor going around that Shayna had recently broken up with Nate. Is it true?"

Katelynn's green eyes hardened. "Who's saying that? Shayna hasn't told anyone, and I only told....oh." Her narrow face settled into a straight line and she slapped her forehead with the palm of her hand as the perpetrator's identity dawned on her. "Stupid me. I should've known better to confide anything to Darlene. I swear the woman is a snake charmer, always getting me to say more than I intend to."

I chuckled. "You're not wrong there. You live over in Lost Canyon, don't you? How do you know Darlene?"

She exhaled. "Unfortunately, we worked together up at the lake for a couple of summers when we were teenagers. We were both lifeguards. It was the most gossipy and backbiting time of my life. Darlene loved to talk about the other lifeguards behind their backs. I'm sure she talked about me just as much when I wasn't around. That summer showed me exactly what kind of a person I didn't want to be, yet whenever I run into her I seem to fall right back into her old trap."

I raised my eyebrows. "Sounds like Darlene hasn't changed much with age. What do you do for work now?"

"Shift work at the mill."

"Here in Pine Bluff?"

"Yep. It's a bigger mill so the pay's better than I can get in Lost Canyon. It's worth the drive, at least for me." She shrugged.

"Glad they make it worth your time." I cleared my throat. "So, back to Shayna and Nate. Is it true then? They had split up?"

Katelynn studied the floor. "Yeah, just last week."

"May I ask why?" We were still alone in the restroom so I wasn't concerned about anyone overhearing our conversation.

"Shayna thinks...thought, Nate might be seeing someone else."

"What made her think he was cheating on her?"

"Because Nate works...worked, all the time and has hardly spent any time with her for a good six months or so. If he wasn't out working in the woods around here, he was off on his trips to log properties where he could get different hardwoods. Shayna says when he was at home, he spent all his time on the phone setting up more jobs, working in his sawmill, or outside practicing for the lumberjack competition. She said there was no time left over for her."

"Could Nate have simply been focused on making a go of his business and there wasn't another woman involved?"

Katelynn threw her hands in the air. "Thank you. That's exactly what I told Shayna, but she was adamant there had to be someone else. I honestly don't think so. Nate wasn't the type of guy to fool around. He adored Shayna and was always so sweet to her. There's no way he was cheating on her."

This girl is not a killer. It might not be the smartest move to completely check her off my suspect list, but it truly sounded like she had liked Nate and the way he had treated her best friend.

"But Shayna convinced herself he was, so she packed up and moved out," I said.

Katelynn shook her head. "She hadn't moved out yet. Like I said, the breakup happened only last week. Shayna can't afford to move out yet, so she moved into another bedroom until she can get the money together to find her own place. Nate didn't want her to go and told her to stay as long as she needed to."

"Where does she work?"

"At the coffee shop in Lost Canyon. She also kept the books for Nate's business. You know, paying the bills and invoicing customers. All the little stuff that needs done in a business. The plan, before they broke up, was for Shayna to transition full time to working for Nate once his sawmill was more profitable. She'd been taking accounting classes online."

"Sure. Having someone you can trust to take care of the paperwork is huge for a small business." I cocked my head and pushed up my glasses. "Do you know how the two of them met?"

"Yeah, at the state lumberjack finals a couple of years ago." Katelynn smiled, remembering. "You've met Shayna. She's one of those people who others are drawn to. Like moths to a flame. From the second they met, Nate couldn't take his eyes off her."

I nodded. "I can see why. There is something compelling about her. State finals, huh? Shayna's doing great today. The woman is skilled with an axe."

"She sure is. The year they met, she actually won the state competition and qualified for world, but her luck ran out when she tore her shoulder muscle in the first round of the world finals."

"Oh no." I sucked air through my teeth. "I've always heard how painful shoulder tears can be. And a fairly long recovery time, if I'm not mistaken. The poor girl. Her injury must've thrown a wrench into her plans."

Katelynn nodded. "Yeah, it took her out of commission for sure, but her budding romance with Nate took the sting out of her disappointment. Once she healed, she got right back into competition but she's never been able to achieve the level of success she'd had before the injury. Winning the Pine Bluff Logging Show would be huge for Shayna, especially now."

"True." I paused as another thought entered my mind. "I wonder what will happen to Nate's house and property now that he's gone. Maybe Shayna will be able to stay there. Do you know if she was on the deed?"

"I don't think she is. Nate inherited his property from his grandfather several years before he and Shayna ever met." Katelynn crossed her arms and narrowed her eyes. "Listen to me answering all of *your* probing questions. You're as bad as Darlene." She turned on her heel and with two long strides left me standing alone in the restroom.

Offended, I stared at myself in the scratched up acrylic mirror over the sink. *Me? As bad as Darlene? Bite your tongue, lady.* I huffed. How rude.

Chapter Thirteen

With the logging competition taking up the better part of the day, April and I treated ourselves to delicious barbeque plate lunches from The Chuck Wagon. The high lonesome sounds of a fiddle, a banjo, and a string bass from a bluegrass trio playing authentic mountain music in the bandstand provided the perfect musical accompaniment for our meal. When the lively strains of "Orange Blossom Special" rang across the park, I couldn't help but tap my feet to the music and sing along. Once our bellies were full, we took a quick cruise through the park and the vendor booths. Under a stand of Aspen trees vibrant with glowing yellow fall leaves, a local artist, Stacey Sannar, was leading a group in open air painting. From what I could see, the painter's canvases were filled with gorgeous nature scenes.

Our local independent bookstore, Literally, had set up a booth filled with both non-fiction and fiction reads featuring trees and nature. A sandwich board announced their next storytime was in five minutes. They would be reading *The Lorax* by Dr. Suess. One of the bookstore employees was decked out in a safety-orange T-shirt and leggings with a walrus mustache made of sunshine yellow yarn somehow tacked above her lips with matching fluffy eyebrows adhered to a pair of glasses. Kids and parents were arriving for storytime and clamoring excitedly for their own Lorax mustache and eyebrows. I kind of wanted a set, too.

Next to Literally's booth, the ecology department from the university in Greenwood had a booth with an eye-catching backdrop of a simple forest scene. A handful of flyers about the program lay on the table next to a small television set that was playing a video about the varying native trees in our forests. A group of people gathered around the professor of ecology, who was giving them an overview of what to expect on the nature hike into the foothills of the Blue Mountains they would be embarking on shortly. The group would be learning about native species of trees and plants growing on the forest floor, as well as learning about the wildlife that lived in our mountains. The hike sounded fascinating. I made a mental note to sign up for the excursion next year.

I stopped by Keifer's Carvings and whipped out my debit card to purchase one of the carved owls I'd been coveting the day before. For an extra ten bucks, Tommy promised to deliver it right to my front door after the market closed for the day. It sounded like a heck of a bargain to me. Without a second's hesitation, I handed over the ten spot and scribbled my address into a notebook below a small list of other buyers Tommy would be delivering carved creatures to.

As April and I walked away from the woodcarver's booth, she slid me the side-eye. "How wise do you think it was to give one of the murder suspects your address?"

My breath caught in my throat. "Whoopsie. The thought didn't even occur to me. You should've knocked the notebook out of my hands."

She shrugged. "I figured you were a grownup and knew what you were doing."

"Well, apparently I didn't." My lunch turned a cartwheel in my stomach. "It's not like he needs to come into the house for anything. I'm sure it'll be fine."

"If you say so." April glanced at me as we walked side-by-side. "Do you want me to make sure I'm at the house with you when he delivers it?"

By her grimace, I was astute enough to figure out my dear daughter had other plans on her agenda not involving babysitting her mother. Did she and our handsome Chief of Police have another secret rendezvous planned?

I appreciated her concern, but didn't want to thwart her love life, so waved her off. "Nah. I'll be fine. I'm honestly not worried."

"Suit yourself," April replied, though her voice showed a hint of relief.

Before we left the rows of vendor booths, I veered off when I spotted a mannequin dressed like a lumberjack. A few years back, someone had donated the mannequin to the Pine Bluff Historical Museum. They'd dressed him up, named him Joe, and adopted him as their mascot to showcase our town's long logging history. Whenever Joe made a public appearance, folks lined up to take pictures with the stone-faced lumberjack. Joe wore the outfit of a bygone era—denim shirt, jeans, black suspenders, heavy black boots, and a flat-brimmed hat.

April nodded her head toward the arena where the lumberjack events were held. "I'm going to go find us a spot while you look. Take your time."

I entered the booth and was immediately greeted by Suzi Terrell, the vivacious president of the museum. "Hi, Dawna. It's great to see you. Thanks for stopping in."

"Wouldn't miss it," I told her. "It's always a highlight every year to see what new display you come up with for the Timber Festival."

"This year we decided to focus on the history of lumberjack competitions and how the skills loggers used in the woods became a competitive sport." With a flourish, Suzi directed me to a glass case. "We've got some of the tools of the trade showcased here, vintage photos over there," she pointed to another display, "and then this fantastic article with all kinds of fun facts about the early days of logging in the Pacific Northwest. One of our members wrote it and his research is impressive. Of course, we had to leave the bigger, heavier items at the museum, but there's a great display you should stop by and check out when you get a chance. We'll have it up for the next two months."

"Sounds like you hatched an evil plan to get people into the museum."

Suzi laughed and flung out her hands. "Hey, whatever works. It gets lonely standing there by myself."

I chuckled. "I'll make sure to stop by."

"You know," Suzi added slyly, "with your interest in history and the fact that you're such a long-time resident of Pine Bluff, you'd make a great addition to the museum's membership. We're always needing more active volunteers." She winked.

Unbidden, a sigh escaped my mouth before I could bite it back. It wasn't the first time Suzi had tried to recruit me for the history museum. "I know, I know. But between the store, family, and my volunteer work with the Women's Service Club, I'm feeling worn a little thin." It wasn't necessarily a lie, but I noticed how much sheer time and effort Suzi put into the museum and I didn't want to commit to something so time consuming. I was protective of my down time. If I volunteered every spare minute, when would I get to read those stacks of books I'd been accumulating for years?

"Shucks." Suzi snapped her fingers in a one-that-got-away motion. "Well, you can't blame a girl for trying, can you?"

"Absolutely not. I wouldn't expect any less."

She sent me a wry smile and turned to a young couple who had entered the museum booth, leaving me free to enjoy the display.

One of the vintage sepia photos showed the image of a massive tree with a crosscut saw that looked as if it must be a mile long. Three loggers stood at each end of the saw as they took a break from falling the giant tree to pose for the camera. Another had two loggers laying head-to-head inside the enormous notch they'd cut out of a tree. Inside the glass case were various rusty tools—a peavey, axe heads, shoe spikes, hooks, clamps, and a few items I didn't recognize. I moved to the end of the case and skimmed through the article.

"It sounds like lumberjack contests came about because loggers lived in remote camps and were bored out of their minds," I said to Suzi while the young couple browsed the photographs on display.

Suzi nodded. "You got that right, for the most part. They needed something to occupy themselves during their time off. They had to have sharp skills to survive in those woods, so what better way to show off those skills then to create games out of them?"

"I had no idea there was a Lumberjack Sports Association clear back in 1905."

"Fascinating, isn't it?"

"Absolutely. I better go catch up with my daughter but I'll stop into the museum to see the rest of the display one of these days soon."

"Great. We'll be waiting for you."

April had dug our lawn chairs out from under the bleachers where she'd stashed them earlier and had set them up in an open spot with a good view of the events currently taking place. This time, we were far enough up a hill to see well without everyone walking in front of us. We watched both the underhand chop and the hot saw competitions before the restless sleep of the previous night caught up with me and I started to yawn. On top of not sleeping well, the heavy, carb-filled lunch I'd indulged in hadn't helped either. I slumped in my lawn chair, energy flagging and broken wrist throbbing.

"What time is it? I ate too much and now I'm ready for a nap."

April glanced at her cell phone. "Ten till three. Do you want me to run you home?"

"Ah, no wonder. The afternoon energy dive has hit hard." I stifled a yawn. "Would you mind? I might be able to sneak in a short nap before I need to be at the theater in a couple of hours."

Two and a half hours later, I was feeling refreshed from my nap, a late afternoon cup of coffee, and half a pain pill to take the edge off the pain in my wrist. It was time to get ready for the play. I changed into a pair of soft and stretchy dark brown corduroy leggings topped with a creamy handknit sweater. Rummaging through a basket filled with scarves in my closet, I found what I was looking for—an orange and brown tartan wool scarf.

After securing my injured arm back in the sling, I clumsily flung the scarf around my neck and draped it over my shoulders to disguise the ugly blue sling as best I could. I stepped back to evaluate myself in the full-length mirror on the back of my bedroom door.

"You'll do, young lady. You'll do."

My husband's signature scent—sawdust and coffee—swept through the room and a faint, low whistle echoed in my head. As soon as the whistle faded, a soft meow took its place.

I peered around the dim corners of the bedroom. "Bob? Is that you? If you're truly here, show yourself." Knowing I was alone in the house and there wasn't anyone else here to make those noises, I was convinced my husband and long departed cat were in the room with me.

The light in the bedroom shifted as a shadow crossed the doorway. The sensation of lips pressed to my forehead caused my skin to tingle, but the scent of sawdust and coffee whirled away as fast as it had arrived. A small white cat rubbed against my leg before she jumped up onto the bed. Lilac purred and kneaded the comforter as if it were bread dough. When she had the blanket arranged how she wanted it, she curled up to watch me through slanted lavender eyes.

I stared back at the cat but addressed my husband. "If Lilac can show herself, why can't you?"

Bob didn't answer but his scent poured fresh into my senses. I held my breath, expecting him to pop into the room in much the same fashion as the cat had done.

The sharp ring of the doorbell intruded, startling both me and any spirits who happened to be hanging around. In a heartbeat, the smell of sawdust and coffee dissipated, and Lilac disappeared from where she'd been lounging on my bed. Disappointed, I sighed and hurried through the living room as the doorbell chimed again. I opened the main door, stepped out onto the enclosed porch and pushed open the storm door. Tommy stood on the wide stone steps, his hand resting on the head of a gorgeous carved wooden owl.

"Owl delivery at your service, ma'am. Where would you like me to put her?"

I stepped outside, surveying the open portion of the front porch. "I'm thinking Harriet should go right there beside the door." I pointed to an open spot on the right.

"Harriet?"

"Yep, Harriet the Owl."

I'd chosen a carving with some color. Tommy had painted the three books at the base in various shades of blue. The owl had been stained a golden brown, then the entire carving had been sealed with a heavy polyurethane to withstand the Northeastern Oregon weather. My wide, covered stone porch provided extra protection and was the perfect spot to showcase my new wooden friend.

Tommy moved the carving to the place I'd indicated and stood back with a smile, studying his handiwork. "She looks good there, doesn't she?"

"Like she belongs." The carving gleamed against the red brick of the house.

After I thanked the talented woodcarver, Tommy bounced down the steps but turned back to me as he reached the bottom. "Hey, you and your daughter were in Timber Creek Saloon the other night, weren't you?"

I gulped and nodded. I'd thought Tommy had been too worked up to notice who had been watching his altercation with Nate. Apparently, I was wrong.

"You know, this whole timber rights ordeal has thrown me for a loop. I don't usually act like such a jerk in public, so I wanted to apologize for my bad behavior."

Not knowing how to respond, I simply went with, "No worries."

"I hope the busybodies of this town can keep their noses out of things. That business was strictly between me and Nate."

Is he calling me a busybody? Did Tommy mean his remark to stand as a warning for me to stop poking around? And if he had wanted the spat to remain private, then he sure shouldn't have made a public spectacle out of it. He had nobody to blame except himself.

He shot me a wry smile. "Sorry to bring ugly nonsense up, but I wanted to clear the air. Enjoy your owl."

Tommy jumped into the driver's seat of his pickup and Mandy and Storm both waved as the Keifer family drove away and left me standing on the porch with Harriet and my thoughts.

I prided myself on my intuition about people and, even with his busybody remark, I hadn't detected one tiny shred of danger radiating from Tommy. But at the same time, his comments needled at me. Did he usually keep his temper tantrums behind closed doors? If he'd found Nate alone, would he have unleashed his frustration on him without an audience watching? I still couldn't picture it, even after witnessing his meltdown in the saloon the other night. My gut feeling was the entire Keifer family were good people. Of course, it wasn't me bringing noisy trucks in to log the land they'd sunk their life savings into. Land and timber rights disputes could send emotions skyrocketing and cause otherwise nice people to commit acts they'd never otherwise consider themselves capable of executing. Tommy remained firmly on my list of suspects.

Chapter Fourteen

"Hi, Judy. Are we ready for tonight?" I stowed my purse in the ticket vestibule of the Emery Theater while greeting Judy Hassin, the treasurer of our Women's Service Club.

"You bet. It's about time someone breathed new life into this old theater." Judy's wild red curls, with a telltale stripe of gray down the center of her part, bounced as she thrummed with enthusiasm for the night's production. She patted an electronic gadget sitting next to the green metal box I'd be using as a cash register. "Do we need to go over the instructions for using the card reader?"

"Nope, I'm good. It's exactly like the one I use at Carpenter's Corner. No worries there." While we'd sold a fair amount of tickets to Paul Bunyan—A Tall Tale during our presale campaign, we still anticipated not everyone arriving to enjoy the play tonight would have purchased their tickets ahead of time. There were still plenty of seats available and I hoped to give the card reader a good workout before the night was over.

"Great. One less thing to worry about." She threw up jazz hands and whirled on her heel, dancing off to make sure all was well everywhere else in the theater. Tall, whisp thin, and ten years my senior, Judy's energy levels were a thing to be coveted. As a retired elementary school teacher, she must've absorbed the energy of the young kids she taught through her very pores. Her energy and enthusiasm had been the catalyst and driving force behind our entire group as we'd organized town members to help us get the Emery cleaned and repaired enough to allow the first production in twenty-five years to take place. Beyond a shadow of a doubt, the rest of us would've pooped out long before we'd made it this far without Judy to cheer us on.

I turned my attention to the ticket booth, excited to see every surface sparkling. During our cleanup efforts, the booth had been my pet project. It'd been a joy to apply my restoration skills to bring it back to the beauty it had been in its heyday when the Emery Theater had been built in the early 1920s. I'd stripped, sanded, and refinished the curved cherrywood counter until it gleamed. Using a brass polisher I carried in the hardware store, I then buffed and polished the green oxidation from the brass fixtures and accents until I thought my shoulders were going to fall off. New red velvet drapes harkened back to the original opulent style of the era. Not only had I applied every drop of elbow grease I'd possessed, but Carpenter's Corner Hardware had donated all the supplies to restore the ancient ticket booth, including the three dozen Edison-style light bulbs circling the top of the booth. We were ready for business, and I was proud of my contribution.

Richard Steinman, a wealthy mill owner, had the Emery built in an attempt to bring culture to the remote woods of Oregon. Even though the theater had been used for various city offices over the years and had been in disuse for some time, many of the original features remained. There was still a ton of work to be done, but our efforts had the surfaces sparkling and the feel of those early days permeated the air. It wouldn't have surprised me one bit to see women dressed in fur-trimmed coats and flapper dresses moving through the theater to find their seats in the auditorium.

"What do you think? Are we going to have fun tonight or what?" Evonne entered through the narrow door of the ticket booth, taking her place on the high stool next to the one I occupied. She quickly glanced at me and then did a double take. "Nice glasses." Her tongue was firmly planted in her cheek.

"Stuff it, lady."

Evonne cocked her head. "Actually, I kind of like them. I think aviators have come back around. You're styling."

"I wouldn't be surprised one bit." I chuckled. "Hold onto anything long enough, and you'll be on the cutting edge of fashion again. Not that I ever was," I added wryly.

"If that's the case, by the looks of my closet I'll be the next top model." Evonne glanced at her watch. "Ten minutes until we open the doors. The line is already getting long out there. And guess who is in line together looking like they're on a date?" Evonne leaned over and nudged me with her shoulder. She wore a soft white, flowing blouse with a navy blue, long cascading vest over a pair of fashionable light denim jeans. Evonne had finished her outfit with a simple strand of freshwater pearls and matching earrings.

"Beats me. Who?"

"Your lovely daughter and our esteemed, and mighty handsome, police chief." She winked. "Why didn't you tell me J. T. and April were finally going on a date? I was beginning to think it was never going to happen."

I narrowed my eyes. "Because April didn't tell me, the little sneak."

I'd grill my daughter later, but for now I grinned. April and J. T. had known each other pretty much their entire lives, and the huge crush April had on him when they were in high school was a thing of legends. I still wasn't sure if J. T. had ever realized how smitten April had been; he'd seemed oblivious way back then. Since she'd moved back to town I'd noticed sparks flying between the two of them on more than one occasion and had been hopeful they'd do something about it. Whenever I brought the subject up, which I did frequently, April denied the attraction vehemently, but the flaming cheeks accompanying her protests told an entirely different story.

I went over the card reader instructions with Evonne, then we both unlatched and attempted to slide open the covers on our ticket wells where theater goers would slide their tickets or payment to us via the small bronze troughs. The cover on Evonne's well opened easily, but mine jammed. I shoved it harder.

"What's the problem?" Evonne asked.

"Beats me." I tried again, but the cover refused to budge. "It worked fine last week when I finished the restoration."

Since I only had one hand to work with, Evonne took over. She prodded around the backside of the cover with her fingers. "Here's your problem."

An Axe Kicker button fell onto the counter, allowing the cover to slide effortlessly into place.

I frowned at Scotty's face smiling from the button. "How did that get there? Weird."

But theater goers descended on us and there was no time to dwell on the arrival of yet another Axe Kicker button. Our little town didn't provide many reasons to get dressed up, so even though Paul Bunyan wasn't a fancy production, it gave us all a chance to change out of our jeans and flannels to hobnob with Pine Bluff's finest. Evonne and I were equally as excited about seeing how well our neighbors cleaned up as we were about watching the play.

As soon as we started taking tickets, the crowd was buzzing with the news about Harris taking top honors in the men's division of the logging contest. The young lumberjack had been named this year's Bull of the Woods. Shayna had won the women's competition and the two of them would both be moving on to state. In the men's division, Matt placed second with Scotty coming in a distant third. Pine Bluffians were saddened our hometown champion had been dethroned, but I didn't sense any rancor in their comments, just mild disappointment for Scotty and deep sorrow for the loss of Nate.

Twenty minutes after the doors opened, the line had thinned out significantly. Just a few stragglers remained. My daughter and her date had managed to finagle their way to Evonne's window, effectively avoiding me so I wasn't able to ask questions and embarrass either one of them like I'd planned. The only thing I'd been able to manage was to shoot April a grin and a thumbs up. She'd blushed as red as a flaming autumn maple leaf, but had looked spectacular in an emerald green velvet dress on the arm of the tall and dapper police chief. J. T. wore a dark gray western-cut sportscoat over a black dress shirt and dark blue jeans. They made a gorgeous couple and I was tickled to death.

In a moment of quiet, I glanced around, my gaze stopping on the portrait of Richard Steinman hanging on the lobby wall near the concession stand. In the vintage black-and-white photograph, the Pine Bluff entrepreneur sported a walrus mustache and a slight smile. He wore a fashionable suit and top hat, and held an ivory-handled cane in the crook of his arm. As I studied the photograph, Richard's image tilted his chin ever so slightly and winked at me.

I blinked and rubbed my eyes. "What in the world? Those pain killers must be stronger than I thought," I muttered to myself.

"What's wrong? Is your wrist killing you?" Evonne asked.

Apparently, my muttering wasn't as quiet as I thought it'd been. "No, my wrist is doing all right, but it looked like Richard winked at me." A nervous edge tinkled in my self-deprecating laughter as I indicated the photograph across the lobby.

"Why wouldn't he? I imagine the illustrious Mr. Steinman is as delighted as we are to have the theater back in business, even if it's for one night only to begin with." Evonne chuckled, not giving any weight to my comment.

It was only a trick of the light, I told myself, yet it wasn't the first time I'd felt like the original theater owner's photograph had interacted with me. I'd mentioned to Evonne before how Richard's eyes seemed to follow me around the room. She'd disagreed, unable to see the same thing I did. I stared at the photograph a moment longer, but when there wasn't even the slightest hint of any further movement, I shrugged. Yep, just my imagination running wild. Again.

A few minutes before, Judy had pulled the doors to the auditorium closed so the Paul Bunyan production could begin. With most people in their seats, the smell of popping corn enticed me now that there was time to notice it.

"I'm going to go get a bag of popcorn. Do you want anything?" I asked my partner in crime.

"Do I ever. Get me a large buttered popcorn, a box of Junior Mints and a Coke, please."

I laughed. "Are you sure it's going to be enough? How about a hot dog and a basket of nachos to top it off?'

Evonne looked over the top of her colorful glasses at me. "Listen lady, I'm working hard here. Don't judge."

"I wouldn't dare."

The two of us had been best friends since I'd moved to Pine Bluff at the beginning of fourth grade. We'd had a few squabbles over the years like all good friends do, but never anything bad enough to damage our relationship. No matter what, I had Evonne's back, and had no doubt she had mine. If she wanted a large buttered popcorn and a box of candy, I was happy to get them for her.

The FFA kids—Future Farmers of America—and their chapter advisor were working the concession stand as a fundraiser. They would use the profits for travel expenses to and from the various events the group participated in throughout the school year. With the bulk of people already settled in for the play, only a short line of customers waited to purchase snacks.

I stood in line behind a young woman whose floral perfume wafted around her and made the end of my nose twitch. She wore a shimmery blouse in various tones of deep rose over a classy black maxi skirt. I lightly touched the woman on the arm. When she turned to me with a question on her face, I complimented her style.

"Sorry to bother you, but I wanted to mention what a beautiful outfit you're wearing." We don't hear compliments often enough, so a few years ago I'd made the decision to hand more of them out, and I liked this young woman's flair.

Her soft brown eyes lit up as she flashed a toothpaste advertisement-worthy smile. "Oh my gosh, thank you so much." She fingered the silky blouse. "Can you believe I found this entire outfit on Poshmark for less than a hundred dollars? The skirt is a Michael Kors and the blouse is Alice and Olivia. I never would have been able to afford them otherwise. Isn't it fabulous?" She spun around to let her flowy skirt twirl.

I blinked and pushed my glasses up my nose. While the woman looked fantastic, she might as well have been speaking Greek to me. "I'm sorry. I don't know who Michael Kors or Alice and Olivia are. Are they friends of yours? Do they live here in town?"

Her tinkly laughter was more delightful than condescending. She patted her brunette updo. "You're so silly. I'm Oriana Francini, by the way."

"Oh, gosh, I'm sorry. It's so nice to meet you, Oriana." I offered my hand. "I should have introduced myself right away. I'm Dawna Carpenter." I was still in the dark about who those other people she'd mentioned were.

Oriana's eyes twinkled as she clasped my hand. "I know who you are. You're the great Dawna Carpenter, a true legend in this town. I'm delighted to meet you."

My mouth fell open in surprise. "A legend? I don't think so, but it's sure nice of you to say so."

"Give yourself some credit. Since I moved to town a month ago, all I've heard about is how Dawna Carpenter saved the townsfolk from a crazed murderer."

I chuckled self-consciously and shook my head. "People do like to exaggerate."

"I've heard it from enough people now to think they're telling the truth. Believe me, your story is what legends are made from." She waved an elegant arm toward the closed doors of the auditorium. "Take Paul Bunyon for example. Did you know a real man gave rise to the legend?"

"Most legends have some truth behind them, but I didn't realize Paul Bunyon did."

"Yep. Google it."

"I just might." I cleared my throat and directed the conversation back to my new friend. "What brought you to Pine Bluff, Oriana?"

"A job and a change of pace. I wanted to be able to save money but rentals are so expensive in the city. Maybe I did things backwards, but I searched for an affordable rental first, then found a job second." She smiled and shrugged. "My parents thought I was crazy, but doing things wrong side up seems to have worked out well for me. So far at least."

"Fascinating. Do you mind my asking where you're working?"

"Moyer Accounting Solutions. I have an accounting degree and Mr. Moyer was hiring. It was my lucky day." The look on Oriana's face said differently.

"Do you like working there? Is Zach a good boss?" It was a nosy probing question, but she didn't have to answer if she didn't want to. I hoped she'd chose to keep talking.

We'd made it to the front of the line and it was Oriana's turn to order but instead, she tugged on my sleeve. The two of us stepped out of line and let the person behind me move forward.

Oriana glanced around, I assumed to make sure no one was within earshot. "When my interview ended up being more Mr.

Moyer telling me everything about himself instead of asking about my skills and background, I knew what type of a boss he was likely going to be."

"He talked about himself instead of interviewing you? What kind of things did he tell you?"

"All about how wonderful his business is and how it's the heart of Pine Bluff. How every business in town, and many in neighboring towns, wouldn't think of going anywhere else for their bookkeeping needs. Then he went on and on about what a great boss he is and how he expects perfection from his employees. How he expects his people to give one-hundred and fifty percent to the company and how they all adore him for it."

"He was wrong about every business using him. I don't."

Oriana smiled slightly. "I know. It was a load of baloney, but he pays well."

"And you've found the money is worth putting up with the baloney, as you call it?"

She shrugged a delicate shoulder. "Sure. Mr. Moyer struts around the office trying to micromanage our work. He's got a short fuse and is a bit...tyrannical, I guess I'd describe it. I know I'm good at what I do, so I've already learned to keep my head down and try not to make eye contact."

"Tyrannical how?" I was more than a little surprised this woman whom I'd met only moments ago was unloading so much on me, but I wasn't about to shut her down. I was all ears.

Oriana must have correctly read my expression, because she clamped her teeth shut and sucked in a sharp breath. "Oh, gosh.

Listen to me rattling on. I probably shouldn't be talking about this, but I don't know many people here yet and haven't had anyone to talk to. It feels good to get some of it off my chest. I'm sorry."

I touched her arm. "No need to be sorry. I understand. Sometimes we keep things so bottled up and then one small thing is said and next thing we know, we're unburdening ourselves to a virtual stranger. I've done it myself. Honestly, I don't mind." With any luck, she'd keep talking. I wanted to find out as much about Zach as I could, and Oriana apparently needed a listening board.

"You're not related to Mr. Moyer, are you? I should've asked first, before I started flapping my big mouth."

I laughed. "Oh, gosh no. Zach and I are neither family nor friends. You're perfectly safe venting about him to me."

Oriana pressed a hand to her heart. "Thank goodness. Anyway, when I interviewed for the job, he made it sound like there were a handful of employees, but counting me, there's only two of us. Mr. Moyer," she held a palm out, "which he insists we call him, seems to take pleasure in berating us and trying to make us feel like idiots. If something isn't done exactly to his ever-changing specifications, he throws a tantrum like a spoiled child. He changes how he wants us to do things on a daily basis and doesn't bother to mention the changes until he's screaming at us about not doing something correctly."

"Screaming at your employees is, by no stretch of the imagination, okay. He doesn't ever get physical, does he?"

"Not with us, but he has kicked a trash can or two and thrown pencils across the room more than once."

Holy cow. It sure sounded like Zach had quite the temper. If he treated his employees the way Oriana described, what would have stopped him from throwing an axe at Nate if he'd felt like Nate was a threat to Scotty winning the lumberjack contest?

Oriana's voice penetrated my musings. "The other day, Mr. Moyer told us our jobs are at stake. He said if someone were to bring in a resume who was more qualified, he would have to hire them and fire one of us." She crossed her arms and shook her head. "I have a bachelor's degree in finance, for heaven's sake."

I was completely taken aback by Oriana's description of her boss. "He sounds like a monster. Why're you putting up with it?"

"I can't say I haven't shed a few tears over it, but I'm new to Pine Bluff. My whole goal is to live cheaply and sock away money to create a nest egg for myself. I want to travel, to see the world, and, like I mentioned, he pays me well. I get three weeks of vacation each year, which really sweetened the deal for me. By this time next year, I'll be able to afford a two-week trip to Italy, and still be able to spend time with my family over the holidays. Believe me, every single morning before work I give myself a pep talk about how it'll all be worth the stress in the long run. And it will. I keep my head down as much as possible and simply do my job."

"Well, honey, for your sake, I hope things improve. I'm not sure all the money in the world is enough to allow someone to treat you the way your boss does." I laid a hand on her arm to show my support. "I've kept you too long. You're missing the play. But if you ever need someone to talk to, you know where to find me."

Not only did I purchase treats for myself and Evonne, I sprang for Oriana's as well. It sounded to me like the poor girl could use a break.

Back in the ticket booth, I handed Evonne her popcorn and Coke, then went back to fetch my popcorn and her Junior Mints. I hadn't thought this one-handed thing through when I'd offered to fetch our snacks. Once I was settled back on my stool, I regaled my friend with what I'd learned about Zach.

Part way through my story, sirens screamed outside the theater windows. We both peered through the windows of our booth, trying to determine what was happening. As we watched like a pair of nosy hens, a sheriff's car flew by, followed closely by an ambulance, a second police car, and a fire truck. They all screeched their sirens as they raced around the corner and up Lookout Hill leading out of town. A chill ran down my spine.

"I hope it's nothing serious." Evonne leaned close to the glass and craned her neck, trying to make out more of the action.

"Maybe they figured out who the killer is and are on their way to make an arrest."

Evonne shot me a skeptical look. "Could be, but you'd think J. T. would've flown out of here if that was the case. And why would they need a firetruck and an ambulance?"

"Good point."

As soon as I caught my breath from the sirens, I launched back into my story about Zach.

Evonne munched her popcorn while I talked. When I finished, she took a sip of her soda and inserted a few remarks of her own. "Okay, so Zach is a pompous, tyrant of a boss who pays his employees well to put up with his atrocious behavior."

"No, he pays them well to do their jobs. Nobody should have to put up with a boss who acts like he does," I said.

"Agreed. I think you took my remark out of context. Let me rephrase. Zach *thinks* he pays them well enough to put up with his atrocious behavior. It sounds like he thinks he's the toast of the town, but my opinion of him has always been quite a bit lower than his own. The guy's a nightmare when he comes to city council meetings, which he does most of the time. I have no doubt what Oriana told you is the absolute truth. I can't imagine working for the man." Evonne shuddered at the thought. "At last month's meeting, Zach was trying to push his agenda to have Pine Bluff sponsor Scotty for the lumberjack competition. He wanted the town to purchase all new equipment for Scotty and to replace all of our downtown fall banners with banners promoting Scotty instead." She tapped the Axe Kicker button. "This was the design Zach proposed. Anyway, we heard him out but let him know in no uncertain terms the town couldn't promote one contestant over the others."

"What did he do?"

"Ranted and raved. Zach's face turned so red I thought his head might blow off. He stormed out of the meeting and slammed the door. We were all relieved to see the back of him. Between you and me, the city council is on the verge of dropping him as our accountant."

I chewed on my lower lip for a second. "When I spoke to Zach today during the competition, he had a handful of these buttons pinned to his shirt and wore a matching ballcap. He said he purchased them himself and had supplied Scotty with new equipment for the competition. It seemed like Zach thought if Scotty won, he would be held up as the town hero for supporting Scotty during the competition. It was kind of strange, but it makes me wonder."

"Wonder what?" Evonne asked between bites of popcorn.

"If Zach was so focused on Scotty winning, would he have killed Nate to keep him from beating Scotty? Was it some kind of weird superfan obsession?"

"Or maybe Zach had some sort of financial stake in Scotty winning," Evonne added.

I frowned. "Like what?"

"I don't know." Evonne shrugged. "It was just a thought."

Our conversation was interrupted by Judy sliding open the door to the ticket booth. "It looks like everyone who is coming is already here. You two should go catch the rest of the play."

"You don't have to tell me twice." I handed Judy the money box and the card reader, then latched the sliding door over the ticket well, and gathered my belongings.

Evonne held her mostly empty popcorn bucket high. "Bear with me a minute. I'm going to get a refill."

With Evonne's bucket full of fresh popcorn, we made our way onto the balcony, finding seats in the farthest row back. The two of us got settled just in time to watch Paul Bunyan belting out a song in praise of breakfast as he flipped a flapjack the size of Wallowa Lake.

Chapter Fifteen

Monday morning, I set to work restocking 2-cycle oil and bar oil on the shelves at Carpenter's Corner. 2-cycle oil was mixed with gasoline and used in chainsaws to keep the engine lubricated and protected from the rigors of a small engine working at high speed. Bar oil kept the blade running smoothly and lubricated the chain to prevent buildup that could slow down the cut. The lumberjacks had depleted my stock of the various oils needed for their chainsaws in the days leading up to the logging competition, which was a good problem to have in my opinion.

April had been in early to load down a metal cart with the items I needed to stock and had sliced open the box tops for me so the task would be easier with my one good arm. As soon as she got me set up, she'd deftly dodged my questions about her hot date the night before with some lame excuse about needing to get to the on-site design job she was working on.

April was working for a local couple who'd hired her to update a three-bedroom bungalow they planned to use as a rental. She'd insisted she didn't have a minute to spare, but the girl was full of baloney; there was plenty of time. Her main goal was to avoid my questions. Unfortunately for her, not only was I her mother, but we worked together. She wasn't going to be able to dodge me forever. *I'll get you, my pretty.* I cackled to myself.

I'd emptied one box and started unloading a second one when the members of the morning coffee klatch started to show up for their daily rendezvous. The first to arrive was Ernie Ford, Evonne's husband. Clad in his signature blue striped shirt and smelling slightly of mechanic's grease, Ernie ambled to the coffee pot and poured himself a steaming mug. At over six feet tall and wearing size huge-by-large clothing, Ernie took up more space than the average man.

"Morning, Dawna," Ernie greeted me after taking a sip of coffee. "Evonne came home chattering about the play last night. Didn't think I was ever going to get any sleep." He chuckled. "Glad you folks had such a great turnout."

"Me too. I was worried when the logging competition got pushed back, but they ended up finishing on time and the crowd exceeded our expectations."

The bell on the front door jangled as Bill Wilder, Bob's old business partner, and Rick Montgomery filed into the store. The men chattered like a trio of rowdy crows as they poured their coffee and plopped into chairs around the small table I kept near the coffee pot for them. These three men had been Bob's closest friends for more years than they could count. They'd been meeting at Carpenter's Corner in the mornings since the day we opened for a cup of my traditionally bad coffee and to solve world problems before they went off to their respective days. Even with Bob gone, they'd kept up the tradition. Mornings wouldn't have been the same without the guys taking up space in the hardware store. I looked forward to seeing them every day and listening to them gossip and carry on.

Ernie owned the gas station and mechanic garage—Ernie's Garage and Gas—kitty-corner across Main Street from my hardware store. Any time my trusty Jeep needed maintenance or repairs, I called Ernie, as did most everyone else in Pine Bluff. He always had me fixed up and rolling down the road again in no time without having to cut off an arm and leg to pay the bill.

Rick Montgomery owned and operated a small land surveying company. He worked all over the state and into Washington. The three men's areas of expertise complimented each other perfectly. For me, I hadn't found myself in need of a surveyor recently, but if I did, I wouldn't think twice before hiring Rick.

Though Evonne was my best friend, I counted both Bill and Rick's wives in my circle of close friends. Kim, Bill's better half, was the friend who'd given me the advice to look at my dusty hardware store with a different eye. Without her nudge, I wouldn't have noticed how complacent I'd gotten and how Carpenter's Corner had needed a long overdue update. My new kitchen nook, which had already proven itself to be a fabulous and lucrative addition to the store, had been thanks to Kim's prodding. Rick's wife, Trisha, had gotten down on her hands and knees, putting all her muscle into helping me and April rearrange and make room for the kitchen nook. When the nook was ready, she'd turned her attention to clearing out the warehouse to create a space for April to refurbish and store her furniture projects. Trisha was never afraid to get her hands dirty. I was forever grateful to have such a great group of friends to rely on. It was a good thing they were all so supportive, since I was taking them up on their offer to help me count inventory in a couple weeks. I'd bribed them with pizza and refreshments, of course.

As the men chatted, I slid a plate of doughnuts onto the table between them from my morning order from Cookie Crumbles Bakery. Ernie didn't waste a second reaching for an apple fritter. Bill grabbed a chocolate glazed cruller and a cinnamon twist, and Rick snatched the two unglazed cake doughnuts. I grinned while internally giving myself a high five. After all these years, I knew them so well and was able to pick out exactly the doughnuts they would each go for. I reached for the maple bar still on the plate, the same as it was every morning, and leaned back against the counter to enjoy my own morning pastry.

"Have any of you heard what all the commotion was about around six-thirty or so last night?" I asked. "A couple sheriff cars, an ambulance, and a firetruck screamed through town."

The guys all shook their heads.

"Which way were they headed?" Bill asked.

I pointed northeast. "Up Lookout Hill and out of town."

"Nope. Haven't heard a word."

They chatted about the new reigning Bull of the Woods, what jobs they were each working on that week, and how soon they predicted snow would fly. They each had their own opinions, and some mornings things got loud around here.

"What do you got going this week?" Ernie asked Rick.

Rick rocked back in his chair and crossed his arms. "Multiple projects. It's going to be a busy week. Top of my list is the construction staking for Bill I better get done before he fires me and hires someone else." They all chuckled. "I had an emergency job I started on Saturday morning, but now with Nate dead, I don't know if the guy will want me to continue it or not."

My ears perked up at the mention of Nate's name. "Whyever not? What does Nate's death have to do with your job?"

"Well, the guy I'm doing the job for bought property from Nate. Apparently, they've been squabbling about timber rights ever since the deed was signed."

"Ah, you must be working for Tommy Keifer then. You did some work for him Saturday morning, you said?" I asked to clarify I'd heard correctly.

"Sure did. Met the guy out at his property before the crack of dawn so he could show me the site."

"Why so early on a Saturday?"

"Tommy said it was the only time he had free. I guess he had his carvings at the Timber Festival and needed to get back to town."

Aha. So Tommy had been headed out to meet Rick when I saw him driving through town. But why was he so secretive about where he'd been? Meeting with a surveyor seemed above board to me. I couldn't imagine why he'd felt the need to lie about something so trivial.

I nodded. "Tommy did have a booth at the festival. I bought one of his adorable carved owls. I named her Harriet."

The guys all looked at me like I was crazy, but, wisely, none of them said a word.

I tapped my chin, thinking about Tommy. "What did he hire you to do?"

"He wants a simple boundary survey so he knows for sure where his property lines are. How'd you know I was doing a job for Tommy Keifer?"

"Tommy and Nate had a public argument the other night in Timber Creek Saloon about those same timber rights you mentioned. I think it's possible he murdered Nate over it."

Rick took the toothpick out of his mouth he'd been chewing on and dropped the front legs of his chair to the floor with a thunk. "No kidding? Is he behind bars?"

"Well, no. It's more my theory than anything else, but I do know the police are looking into him as a suspect."

Bill huffed and crossed his arms over his stocky chest while he leveled me with a disapproving look. His posture told me he was about to deliver some unsolicited advice.

"Now Dawna, you stay well away from any investigation the police are doing. I'm sure J. T.'s handling the situation just fine without your help. We don't need you getting yourself in hot water by thinking you need to jump in and figure this out for yourself." He waved a hand at me. "You've already gone and gotten yourself hurt. Keep your pointy little nose out of it."

"My nose is *not* pointy." If I didn't know Bill was only worried about my safety, I would've been offended at his proprietary tone. I huffed anyway to show my irritation. "And my broken wrist doesn't have a thing to do with Nate's murder."

Bill raised his gray eyebrows and stayed silent. The whole meddling lot of them stared at me until I felt like I needed to clarify my statement.

"Fine. I suppose it *was* directly related, but only because I tripped over his feet, not because I was snooping around."

Ernie and Rick both chimed in with their own concerns. I shook my head, disgusted they all thought they needed to protect me from myself. They were like a bunch of big, gruff mother hens. I swear these guys worried more than any woman I'd ever known, but if I were to mention that one tiny little fact, they'd get their feathers ruffled.

I held my hand up in surrender. "Hey, I promise you I'm not getting involved in the police investigation." Okay. Maybe a weensy bit. My investigation and the police investigation were two different animals, but I wasn't about to point that out to my group of protectors. What they didn't know wouldn't hurt them.

I turned back to my restocking and let the men think they'd won the argument. They hadn't. Not by a long shot.

"Dawna, what do you need there?" Rick jumped to his feet and grabbed a box of bar oil off my cart. "Why don't you let me stock the shelves for you this morning?"

"Thanks for the offer, but I'm good. Honestly, my pain level is next to nothing this morning and April got me all set up before she left. Plus, there's only room for one person to work right here. We'd be in each other's way."

He blew out a breath and plunked the box back onto the cart. "Why don't you at least let me call Trisha and see if she could come in to help you out today?"

I chuckled, grateful once again for my caring friends. "I'll tell you what, if I get tired or this darn old wrist starts aching before April gets back, I'll call Trisha myself. Deal?"

"Fine. But I don't know why you have to be so gosh dang stubborn all the time." Rick poured himself another cup of coffee and leaned against the counter, clearly not pleased with my rejection of his offer to help.

"Look at the pot calling the kettle black." I turned my back on the guys and continued restocking.

It wasn't long before a handful of customers wandered in and needed my attention at the register. I was ringing up a roll of metal sheeting for one of my regulars when Luther Voss entered the store. While Luther's appearance might scare the holy living daylights out of people he'd never met, in reality he was a teddy bear. Every square visible inch of the man was tattooed, except for his face, if you didn't include the permanent eyeliner and a hint of baby blue tattooed eyeshadow. As far as I knew, no one had ever had the nerve to ask him about his permanent makeup; we'd all simply accepted it as one of Luther's many quirks. In the twenty plus years he'd been in Pine Bluff, I'd never seen the guy dressed in anything except black leather pants with a matching biker vest over a black T-shirt; short-sleeved in warmer months and long-sleeved in the winter. He sported a horseshoe mustache to top off the bad dude biker look. More than once I'd witnessed people crossing the street to avoid Luther. In every single instance, it was either a visitor or someone new to town who hadn't had the pleasure of getting to know him yet.

"Morning, Dawna. How's the family?" Luther politely asked.

I told him all was good on my end and, in return, enquired after his wife and kids.

"They're crazy as a box of frogs." He chuckled but his eyes twinkled. "Did my order come in yet?"

Luther owned and operated Iron Horse Plumbing and was one of my wholesale customers. Sometimes if the job he was doing was small enough, he'd load up the saddlebags on his Harley with the tools and supplies he needed and roar through town with his pistons popping. Today, though, one of his fleet of three vans was parked at the curb.

"It sure did. April has it all loaded on a cart for you at the warehouse door if you want to pull around and load up." I pointed at my injured arm. "Sorry I can't help you load today." He never let me help anyway, but I liked to offer. I slid his invoice across the counter.

"No worries." Luther signed the invoice, a thick skull ring on his pinkie finger flashing under the overhead lights. "Did you hear about the wreck on Tuekakas Grade last night?"

"No. Evonne and I watched the emergency vehicles fly through town, but we didn't know what was going on or where they were headed."

"Well, let me tell you then." Luther folded his copy of the invoice and stuck it into his vest pocket. "You know the little gal who won the women's lumberjack title? Can't think of her name off the top of my head."

"You mean Shayna Granberg?"

He pointed a sausage-sized finger with a black polished fingernail at me. "Yes, that's the one. Apparently, she drove off the road and straight into the canyon yesterday evening."

I gasped and covered my mouth with my good hand. "No she didn't."

"Oh yes she did," he replied.

"Holy fright. Is Shayna okay? Did she die?"

Luther shrugged his enormous shoulders. "Beats me, though I can't imagine anyone going into the canyon and surviving. Can you?"

A shudder ran through my body. I absolutely could not.

The coffee klatch had gone silent as they listened to the exchange and every customer in the store had stopped what they were doing to listen to Luther's bit of gossip.

Vicky Snider, a clerk at the local pharmacy, chimed in from where she'd been perusing the paint chip cards. "Shayna's not dead, but from what I gather, she is in critical condition. They took her by ambulance to the hospital in Greenwood last night." Vicky slid the paint card she'd been looking at back into the rack and stepped up to the counter to address her rapt audience. She placed a hand over her heart and rapidly blinked her eyes as she got emotionally involved in the story. "It was touch and go for hours, the poor thing. They thought they'd lost her more than once. The family even called their minister to her bedside, but each time they thought she'd taken her last breath, little Shayna rallied. She's not out of the woods yet, but we are hopeful. The woman's injuries are atrocious. If she does make it, she will have a long road to recovery. She may never walk again. It's all so awful." A tear dripped down Vicky's cheek as we all hung on her every word.

When Vicky took a breath, I jumped in, assuming she and Shayna were family. "I'm so sorry for Shayna, and you and your entire family. Is there anything I can do at this point?"

She swiped at her misty eyes. "Oh, heavens, I don't know. I've simply been kept apprised of the situation through my husband texting with a family member."

"So, Shayna and your husband are related?" You couldn't sneeze in a town the size of ours without hitting someone's cousin. It was hard to keep it all straight at times.

"In a roundabout way." She tapped her lips with a finger. "Let's see...we heard about the accident through my husband's sister's ex-boyfriend's mother-in-law, who is a third cousin twice removed to Shayna's father. No, no, stepfather, I believe. Or maybe it's a second cousin three times removed." Vicky flapped her hand. "Anyway, you see the relation and understand why I'm beside myself over this. Truly devastating to the entire family."

I shoved my glasses up the bridge of my nose and blinked several times, fairly certain my resemblance to a confused owl was on target. A deafening peal saved me from having to put together an acceptable answer. Thank goodness for Ernie being hard of hearing and having his ringtone set at a volume competing with the sound barrier. When Vicky whipped her head around to see who'd interrupted her attempt to gain misplaced sympathy, I took the opportunity to redirect my focus to helping another customer and Luther slipped out the back door. No longer having our attention turned her way, Vicky sniffed and left the store, her painting project apparently abandoned. I decided not to remind her.

I truly felt terrible for Shayna, and for her real family. Had anything Vicky told us even been remotely true, or had she made most of it up to make herself appear important to the situation? The woman had a reputation around town for inserting herself into various scenarios in an attempt to garner attention. I had no doubt if television news cameras ever got anywhere near Pine Bluff, Vicky would be front and center to tell her side of whatever the breaking story was.

As I rang up customers and they scurried out the door, my coffee klatch broke up. Rick and Bill scraped their chairs back, gathered any detritus they'd created, washed out all three of their mugs and hung them back on the hooks above the coffee pot, while Ernie finished up his phone call.

Ernie pushed to his feet and dropped his cell phone into the front pocket of his work shirt. "Well, at least some of what Vicky said is true."

"Which part?" I inquired.

"Shayna did drive off into the canyon yesterday evening. The phone call I got was from the sheriff's office requesting my towing service. From the sounds of it, she went over in the best place possible, if someone's determined to drive off the cliff. I'll need my big tow truck and will have to use the hoist to get her rig out of there, but I'm sure it can be done."

"Did they say anything about Shayna's condition?"

"No, only about her vehicle. She drove a mid-size Ford Ranger. Apparently, it's flipped on its head, from the sounds of things. Can't be good."

I shook my head. "No, it can't. Be careful getting the truck out and let me know if you hear anything about Shayna please."

"Will do."

The rest of the morning was spent restocking and helping customers. During any quiet moments, I tackled inventory prep, making sure items were on the shelves where they belonged and hooks were in their proper places to make counting easier.

Shayna was never too far from my thoughts as I worked. The weather the day before had been clear and mild. We hadn't had any rain, no early snow, not even a hint of fog. Why had Shayna gone off the road and into the canyon? Some of those corners on the way to Lost Canyon were hairpin and treacherous on the best of days, so it could have been an honest accident, though Shayna didn't strike me as a careless person. Was it possible she was so distraught over Nate's death to have driven off the cliff on purpose? From what I'd seen of her behavior over the weekend, she seemed to be handling it well, but you never know what's actually going on in someone else's mind. Shayna had won the women's lumberjill competition and qualified for state, so it seemed odd to me she'd try to kill herself. Unless...

With what Katelynn had told me about Shayna and Nate's split, maybe Darlene was right and Shayna had killed her ex in a fit of jealousy. Katelynn had mentioned how Shayna thought her boyfriend had been seeing someone behind her back. Could she have discovered she was right and thrown Nate's axe at him with the powerful arm we'd all seen in action over the weekend? If Shayna had killed Nate in a moment of passion, she might've been overcome with distress over her own actions and made the split-second decision to drive herself off the cliff.

The store phone rang, interrupting my thoughts. "Carpenter's Corner Hardware and Building Supply. How may I help you?"

A man cleared his throat. "Dawna Carpenter? Frank Stockwell here over at Elkins National Bank in Greenwood."

I slammed the receiver down with a satisfying thunk, glad I still had a landline in the store so I could hang up on someone properly. I was fed up to the rafters with the calls from that darn bank.

Chapter Sixteen

Mid-afternoon I stepped out on the sidewalk to watch as Ernie's big blue tow truck driven by one of his hired mechanics, pulled into the parking lot at his garage. Ernie followed with a dark gray pickup on his flatbed that had been smashed to smithereens. The truck was so destroyed, if I hadn't known he'd been called to hoist Shayna's truck out of the canyon, I wouldn't have been able to tell what kind of a vehicle it had been.

"There's no way Shayna made it through her accident alive," a voice whispered over my shoulder.

I turned to find Darlene had joined me and a handful of other looky-loos who'd gathered on our corner. In all the years I'd known Darlene, I'd never heard her speak softly or have a note of compassion in her voice. Maybe there was hope for her after all.

Before I had a chance to reply, she flung her hands out. "Probably for the best. How a simple barista was going to afford to live on her own was beyond my comprehension anyway."

So much for the flicker of compassion I thought I'd heard in her voice. I shoved my glasses up the bridge of my nose. "For your information, Shayna is alive."

Darlene's bright red lips formed a shocked O. "No way. Really?"

I nodded.

"Bet she's wishing she wasn't." Darlene pointed a pumpkin-colored manicured nail at the smashed truck. "Damn, that had to have hurt."

Ernie backed the flatbed truck into the garage. With nothing left to see, the crowd of rubberneckers dispersed, and I scooted back into the hardware store, leaving Darlene standing alone on the sidewalk.

"You're sure she's still alive?"

I jerked around. The dratted woman had followed me inside. Didn't she have customers of her own in Lipstick and Lace to deal with? I glanced around my own empty store. Maybe not. Mondays were always the slowest day of the week, and after a festival weekend, my guess was most people were back to work and resting up from the festivities. They'd be saving any home improvement projects and clothing shopping for their next days off.

"As far as I know, she is. Though the source we heard the news from wasn't the most reliable." I sighed, thinking about Vicky's husband's ex relatives a thousand times removed. "Aren't you and Katelynn friends? Maybe you should give her a call. She would probably know for sure."

"Why didn't I think of that? Sometimes you *are* good for something." Darlene spun on her heel and trotted out of my store.

"Let me know what you find out," I hollered after her.

I didn't have long to wait.

Fifteen minutes later, Darlene was back and ready to spread the gossip. She leaned against my checkout counter then eyed it with a disdainful sniff. Apparently deeming the counter too grungy to touch, she straightened her posture. "Ew, don't you ever clean in here?"

I rolled my eyes. "It's perfectly clean. You realize this is a hardware store, not a fancy clothing boutique, right?"

"For now." A Cruella deVil smirk lifted the corners of her ruby red lips.

"What in the world do you mean by that comment?"

The Cruella smirk morphed into a Cheshire cat grin. "Oh, nothing to worry your little head about. Now, do you want to know what I found out about Shayna or not?"

I forced a smile of my own, certain my attempt resembled a deranged jack-o-lantern. "Yes, please, your highness."

"Fine. Katelynn says Shayna's in a coma. She's suffered a fractured spine, broken both legs, an arm, and a few ribs. It doesn't sound good. Apparently, they won't know the extent of her injuries until some of the swelling goes down. The doctors told the family it's possible Shayna may never walk again."

Vicky's weird comments had some of the facts correct, at least. "That poor girl."

Darlene forgot all about the dirty counter and leaned in. "Oh, but you haven't even heard the best part yet."

Best part? What kind of person thought someone's life threatening injuries could possibly count as the best part of anything?

"Katelynn hinted about Shayna liking to tip the bottle, if you know what I mean." Darlene pantomimed drinking from a bottle. "My guess is she had a few too many and ended up driving off the cliff."

"Your guess, or a fact?"

Darlene tossed her dark hair over her shoulder. "Well, it's not too far of a stretch to imagine Shayna had a celebratory drink or three before she headed home. And Katelynn also said she saw Shayna having an up close and personal conversation with Scotty. Most likely it wasn't Nate having the affair." She batted her long eyelashes. "I mean, none of those lumberjacks are my cup of tea, but if I was going to go for one of them, Scotty would definitely be my first choice."

"Scotty and Shayna? No way. He and Nate were best friends since they were knee-high. I don't believe it for a second. Scotty is happily married and, even if he wasn't, he would never have backstabbed Nate."

Darlene tilted her head. "Dawna, you're so naive. People have affairs all the time without a second thought to who they're hurting. There's no such thing as loyalty when it comes to love."

"Well, that's not ever been true in my experience." And I felt sorry for Darlene and the world she lived in if she thought the words she'd spoken held the truth.

She looked down her nose at me. "You got married, what, a gazillion years ago? Things aren't the same as they used to be back in your day. Believe me."

With someone like Darlene, there was no point in arguing. It would get me nowhere.

When I didn't reply, she smirked and flicked a finger my way. "See? You have nothing more to say, do you? Because you know I'm right. Katelynn witnessed Scotty and Shayna locked in an embrace. I guarantee you they were having an affair."

"Or comforting each other over their mutual loss, perhaps?"

Darlene blew a raspberry. "I seriously doubt it."

I sighed. It seemed like Katelynn had spilled all her inner thoughts to Darlene again, and I was the one who had sicced the piranha on her. "It sounds to me like this is all speculation and we should keep it to ourselves until the facts surface. No reason to add to the family's distress."

"Keep it to myself? Not on your life. I'm going to call my girl-friends right now. This is too juicy not to share. Oh, and add this to my tab." Darlene grabbed a pack of the Big Red cinnamon gum from the display I kept on the counter, winked and waved three fingers at me as she headed back to her boutique.

When I got home later, Smitty, the eighty-eight-year-old woman who rented my carriage house, was being dropped off by her son. Tiny and as thin as a toothpick, Smitty ran cold on the hottest of days. This afternoon she was bundled up as if it were midwinter instead of early October. Watery blue eyes behind round glasses were the only part of her visible between the tightly cinched hood and the purple parka she had zipped to her chin. As her son carried two bags of groceries into the house for her, Smitty and I stopped to chat for a moment.

She was lamenting the price of groceries these days when I noticed the Axe Kicker button pinned to the front of her heavy winter coat.

"I see you have one of Scotty's buttons. You must be a client of Moyer Accounting Solutions."

Smitty looked at me quizzically. "Moyer who?"

"The accounting firm downtown. Do they do your taxes?"

"Heavens, no. I haven't had to worry about filing taxes for years, dearie. Not living on social security like I do. Why do you ask?"

I once again gestured to the button. "It was Zach Moyer's office who were handing out those buttons like the one you're wearing."

Smitty's mouth formed an O. She patted the button. "Oh, no. This was lying under the rose bush. Someone left it there for me." She pointed to the base of the rose bush where far more leaves lay on the ground than clung to the bare branches.

Smitty's son held open the front door to the carriage house. "Mom, come on inside. I don't want you to catch a chill. Your soup is heating up on the stove."

I left Smitty to her meal and went inside my own cozy home. I decided to put some eggs on the stove to boil so I'd have an easy grab-and-go breakfast option for the next couple of days. Placing four eggs in a medium-sized stainless-steel pot, I filled it with water, added a shake of salt, and turned the burner to high. I'd turn it down once the water started to boil.

While I waited, I paced around the kitchen, contemplating Nate's murder and Shayna's accident. Wanting to make some notes on what intelligence I'd gathered so far, I headed for Bob's office. After the kids had all moved out, he'd converted the small corner room tucked between the bathroom and the upstairs staircase into a home office. In the three years he'd been gone, I'd kept the room on my weekly, okay...more like monthly, dusting schedule, but still hadn't moved a thing. His big wooden desk still sat in the middle of the room, facing the windows with a view of the backyard. The last ledger Bob had worked on before his death still lay open on top of the desk. I flipped the ledger closed, pushed it aside, and took a seat in the squeaky office chair, wiping dust off the top of the walnut desk with the sleeve of my sweatshirt. All around me the house remained still and quiet. I soaked up the peacefulness for a moment, then slapped a hand on the desktop to give myself a jumpstart.

"Come on, Dawna. Get to work and figure this out. Time's a wasting."

I grabbed an ink pen out of the white Carpenter's Corner coffee mug Bob had used for a pen holder. Paper. I needed a sheet of paper. I pulled open the top drawer on the left side of the desk, but it stuck before I had it open far enough to get anything out. Impatient, I tugged harder at the drawer. It didn't budge. "You're jammed good, aren't you?" I muttered to the obstinate drawer.

A silver-handled letter opener jutted out of Bob's pen mug, so I grabbed it and made an attempt to get my arm far enough into the drawer to dislodge whatever had it jammed up. It was no easy task with only one working arm. After flailing around for a few minutes, I retrieved a flashlight from the closet and got down on my knees to peer into the depths of the drawer. Yep. Somehow a bunch of paper had gotten pinched between the far back corner of the drawer and the metal track. I contemplated the letter opener. It was too flimsy. This job required a longer and sturdier tool. I heaved myself to my feet and went in search of the right apparatus, but what? I snapped my fingers. A pair of kitchen tongs might work rather nicely.

With tongs in hand, I propped the flashlight up to shine inside the drawer, then got back down on my knees, squeezed my arm into the drawer, and grasped at the papers with the tongs. When I got a grip on them, I pulled hard, only to feel the corner rip away while the rest stayed firmly wedged inside the drawer. After several more attempts, the papers finally gave up their stronghold and I was able to pull the drawer fully open.

Laying the rogue bundle of papers on the desk, I smoothed out the top, crumpled page. The words on the first document leapt off the page, causing me to scoot to the edge of the chair as I stared at them. "What in the name of..." My breath caught in my chest and a freight train roared in my ears as my brain tried to catch up and make sense of what I was reading. I jerked to my feet, sending the chair flying backward. It tipped sideways onto the hardwood floor with a resounding crash.

A promissory note listing Elkins National Bank as the lender and Robert C. Carpenter and/or Carpenter's Corner Hardware and Building Supply as the borrower lay in front of me. As I read through the document, my confused brain picked up on a few important details. The principal sum of the loan was twenty thousand dollars. It was a single payment loan with a maturity date five years after the signing date. My eyes raced down the page. Yep, like I feared, there was Bob's handwriting on the signature line at the bottom of the document. I stared at the date he'd signed, my brain quickly doing the calculations. Holy fright. It'd been five years and...fifty-eight days. I was in deep trouble. I needed some answers quick, and there was only one man who could provide them to me.

"Bob," I yelled to my empty house. "You have some explaining to do!"

The house remained eerily silent. For all of two seconds.

An explosion that sounded as if it came from the direction of the kitchen sent me jumping a foot into the air. Once I came back to earth, I sprinted toward the sound. As I rounded the corner into the kitchen, the smoke alarm screamed to life with a sharp, repeating chirp loud enough to scare the rest of the leaves off all the trees in a mile radius.

The smell filling the house reminded me of the bubbling geothermal hot springs in Yellowstone National Park. Or what I imagined the depths of hell to smell like. White and yellow splats of eggs and shells clung to the ceiling and lay scattered around the room like buckshot. I grabbed the smoking pot off the stove, but it was too late to save it. Not only had I forgotten all about the eggs, I'd left the kitchen before turning the element down. When the pot boiled dry, the eggs exploded, sending boiled egg shrapnel in every direction. What was left in the bottom of the pan resembled The Blob from the old B-horror film with the same name. It wasn't clear if the stainless steel itself had burnt and started to melt, or if the goop was all charred egg. What was clear was I was down one 2-quart saucepan. I tossed the pot in the sink and grabbed the broom, swiping at the shrieking smoke alarm until I finally managed to knock it onto the floor and shut the wretched thing up. I almost stomped on it for good measure but figured I would only end up hurting myself with my temper tantrum.

I studied the egg stuck to the ceiling. Boy, was that mess ever going to be a bugger to get off. And with only one hand, it was going to be next to impossible.

"I wonder how much April will charge me to clean up this mess?"

I switched off the kitchen light and went to bed.

Chapter Seventeen

"I'm probably not supposed to share this information, but I know it won't leave this room, right Dawna?" Ernie hit me with a look the next morning as the coffee klatch sat around the table in Carpenter's Corner. It was early and no other customers had come into the store yet.

"Cross my heart and hope to die." I made an exaggerated X across my chest but winced as I attempted to cross my fingers on my injured hand hidden inside my sling.

Ernie frowned my direction, as if to say I was full of baloney and cheese.

"What?" I stared back, wide-eyed to prove my innocence.

Unable to find anything amiss, Ernie settled back in his chair with his arms crossed over his chest and his hands tucked into his armpits. "You all know the sheriff's office called me to bring Shayna's wrecked rig in, right?"

When he paused, we all nodded.

"It's not the first time the sheriff's office has hired me to inspect wrecked vehicles. They've been happy with my work so they asked me to inspect Shayna's once I got it back to the garage." Ernie reached for his mug and took a loud slurp of coffee.

The long pauses were killing me. I bugged my eyes out at him. "Okay, and? Don't keep us in suspense."

Rick and Bill echoed my impatience.

"I'm getting to it. Sheesh, simmer down." Ernie set his mug back on the table while I scowled at him. "It wasn't the easiest task since the truck was so smashed up. How Shayna survived her wreck is beyond my limited understanding. It's a gosh dang miracle, if you ask me. You know, I haven't seen a person live through a smash up like that since 1982 when Harry Sheridan fell asleep, went over the canyon, and ended up right side up in the middle of the river. You guys remember when he drove into the river? The doctor said being asleep at the wheel was probably what saved his life 'cause he was loose and limp on impact. Slamming into the cold river sure woke him up, alright. The old coot climbed out of the canyon and flagged down help before..."

"Sure, we all remember Sheridan going in," Rick interrupted Ernie's story. "Would you hurry up and get to what you found with Shayna's truck? We're burning daylight here."

"Geez, you're all so impatient. Fine. Shayna didn't drive off the cliff on purpose, I can tell you that much."

"How do you know for sure?" I asked.

"Because somebody cut her brake line."

I gasped and stumbled backward, catching myself on the counter. "Cut her brake line? Are you sure?"

Ernie nodded. "Couldn't be more positive. It was a clean cut straight through the brake pipe. Definitely intentional."

Car maintenance had never been my strong suit. Or anywhere even close to my wheelhouse. "Is the brake pipe easy to access? What kind of tool would it take to cut it?"

The three of them talked over one another as they explained to me the dynamics of cutting a brake line. I stopped paying attention about three sentences in and finally cut them off when they started throwing words around like caliper and master cylinder.

"Okay guys, I don't need an in-depth lesson. Just tell me the simple bones of what it would take to get the job done."

"Anyone with a pipe cutter could've shimmied under Shayna's truck and cut the line," Rick finally answered my specific question.

"Holy fright. Someone was trying to kill her." I shoved my glasses higher up the bridge of my nose and stared at my friends.

Ernie nodded. "Yep. My educated guess would be the same person who murdered Nate cut Shayna's brake line. Lord knows why anyone would want to kill either one of them, let alone both, but they sure did."

My mind flashed to the pipe cutter April and Thor had found in the river. She had said she'd thought she'd seen someone throw it in. I raced to the phone on my desk and dialed my daughter's cell phone number.

"April," I barked when she answered. "Bring the pipe cutter you found in the river and meet me at the police station as soon as you can get there."

Telling the guys to leave their coffee cups for me to clean up later, I shooed them out of the store, flipped the open sign to closed, locked the door, and headed over to the station to share April's find and my suspicions with J. T.

Chapter Eighteen

"How did you find this?" J. T. sat behind his nondescript beige metal desk, studying the pipe cutter from inside the clear plastic evidence bag he'd placed it in. Day old stubble darkened his face and a hint of fatigue rimmed the police chief's crinkled blue eyes. A chocolate-colored felt cowboy hat perched on top of a file cabinet tucked in the corner behind his desk, and a dark brown canvas jacket hung from the back of his chair. A half dozen framed photographs of J. T.'s pre-teen daughter, Chandler, stood out against the otherwise stark white walls of his office. Chandler lived full-time in Idaho with J. T.'s ex-wife, visiting her dad in Pine Bluff during the summer and on some holidays.

"Thor and I took a walk beside the river. You know, the trail coming from Steam Engine Park? Like usual, Thor was taking his time, sniffing every rock and blade of grass he could get his nose on. I swear he could spend hours inspecting the same ten feet of shoreline."

"He's a busy guy." J. T. chuckled. "And what were you up to while Thor was doing his thing?"

"Looking for crystals in the water."

"Find anything?"

"A couple, but the water was too cold to dig around much. I'm more of a fair-weather rockhound. Anyway, I heard a noise and looked up. One of the lumberjacks was up near the bend in the river. He threw what I thought was a rock into it, then turned and left. When Thor and I finally made our way to where the guy had been standing, Thor pulled me right into the river. I got soaked to the knees, but the river is clear enough, it was easy to spot the pipe cutter in the water."

"Why do you think it was one of the lumberjacks who threw it in?"

April shrugged. "The red-and-black shirt. But honestly, I wasn't paying close attention and only saw him for a second."

"Could it have been one of the lumberjills?"

"Maybe. I guess so, yeah."

"And you're sure whoever it was threw this tool into the river?"

"Well...no. I think so, but I can't be positive. I didn't actually see it go in, but the pipe cutters were in the water at roughly the same place the person was standing."

"And why are you bringing the cutters to me?"

April glanced sideways at me. "Mom told me to."

"I thought it was relevant, given how Shayna's wreck was no accident."

J. T.'s eyebrows shot into his hairline. "Ernie supply you with that information?"

Whoopsie. Ernie did tell me to keep the information to myself, didn't he? And I'd even crossed my heart, though I'd crossed my fingers, too. Ernie had been right not to trust me, since I'd apparently thrown him under the bus the first chance I got. Accidentally, of course. I clamped my lips shut.

"Wait a minute. Shayna's wreck wasn't an accident?" April swiveled her head between me and J. T. "Nobody told me."

"We just found out, though it sounds like Ernie told your mother almost before I had the report in hand." J. T. stared at me for a beat, then placed the evidence bag onto his desk and reached for a pad of paper. "I suppose if he hadn't spilled the beans, you wouldn't have known to bring this in." He jotted down a couple of sentences then glanced up at us. "Anything else I can do for you ladies?"

April started to shake her head no, but I cleared my throat and settled back into the uncomfortable guest chair. "There are a few things I've been thinking about I wanted to run by you, if you've got the time."

J. T. tapped his pen on the desk. "Shoot."

Since Tommy was already on the police chief's radar, I launched into my suspicions about the accountant, Zach. I filled J. T. in about finding one of the Axe Kicker buttons when I picked up my scattered cookbooks, and then told him how crazy Zach had been acting at the logging contest about Scotty's losing streak.

J. T. leaned back in his chair and crossed one lanky leg over the other at the knee. "Where's the button, and why are you just now bringing it to my attention?"

On instinct, I patted my pockets in search of the button. "Ah, I think it's in my coat pocket. I didn't think to mention it before because it didn't occur to me it might be a clue. But when Zach had a few pinned to his shirt and was acting as if he owned Scotty, I wondered if he would stoop as far as killing Nate to rid the competition of Scotty's closest competitor. Zach seemed to take it as a personal afront that Scotty was grieving and not throwing his best this weekend. He said Scotty was ruining Zach's reputation." I paused. "And, honestly, I've found a handful of the Axe Kicker buttons since. They keep turning up everywhere. I'm sure it's nothing."

April, who had been quiet during my Zach tirade, piped up. "I found one, too."

J. T. chewed on the cap of his ink pen as he contemplated my words. "I'll admit Zach as the killer isn't an angle that had occurred to me, though tracking down the person who lost the button near Nate's body would be like trying to find a needle in a haystack." J. T. opened his top desk drawer and slapped an identical Axe Kicker button onto the desktop. "Zach handed out quite a few of these things."

"Two hundred to be exact."

"Like I said, impossible. Well, bring it in and with any luck they'll be fingerprints on it to lift."

"Will do. Do you have any other suspects? Besides Tommy and now Zach?"

J. T. puffed out a breath. He scrubbed a hand over his face and shook his head. "To be honest, we've got a thousand suspects. Everybody who was anywhere near the park Saturday morning at the time Nate was killed. But I gotta tell you, there's not a single person who stands out yet. Everyone we're looking at seriously has solid alibis. Nate's fingerprints are the only prints on the axe. He was a great guy. Everyone I talk to liked and respected Nate; even Tommy, though he's twisted up over the timber rights. Now with the circumstances surrounding Shayna's wreck, things are even muddier."

I pushed my glasses up. "Sounds like you could use a little help."

"Mom," April started but I shut her down with one look. Good to know my Mom Look still had some power behind it.

The police chief stared at the ceiling for so long I thought he'd forgotten we were there. Finally, he spoke. "Your observations were helpful in the past, and I'll admit our small police force is stretched a little thin on this one. The last thing I want is for either one of you to get hurt because you're snooping around where you shouldn't be." He looked back and forth between April and me. "But if you could keep your eyes and ears open and report back to me anything you hear, I'd be grateful."

"Will do. Right, April?" I nudged my daughter with my elbow.

She reluctantly nodded, then added her own little tidbit. "I think there's maybe one more person you don't have on your radar."

"Who?"

"Katelynn Norris," April said.

J. T. lifted one side of his lips in a dismissive gesture. "We talked to Katelynn. She didn't strike me as a murderer and was forthcoming about her whereabouts during the time of the incident."

"Okay, so she told you Shayna broke up with Nate last week, then?"

J. T. sat up straighter and cocked his head. "Uh, no, she didn't mention that particular detail. Neither did Shayna." He tapped his pen against the desk. "Who did you hear this from?"

"Mom heard it directly from Katelynn. She can tell you about it better than I can." April tilted her head my direction.

"First I heard it from Darlene, who had heard it from Katelynn." I filled J. T. in on the conversation Katelynn and I had at the logging competition. "And I've been thinking about her. The morning Nate was killed, Katelynn came from behind the log stack, which is exactly where I saw someone vanish right before I fell over Nate's feet. When I talked to her the other day, she made it sound like she liked Nate and I got the impression she thought Shayna was overreacting, but what if it was all a cover? Katelynn and Shayna are obviously close. There could be a possibility Katelynn killed Nate in revenge for him cheating on her best friend."

J. T. riffled through a file on his desk before jotting down some notes. "It's a feasible theory, for sure, but Shayna's accident, well, the sabotage of Shayna's vehicle, throws a wrench in things. Why would Katelynn commit murder for her best friend, then turn around and try to kill the very friend she was protecting?"

"True. The information about someone tampering with Shayna's brake line is so new I hadn't had time to process it yet. I'll mull it around and get back to you." I reached for my bag, then set it back down and leaned forward. "There is one more thing I'd like to discuss before we go."

J. T. raised his eyebrows. "Which is?"

I glanced between him and April. "You two went on a date and didn't bother to tell me it was happening. My feelings are hurt." They weren't, but I wasn't above using emotional trickery to get the two of them to talk.

The police chief's cheeks flamed, and his lips twitched as he tried, unsuccessfully, to hold back a grin. His gaze lingered on April's face as if he was waiting for her to address my comments.

April fidgeted in her chair and tucked a strand of red hair behind her ear before she turned and scowled at me. "Maybe not every little thing is any of your business, Mom. Did that ever cross your mind?"

"Yikes. Shots fired!" J. T. grinned as his head swiveled between me and April.

I ignored him and zeroed in on my daughter. "It most certainly is my business. You're my daughter, and I've known J. T.," I flung an outstretched hand his way, "his entire life."

"So what? We went to a little play together. It's not a crime, is it?" Embarrassed, April jumped to her feet.

"Not in my book," I answered with a grin.

"Mine, either," J. T. agreed, his smile about to split his face in two. "In fact, how about I pick you and Thor up at six for another walk by the river?"

April bit her lip and finally made eye contact with J. T. "I've got a soccer game this afternoon. Raincheck?"

Chapter Nineteen

"**A**re you going to stop by the hardware store today?" It was high time I got back to Carpenter's Corner, but it was more important to me to get the scoop on April and J. T.'s date.

"Nope," my daughter replied with a sly grin. "Remember, I told you we have a game in North Powder this afternoon. We're leaving right after lunch."

Dang. Foiled again.

April was the assistant girls' soccer coach for the high school team. I'd caught as many home games as I could but didn't usually travel to the away games.

"Fine. I guess I'll wait. Tell the team to have a great game. Go Timbers!"

April went one way from the police station and I went the other. I wasn't happy about not getting the deets, but there wasn't a thing I could do about it. The girl was certainly good at being elusive when she wanted to be. Two days had already passed, yet I hadn't been able to squeeze a single drop of information out of her about her and J. T. showing up at the Paul

Bunyan play together, dressed to the nines and looking pleased with themselves. I huffed and carried on my way.

Back at Carpenter's Corner, two local customers were sitting on the bench below the front window waiting for me to get back and open the store. I apologized and they both followed me through the door as I unlocked and pushed it open.

"What can I help you find?"

"I need a roll of weatherstripping and a tube of heavy-duty caulk. The wife says it's time to get those doors and windows sealed before the wind and rain pick up and it's too late." The forty-ish man ran a hand through short curly brown hair.

"She's right. You don't want drafty, leaky windows." I pointed to the area of the store where he would find his supplies. "Let me know if you have any questions."

When I turned to address the needs of the second customer, a woman I knew from yoga, she was nowhere in sight. After a quick jaunt around the store, I found her in the kitchen nook. She stood in front of the small appliances, debating the merits of two different air fryer toaster ovens.

"Those things are incredible. I love mine," I told her.

"Do you? Is it worth the cost?" She turned back to read about all the various features displayed on the box of the more expensive model. "I've been wanting to get one for eons now but didn't want to spend the money. My parents sent me a Visa gift card for my birthday, and I think it might be time to splurge on a new kitchen gadget."

"Happy birthday. And yes, I use mine all the time, even though I'm pretty worthless in the kitchen. But the air fryer is amazing for crisping up leftovers and giving you the crunch of fried food without using all the grease. Heart healthy, right?" I winked.

"Exactly." She glanced over at me. "I never cook with oil anymore if I can avoid it. Have you made homemade chicken strips in yours? I miss them more than I can tell you, and a friend told me hers come out great in her air fryer."

"Uh, no. But I can tell you they do a fabulous job crisping up the strips you can buy in a bag from the freezer section." I chuckled at myself, but only received a confused glance from my customer in return. "Plus, with the toaster oven feature, you can make toast, cook a pizza, and rumor has it you can even bake a cake without turning on the big oven." I shrugged. "I wouldn't know about that last part." I guessed she probably didn't care to hear about the frozen burritos I threw in my air fryer on a regular basis.

When she hefted the box with a grin and carried it to my checkout counter, I wasn't under any delusion that her purchasing decision was based on anything I'd said. She placed the fryer on the counter, then went back for a set of potholders adorned with autumn leaves and a cute big-eyed owl.

"Thank you so much for shopping in Carpenter's Corner's new kitchen nook. I'm glad you were able to find what you were looking for today." I swiped her gift card through the card reader.

"Me too. When my birthday card came, I wanted to go shopping but didn't feel like driving to Greenwood today. Then a friend reminded me you'd started carrying kitchen items." She glanced back toward the kitchen nook. "Honestly, I thought you'd only have a few random items, but you have a great selection. You can bet I'll be back for a few things for myself, and to buy gifts for Christmas."

"Glad to hear it." I handed over her receipt. "Tell all your friends."

The morning wasn't necessarily busy, but a steady stream of customers came in for supplies to tackle those outside chores they'd been putting off. Here in the Blue Mountains of Oregon, snow could come early and we all liked to be as prepared as possible. Winters weren't as harsh as they used to be when I was a kid, but I remembered plenty of years where there'd been snow on the ground by Halloween. Some years we didn't see the ground again until Easter. Nowadays, our first snow generally fell sometime in November, but an October dusting wasn't out of the question.

By mid-afternoon, the number of customers had dwindled, and those loan documents I'd found the night before in Bob's desk at home were a flaming image burning a hole in my mind. The mere thought of them was making me even more anxious than finding a dead body had done. With my heart pounding in my temples, I finally sat at my desk and dialed the number for Elkins National Bank. Might as well get it over with.

"Frank Stockwell isn't available at the moment. May I take a message?" A pleasant but professional sounding woman answered my inquiry.

Relief washed over me at the reprieve of another few minutes at least. "Yes, my name is Dawna Carpenter and..."

"Oh, Mrs. Carpenter!" The receptionist's voice rose an octave as she interrupted. "Frank has been hoping to hear from you. I've been under strict instructions to set up a time for you to come in and chat as soon as we heard from you. When would be best for you? The sooner the better, for obvious reasons. He's available at four this afternoon."

Chat. Yeah, right. Start foreclosure proceedings on my store, more like. The meeting couldn't be put off forever, but maybe just a hair longer. "Does he have an opening for tomorrow afternoon?" I asked hesitantly. Both April and Westen would be working in Carpenter's Corner, so I could get away for an hour or two without too much finagling.

"Tomorrow afternoon is perfect. Frank has a two o'clock open."

"Pencil me in please."

She hung up with a cheery, "See you tomorrow!"

Though I was glad the receptionist was happy about getting the meeting scheduled, for me, tension rose into the top of my head like I'd been handed a death sentence.

To get my mind off the imminent demise of my beloved hardware store, I turned my attention to murder. Mindlessly restocking shelves provided the opportunity to think about what

I'd learned so far about Nate's death and the various people on my suspect list.

With Shayna's wreck established as not having been an accident, it seemed like I could reasonably scratch her off the list. Her brake line had been cut, so it wasn't a far leap to think whoever had killed Nate must've gone after Shayna as well. Not many people knew about Nate and Shayna's recent breakup, and with J. T.'s question about why in the world Katelynn would protect her friend only to try to kill her later, my gut told me Shayna's best friend was not the culprit. I mentally crossed her off my list.

What could Nate and Shayna possibly have been involved with to make the killer come after both of them? Tommy was the logical suspect, in my opinion. Did he assume Shayna had been in on Nate's decision to cut the timber on Tommy's land? And maybe she was. Tommy had made it clear at Timber Creek Saloon the other night that he wasn't anywhere near ready to let the matter drop. If Tommy wasn't getting the response he wanted from Nate, he might've taken things into his own hands. He'd hired Rick for the boundary survey and the two of them had been together early Saturday morning out at Tommy's place, but, from what Rick said, they had been there less than an hour. Was there enough time for Tommy to get back to Pine Bluff, kill Nate, then pick up his family in Greenwood and be back to Steam Engine Park by mid-morning when they were finally setting up their booth? I might have to take a drive and find out how long it would take to accomplish all that.

Then there was Matt. He'd been right beside me at the scene and had been super helpful picking up my spilled cookbooks, which was out of character for him. Was his helpfulness all an act to cover up his role in Nate's murder? From Matt's snarky comments at Timber Creek the other night, it was obvious he hadn't cared for Nate one bit. But from what I understood, Matt didn't get along with anyone, especially loggers he'd worked with in the past. It wasn't unusual for Matt to be the loudest and meanest voice in the room, blaming everyone except himself for his troubles. Nothing unusual there. Nate's death had allowed Matt to move up the list to be able to compete in the lumberjack contest, but he was a longshot to win and hadn't, so I didn't see how the contest could possibly be enough of a motive for him to murder Nate. And why would he sabotage Shayna's pickup? Plus, there was the problem of clothes. I knew beyond a shadow of a doubt the person I'd seen hightailing it away from the murder scene was dressed in red and black. Matt had been wearing blue jeans and a green plaid flannel shirt under a forest green coat before Chad told him he'd be competing. I didn't feel like there was much to go on with Matt for motive, but I'd leave his name on my suspect list for now.

My thoughts drifted from Matt to Zach. Talk about a nasty person. From what I'd learned from Oriana, Zach even put Matt to shame in the crappy person department. And with Zach's obsession over Scotty winning the competition, and his unrealistic tie to the success of his own accounting firm, was it a far stretch to think Zach had taken it upon himself to wipe out the competition? It wouldn't be the first case of a rabid super fan mercilessly attacking someone they deemed to be standing in the way of their hero. Zach had even been wearing a red-and-black buffalo check shirt in solidarity with Scotty, so he checked the box on the clothing color card. Evonne had mentioned how the city council had shot down Zach's request to sponsor Scotty. Had he taken the matter into his own hands? But, like Matt, what would be Zach's reasoning for trying to kill Shayna? As hard as I racked my brain, I couldn't come up with a plausible motive.

The last person on my list was Scotty, and he was only there because of his attire. Scotty and Nate had been attached at the hip since the two boys were in kindergarten. When Scotty learned of Nate's death, he was truly stunned. His reaction had been immediate, and I couldn't imagine anyone being able to force the kind of response Scotty had shown. Friday afternoon, he'd been all smiles, raring to go and ready to win the entire competition. The rivalry between the two had always been just a bit of good-natured fun as far as I knew. What if things hadn't been as amiable as they had appeared to be on the surface? But, after Nate's murder Scotty had been off his game all weekend, throwing like an amateur. Unless I read him all wrong, he was genuinely grieving the loss of his best friend. Then there was Darlene's report that Katelynn had witnessed a tender moment between Scotty and Shayna. Was it possible they were having a secret affair like Darlene suspected? I shook my head. No way. *They're two grieving friends who were comforting one another. End of story.* Unless actual hard facts came to light, I refused to believe anything else. Besides, if Shayna and Scotty were involved, he wouldn't try to kill her, would he? Nothing made sense, but as he was Nate's best friend, I should probably make a point of talking to Scotty. He might know something important about one of the other suspects that could steer me in the right direction.

With all the suspects swirling around in my head, I realized I wasn't going to figure anything out without more investigation. And since our esteemed police chief had given me the go-ahead, I didn't feel any guilt about planning my next steps.

Picking up the phone, I dialed Evonne's number. "Are you up to going for a drive after work?"

"Absolutely." Because that's what true best friends did, Evonne agreed without asking a single question. She was my ride-or-die human being; the person I could count on to always have my back no matter what. I never had to worry about Evonne's loyalty or her talking crap when I wasn't around. Whatever she had to say, she'd say directly to my face.

"Great. We won't have a ton of daylight, so can you get out by five?"

"Shouldn't be a problem."

"Good deal. Oh, and I'll need you to drive. You know, the broken wrist and all."

"I figured. I'll call Ernie and ask him to top off my gas tank."

Chapter Twenty

Two hours later, I set the timer on my phone as I climbed into the passenger seat of Evonne's Nissan Rogue. She pointed the sunset-colored SUV up Lookout Hill and out of town.

"What do you have there?" my best friend asked, eyeballing the cardboard drink holder I balanced on my lap.

I handed over one of the two takeout cups of piping hot apple cider I'd raced down to Rocking M Coffee Company to get.

"Careful. I already burnt my tongue on mine," I warned.

After she'd taken a tentative sip and placed the spicy cider into the console's cup holder, I offered Evonne one of the leftover doughnuts from my morning order I'd had the forethought to bring along. After all, you can't have a road trip, even a short one, without snacks.

"Do you mind telling me exactly where we're going, since I seem to be the getaway driver?" Evonne took a bite of a maple bar and glanced quizzically my way. "I'm assuming we're about to do some investigative snooping. Am I correct, Miss Marple?"

"Mmhm," I mumbled around a mouthful of a raspberry-filled pastry. I swiped red jelly from my chin, then sucked it off my fingers. "I want to determine how long it would take a person to drive from Pine Bluff to Keifer's property out at Lost Canyon, from there to the Starlight Inn in Greenwood, then backtrack to Steam Engine Park."

"Okay, seems a bit convoluted to me, but I'm game for whatever you want to do."

"Don't worry. There is a method to my madness."

"I don't doubt it for a second."

We munched on our doughnuts and sipped our ciders while we enjoyed the drive through the countryside. Farmhouses and red barns dotted the landscape, pressed up against the timber line and surrounded by wheat and hay fields gone fallow ahead of the upcoming winter. Brown and white Hereford and Black Angus cattle dotted pastures where the remaining grass was yellow and gold from the summer heat. The fall rains and cooler temperatures were beginning to bring a hint of green back to the fields. A picturesque, centuries-old, white clapboard church sat under a stand of towering Ponderosa Pine trees, its sharp steeple stretching to the sky.

After swallowing the last bite of my doughnut, I filled Evonne in on the confrontation in Timber Creek between Tommy and Nate and my theory that Tommy might be the killer. "He was driving through town Saturday morning when I was on my way to yoga. Rick says he met Tommy out at his property and they spent close to an hour together. But Tommy thought I was in charge of the vendors at the park and told me he was late setting up because his truck wouldn't start, which turns out not to be true. What I'm trying to determine tonight is if he would've had enough time to stop at the park and murder Nate before picking up his wife and son in Greenwood and getting back to the park by eleven to set up his booth."

By the time I finished my dissertation, Evonne was steering the SUV around the sharp corners of Tuekakas Grade and down into the chiseled canyon. The steep route was the only way to get to the small town of Lost Canyon. Far below the gray stone sides of the deep canyon, I could barely make out a glimpse of the Tuekakas River. With each switchback, the river got closer. On the far side of the river, dense patches of evergreen trees covered the hills, stretching down to the waterline.

Evonne and I both gasped as we came around a hairpin turn near the bottom of the grade. Mangled and dented guard rails clung precariously to the posts with a ten-foot-long chunk missing altogether. Evonne slowed the Nissan to a crawl.

"Holy fright. This must be where Shayna went over the edge." I shuddered. "I can't even imagine how scared she must've been." A sudden swirl of vertigo hit me as I imagined Shayna frantically trying to pump brakes no longer working, only to have her pickup fly off the road and into thin air before tumbling down the rocky face of the canyon. "She had to have been absolutely terrified."

Evonne's knuckles were white as she tightened her death grip on the steering wheel. "I can't look." Her voice fluttered and cracked.

"Please don't."

I glanced over at my driver. Her face had blanched as white as a glob of Elmer's glue.

The road had been widened once or twice since 1922 when my great-grandfather had worked on the crew that had pushed the road into the rugged and remote mountain range. Despite the upgrades, there were still plenty of sharp corners and drop-offs that could be treacherous to the driver not paying close enough attention to the road. Following Shayna into the bottom of the canyon was definitely not on my to-do list for the evening.

At the bottom of the grade where the river curved and the road flattened out, a Forest Service outhouse provided respite for fisherman and travelers alike. A one-lane wooden bridge stretched across the river, providing access to a fishing lodge perched on the far bank. A trio of small matching cabins dotted the hill overlooking the rushing river.

Evonne wheeled into the gravel parking area near the outhouse, shifted her car into neutral, and lowered her head onto the steering wheel. "Sorry, I need a minute."

"No worries." I twisted in my seat enough to reach across with my good hand and rub her back. "If I'd known it would bother you this bad, I never would've asked you to drive me out here."

"Going over the side of the canyon has always been one of my biggest fears, ever since I was a little girl. My dad used to bring us all down here to the river a lot in the summer. He'd fish while us kids played in the water and Mom usually sat on the bank and read a magazine. I'm not sure how Dad managed to ever catch a fish with the four of us kids splashing around." She chuckled. "Anyway, I remember one day Dad pointed out a place where an entire family was killed when a tire blew out on their car and sent them careening off into the canyon. Suffice it to say, I had nightmares about the same thing happening to my own family for years afterward. Still do, if I'm honest."

"It's amazing what we parents say in all innocence that traumatizes our kids for the rest of their lives, isn't it? April freaks out if she's forced to drive behind a truck carrying any type of irrigation pipes because of a story I told her once."

Evonne turned her head and eyed me. "What story?"

"Uh-uh, nope. Not telling you. I already traumatized my kid; I'm not going to layer another level of trauma on you. Sounds like you have enough of your own to contend with." I reached into the box balanced on my lap and held out a plain old-fashioned doughnut. "Here, you need some more sugar."

She scowled at me. "Put that plain jane back and dig me out the chocolate sprinkled one instead. I deserve it." She threw the car into drive and steered back onto the road, munching on her doughnut.

After paralleling the river for another five miles, we came to the charming small town of Lost Canyon, surrounded by pastural farm country and sitting beneath the majestic peaks of the Wallowa Mountains. A sign greeted us—Welcome to Lost Canyon, population 846—as Evonne pulled into town. We passed the Dairy-Made drive-in with a statue of a life size black and white Holstein cow standing tall on the flat red roof of the burger and ice cream joint. Taillights shown in the early evening light as several cars waited in line at the burger stand to pick up their dinners. The drive-in sat on the corner where the highway curved and headed into downtown, forming Lost Canyon's main artery. We cruised past the high school, town library, a pharmacy, a mom-and-pop diner lit up and bustling, a feed store, and a corner grocery store.

I swiveled my head as we passed a coffee shop with a wooden sign announcing the name of the shop—Mudslingers. A sign on the door was flipped to "Closed." I pointed at the shop. "I bet that's where Shayna works."

"Must be," Evonne agreed. "I think Mudslingers is the only coffee shop in town. And boy, do they ever make the best caramel rolls. We'll have to drive back up for one soon."

"It's a date."

At the far edge of town, I directed Evonne to swing a left onto Kingfisher Road. I wasn't a hundred percent sure where the Keifer's acreage was, but from what I understood it butted up to Nate's property. If we timed the drive to Nate's driveway, we should be close enough for my purposes.

Dusk had settled in, and with the towering trees overhead, the road was thrown into deep shadow. Evonne flipped her headlights on and we slowed to a crawl as we checked the scattered mailboxes for one reading "Durand." When we found it, I stopped my timer and Evonne pulled into the circular driveway. A boulder the size of a small cabin sat in the middle of the turnaround. A two-story log home with a covered front porch held up by enormous log pillars sat majestically in a clearing. The large clearing allowed enough daylight in to make it still fairly easy to see. The sky had shifted to the lavender and blue ombre of evening descending into night.

A small light gleamed from somewhere deep inside the house and the porch light had been left on to welcome home the couple who would never walk side-by-side up the wide stone steps again. The house was surrounded by a split rail fence and a trio of Aspen trees sporting gorgeous bright gold fall leaves whispering in the gentle breeze. A wooden swing and a pair of rustic benches took up residence next to a fire pit made from a ring of large gray river rock. The rugged landscaping comple-mented the natural surroundings beautifully. The entire place was well cared for and inviting. I swiped a tear from the corner my eye that had pooled as the loss of Nate and the long road ahead for Shayna, if she managed to survive, hit me hard again. A lone hawk soared on the wind overhead, letting out a sharp cry before flapping away and leaving us to our own devices.

I slowly swiveled my head, taking in the sight of the beautiful home and grounds the couple had shared. About two hundred yards from the house, a barn-like structure loomed at the far edge of the clearing. A shoot-off from the gravel driveway ex-tended to the large sliding wooden doors. A long sign proclaim-ing the building "Durand Sawmill" hung over the doorway, lit by two arched outdoor lights placed strategically above the sign.

Two logging trucks were parked to the left of the building, one still loaded down with logs.

Evonne and I sat in silence for a few moments, each of us lost in our own thoughts. "Are you ready to go?" she asked as she swung the car around the enormous rock in the circular driveway.

I nodded and restarted the timer on my phone, but when I looked up a bright orange marking I hadn't noticed before drew my attention. "Wait. Stop the car!"

As soon as Evonne slammed on the brakes, I shoved open the passenger door and jumped out of the car, making a beeline for the large boulder sitting in the grassy middle of the circular driveway.

"Where are you going?" Evonne yelled.

I pointed at the rock. From the far side of the circle, we hadn't been able to see it, but as soon as we'd swung around the driveway, the words painted on the boulder were loud and clear. In safety-orange spray paint, someone had written "THIEF" across the boulder. With the October light waning, and me staring down at my phone, I'd nearly missed it. I thumbed open the camera app on my cell phone and snapped a few pictures, texting one to J. T. immediately.

"Thief?" Evonne's eyes flared. "What in the world did Nate steal?"

I stared at her. "It's got to be Tommy, don't you think? In his mind, Nate was stealing his trees, even though Nate held the timber rights. It was all perfectly legal, but I'm certain Tommy doesn't see it that way."

We both stared at the offensive graffiti for a moment as I racked my brain in search of any other suspects with a motive to name Nate or Shayna a thief. I came up blank.

"I might be wrong, but I think the paint is still wet." Evonne pointed at the markings. "See there? It's dripping."

I gasped. She was right. A trail of paint ran down the boulder, elongating the "F." Someone had painted the graffiti only minutes ago, and long after Nate was already dead. The message didn't make any sense. The tiny hairs on the back of my neck stood at attention. I scanned the tree line with the uneasy sensation that something, or someone, sinister was watching us. Wide-eyed, Evonne and I didn't waste another second before hustling back to her car. As soon as we were inside and had slammed the doors tight, Evonne pressed the lock button. I'd never been so happy to hear that little click in my life.

While we drove back up the steep Tuekakas Grade, full dark set in. Evonne turned on her brights and kept her eyes glued to the road, hugging the side of the cliff as we crept past the location of Shayna's wreck. I bit my tongue and didn't say a word about the torturous twenty-five miles an hour my friend was driving. For nearly the entire way, a pair of headlights rode our tail through the harrowing turns. The unbroken strips of yellow paint in the middle of the road marked the entire uphill side of the grade as a strict no passing zone, but the annoyed driver behind us finally got fed up enough with Evonne's snail pace. The idiot took all of our lives in their hands and burned rubber as they sped around us, blasting their horn the whole way. For a split second while the other vehicle was in our headlights, we had a clear view of a faded avocado green Ford pickup that had seen better days. The tailgate, clearly a salvage replacement, was brown and didn't match the rest of the ancient paint job on the truck. The pickup was scarred and dented, and the rear bumper was all but rusted away.

"You go right ahead, mister. Be my guest," Evonne remarked. "Sorry to slow you down."

"He's sure in a big hurry for someone who looks like his truck might rattle apart at any given moment," I added.

"You don't think that impatient driver could be the person who painted the graffiti at Nate and Shayna's house, do you?" Evonne asked.

I pursed my lips, contemplating her theory. "I suppose it could be, but it wasn't Tommy's truck. Unless he has more than one."

"Probably not, anyway. It would be way too much of a coincidence."

I agreed.

Once we topped out of the canyon and hit the area known as Coyote Flat, Evonne let out an audible sigh of relief and put her hammer down on the gas pedal. At least after the slow climb out of the canyon it felt like the hammer was down. A quick glance at the speedometer informed me we were still traveling a fair amount under the speed limit. Stars twinkled overhead in the deepening cobalt sky.

We moseyed through Pine Bluff, then headed out the highway toward Greenwood. Evonne pulled into the convenience store across the street from the Stardust Inn, whipped around and scuttled back to Pine Bluff and Steam Engine Park. With my stopwatch reflecting a total driving time of two hours and three minutes, Evonne pulled up in front of my house and threw the car in park.

"So, what do you think, investigator? Could Tommy be the murderer?" Evonne asked.

I shivered as the image of Nate's body stretched out on the ground flooded my mind. "It's more than possible. The graffiti points straight to Tommy, in my opinion, and he had plenty of time. Almost an hour to spare, by my calculations." I paused and tapped a finger against my chin. "I think Tommy could've easily killed Nate and been at the park to set up his tent by eleven, even at our speed. And I'd bet you a million bucks Tommy drives faster than Slowpoke Rodriquez."

"Hey! I did my best. Beggars can't be choosers." Evonne sent me her best mean-mug. "I got you home safe and sound, didn't I?"

I grinned at her. "Yes, you certainly did. I owe you one."

Evonne touched the tip of her nose, then pointed at me. "Big time."

I made a mental note to call the salon tomorrow and set us both up with pedicure appointments. My best friend could use a good pampering.

Chapter Twenty-One

With the doors locked against the dark, and me feeling cozy in my flannel pajamas, I stared at the two frozen burritos thawing and getting deliciously crispy inside my air fryer.

"When was the last time you ate a vegetable?" The voice in my head, at least I thought it was in my head, was Bob's.

I spun around and sniffed the air but if there was a slight smell of coffee and sawdust, the stronger scent of bean burritos cooking overpowered it. I glared around the room anyway, in case my deceased husband was haranguing me about my eating habits. With a put-upon sigh, I jerked open the freezer door and pulled out a bag of frozen broccoli. How an imaginary comment from a man who'd been gone for over three years could still manage to make me feel thoroughly chastised was beyond me. Dumping a handful of the stupid green vegetable into a small pot, I ran cold water over the stalks and set the pot on a burner to heat up.

"There. Are you happy now?" I asked the room at large.

For good measure, I wrenched open a new jar of salsa with the help of my handy dandy jar opener mounted under the cabinets, then made a mental note to add a few jar openers to my next order for the kitchen nook. Next, I wrestled the lid off of a plastic container of guacamole. *Look at me go.* Two green items on my plate. I was getting healthier with every passing minute, all while figuring out how to accomplish simple tasks one handed without breaking everything in sight.

The air in the kitchen sparked with electricity as a low chuckle thrummed through the room. With a spoonful of guacamole halfway to my mouth, I froze. "Bob? This time I know it's you. I'd recognize your chuckle anywhere."

A movement in my peripheral vision spun me around, but the second I turned, the figure was gone. Disappointed, I clinked the spoon onto my plate. "Oh, come on, Bob. Why so shy? It's not like you."

Thinking back to my experience with my ghostly childhood friend, I realized either I was getting crazier, or Bob's spirit was truly here. I wasn't ready to contemplate the crazy part, so both his spirit and my lost ability to see ghosts must be getting stronger. Karen had been as real to me as my own siblings, even though my mother had insisted she was imaginary. No, Karen hadn't been a figment of my imagination, and Bob wasn't either. Sure, his sawdust and coffee scent filled the house from time to time, and I'd imagined his voice before—I'd even go as far as to swear he'd been sitting next to me a time or two—but I was always in a half state of sleep when Bob had seemed almost tangible in the past. This evening, I was as wide awake as I'd ever been. And I hadn't taken another pain pill for my broken wrist since the half dose I'd swallowed on Sunday afternoon, so it couldn't be affecting my brain. No, there was most definitely a bit of ghostly activity going on at the Carpenter residence, no matter what anyone else thought. Even April had admitted to feeling her dad's presence around the house on more than one occasion.

And then there was Lilac. The cat had made an appearance more than a handful of times when I hadn't been anywhere near sleepy. To prove my point, a tiny squeak of a meow sounded as the soft whisper of fluffy fur twined around my legs. I looked down in time to catch the tip of Lilac's white tail disappearing around the corner into the dining room. Instantly, I followed her, but the ghostly cat was nowhere to be found and my broccoli had started to boil. Not wanting a repeat performance of the exploding egg incident, I went back to the kitchen to stare into the pot until the vegetable was ready. *Does broccoli explode, anyway?* I eyeballed the gleaming ceiling where April had done a stellar job of cleaning up my mess. She'd only complained a little when she'd realized the entire thing needed to be repainted. I'd better remember to tell her how good it looked or I'd be in trouble with my daughter.

The rest of the evening proved to be uneventful. I ate my dinner in front of the television and cackled at the over-the-top antics of the characters in the sitcom *Ghosts,* successfully keeping my mind off the meeting at the bank the next afternoon. I idly wondered if Bob was camped out on the couch watching with me. As soon as I switched off the TV, the loan forced its way back into my thoughts as if it hadn't been gone.

"Why in the name of all things holy did you not tell me about this loan?" I implored my husband. "Not to be accusatory, but you never once mentioned the store was in a financial bind, or that we needed twenty-grand for anything. What were you hiding from me? Did you have a secret life I didn't know about?" I took a breath before I continued chewing Bob's butt. "What were you thinking? We never kept secrets from each other, not in all of our forty years together. Except maybe you did, and I was an overly trusting idiot. What was the problem, Bob? Drinking, gambling, drugs, loose women?" I cringed at my own words. Bob had never had any type of addiction I knew about, and nothing except this crazy loan to indicate anything was amiss. "I trusted you!" I yelled.

I tried to calm myself down while I waited for him to answer, but Bob wasn't talking. Not even a shimmer in the air or the hint of sawdust. Frustrated, I stomped to the kitchen and brewed a mug of lavender chamomile tea, then took it to bed to sip on while I lost myself in my current read. My mind was so twisted up between the money and the murders that sleep proved to be evasive. I finished the cozy mystery I was reading, without figuring out who the killer was before the big reveal, then made a sizeable dent in the next book on my nightstand—a mystery with an Irish setting titled *The Drowning Sea*. I finally put the book down and drifted off to sleep in the wee hours of the morning.

While I slept, rain and wind moved in. I awoke to the melodic patter of raindrops against the window, but while it was cozy and warm in my bed and I could've happily stayed there for another hour or two, the hardware store wasn't going to open itself. I padded to the sunroom and pulled the curtains back.

"Crap!" A puddle the size of a small lake pooled and swirled on the street directly in front of my house. The unexpected wind had knocked loose bunches of dry leaves from the huge elm tree in my front yard. The leaves had blown into the street and been swept into the stream of rainwater before getting caught up and plugging the storm drain. It tended to happen every fall along with the first big wind and rainstorm. I sighed and pulled on a pair of sweats and a sweatshirt. Leaving the sling for my wrist behind, I zipped on a hooded rain jacket before heading outside to deal with the drainage problem.

Twenty minutes later, I'd managed to free the drain and had carted two wheelbarrows full of leaves to my compost pile. I was sopping wet, bedraggled, and had a leaf or two stuck to my clothing, not to mention the raking and scooping hadn't done my wrist any favors. The good news was that I'd planned a weekend sale while I'd been carting off leaves. Leaf rakes and biodegradable leaf bags would be twenty percent off at Carpenter's Corner today through Sunday.

Instead of my usual walk to work, I drove my Jeep, pulling into line behind three other vehicles waiting for their turn at Rocking M Coffee Company's drive-up window. J. T. was one car ahead of me. When he got his coffee and pulled out, he wheeled back into the parking lot and motioned for me to join him.

At the window, I smiled at the coffee shop owner. "Good morning, Lily Anne. May I please get a medium pumpkin spice latte?"

"Sure thing, Dawna. How's your morning going so far?"

I regaled her with my morning leaf adventure while Lily Anne created my coffee. Once finished, she handed the coffee out the window to me and I attempted to hand her cash in exchange.

Lily Anne waved my money away. "It's been taken care of."

Taken aback, I blinked in surprise. "Taken care of? By whom?"

She cocked her head toward the police cruiser idling in the parking lot. "That irresistible police chief of ours."

"Huh. Well, it was awfully nice of him." I stuffed the five-dollar bill into Lily Anne's tip jar instead and wished her a nice day.

Popping the chocolate covered espresso bean from the top of my cup into my mouth, I flipped around and steered my Jeep up next to J. T. He rolled his window down so we could visit without standing in the rain.

I raised my cup in a toast. "Thanks for my coffee. It was an unexpected surprise."

"You bet. You were first on my list to visit today, anyway, and now you've saved me a trip." Wearing a navy-blue police jacket against the October chill, J. T. hung his elbow out of the open window, apparently unconcerned with the raindrops pelting his sleeve.

"Did you get the picture I texted to you last night?" I asked.

He scowled. "Sure did. What were you doing out at Nate's house, anyway?"

"I wasn't exactly at Nate's house, per se."

He bugged his eyes out at me. "You said the picture of the graffiti was taken in Nate's driveway, and I can clearly see his house in the background." J. T. swiped through photos on his phone, then held it up to prove his point.

"It was taken there, but Nate's house wasn't the place I meant to be."

J. T. clenched his jaw. "Dawna, stop beating around the bush. Where did you mean to be?"

"Well, I was testing a theory, so Evonne and I wanted to drive out to Tommy's property. I'm not one-hundred percent sure where the Keifers' driveway is, so we thought Nate's place was close enough. That's why we pulled into the driveway and how we noticed someone had painted "Thief" on the big rock in the middle of his turnaround."

"Okay, so what was your theory? Did it pan out?"

"I wanted to see if Tommy had enough time to get back and forth from Greenwood to his place, stop in the park to kill Nate, then hustle back to…"

"Stop. I'm following your line of thinking here. You don't need to spell out the entire route for me again. And did he? Have the time I mean?"

I nodded my head vigorously, causing my glasses to slip down my nose. "Yeah, with time to spare." The fact the chief was taking my theory seriously had me excited. I raised my hand to push my glasses back but ended up spilling a drop of hot coffee on my nose. For crying out loud. Maybe I didn't have this one-handed thing down as well as I'd thought.

J. T. ignored my yelp and chewed on his lower lip. "And how do you think Tommy got his hands on Nate's axe and knew where Nate would be at precisely the right minute to kill him?"

Good question. I hadn't thought of that, but where there was a will, there was a way. "Tommy had plenty of time. Maybe he lay in wait behind a pine tree or something. Nate could've been carrying his axe, since he was getting ready for the competition, and Tommy lured him behind the log stack..."

"Lured him with what? A donut on a string?" His eyes twinkled in mirth.

"You don't have to be so sarcastic." I huffed. "I don't know with what exactly, but it's worth thinking about."

"You're right. It's a long shot, but still a possibility." By his skeptical tone, it was clear he wasn't buying my theory.

"As far as I can tell, Tommy is the only one with a reason to call Nate a thief."

J.T's grunt was noncommittal.

"The graffiti was still wet. There's no way you knew about it before I sent you the pictures."

"You are correct. I did not."

Score one for me. If I was keeping track. Which I wasn't. "Who do you think the graffiti artist was?"

"You and Evonne are my top suspects."

"What?" I nearly choked on the sip of coffee I'd just taken.

He stared at me, deadpan. "Makes sense, doesn't it? I can place you at the scene of the crime, Evonne fairly near it, and both of you at Nate's house with dripping, wet paint."

"It's a complete coincidence we were there and you know it." My voice rose in outrage.

"There's no such thing as coincidences in police work."

"You can't be serious." But a knot had formed in my belly.

He chuckled. "Of course I'm not."

I glared at him and shook my head. "Not funny."

"Well, it was kind of funny. You should've seen your face. Besides, the graffiti is far from art, and you know I can't divulge any information about who I think might have painted it." J. T. stared straight ahead, appearing highly vigilant as cars splashed through the puddles on Main Street.

"Can't, or won't?"

"One and the same, though it's not a leap to think the graffiti, Nate's death, and Shayna's accident are all connected."

His words validated my own thoughts and gave me hope we were another step closer to finding the killer.

"Is there any news on Shayna's condition this morning?" I asked.

"Oh, you didn't hear?"

I shook my head. "Hear what?" My stomach dropped into my toes. Had she succumbed to her injuries?

"Apparently late yesterday Shayna started to show signs of responsiveness. Her doctor is hopeful she'll be fully alert sometime in the next few days."

"Thank goodness! Her family must be thrilled." My stomach took the first elevator back to its rightful place.

"I'm sure they are. Well, thanks for your help, Dawna." He saluted me with his coffee cup. "We'll talk soon."

Chief Dallas drove off toward the Pine Bluff police station. He hadn't divulged a single thing in our conversation, except to yank my chain. However, the report about Shayna appearing to be on the road to recovery was welcome news.

Chapter Twenty-Two

Focusing on setting up a display for my fall leaf clearing sale and helping customers find the right supplies for their other home repair and improvement projects was a welcome distraction from thinking about a killer running loose in our town or the upcoming meeting at the bank. In a few short hours, I'd be sitting across from a loan officer, finding out the fate of Carpenter's Corner. Before leaving for work this morning, I'd placed a copy of Bob's death certificate in a folder to deliver to the bank. With any luck, Bob had the foresight to purchase death protection when he'd taken out the loan. If he hadn't, maybe the bank would grant me some type of a mulligan since I hadn't been aware of it. And I wasn't even sure the loan was legal. How could Bob possibly have taken out a loan on our hardware store without my signature?

"Arrghh!" I shook myself to rid my head of all the negative thoughts and pulled two cans of paint I was mixing for a customer off the paint shaker. The lavender Himalayan Poppy she'd chosen would be beautiful in the woman's home office.

Ten minutes after noon, April arrived in a shower of raindrops. "The Schoonover's rental is finished and ready for their new tenants," she announced. "And I bet you're past ready for a break."

"It'll sure be nice for them to have the rental income. I bet they're feeling the pinch with all three kids in college this fall. And you're right. I wouldn't say no to a chance to use the restroom," I agreed. "By the way, I do need to leave in about an hour for a bit. Westen will be in after school, so you'll have some backup while I'm gone."

"Yeah, no problem." April stowed her purse and jacket behind the counter. "Where are you headed?"

"Oh, just to an appointment in Greenwood. I'll probably be gone a couple of hours." April would be mad as a hornet when she found out I hadn't told her about the loan, but there was no sense getting her riled up until I got all the details.

"An appointment for your wrist? Do you need someone to drive you?" Her brow furrowed in concern.

"Nah, I'll be fine. I'll take it slow and easy." The last thing I wanted was for April to insist on taking me. "Where I really need you is here minding the store."

She continued to frown but agreed in the long run. "Okay, but I thought you didn't have a follow-up until your appointment with Dr. Carla next week."

I shrugged and headed to the restroom, effectively avoiding answering her questions. By the time I got back, April was immersed in helping a customer pick out the right hinges and handles for their new bathroom cabinets. An hour later, I grabbed my purse and headed out the door with a quick wave. My daughter wasn't the only one adept at avoiding questions.

"Frank is tied up on a phone call at the moment, though he shouldn't be long. Please take a seat and I'll let him know you're here." The woman at the reception desk at Elkins National Bank waved a cordial hand toward a trio of chairs lined up against the wall outside a glass-walled office with "Frank Stockwell, Vice President" etched in white lettering on the door.

As directed, I took a seat and studied the man yakking on the phone. Dark hair with a few silver strands framed a thin, pleasant face with a large beaked nose. Even seated behind the desk, it was clear Frank stood over six feet tall with the long, lanky arms to prove it. As I watched him, I couldn't help but be reminded of the Disney version of Ichabod Crane in the old *Legend of Sleepy Hollow* cartoon. The banker appeared relaxed and approachable as he finished up his phone call. A few muted words made their way to me through the glass.

"Tee time...not long...last appointment...see you at the club."

Ah. He'd be out on the golf course later in the afternoon. No wonder he was happy and relaxed. Hopefully his good mood would transfer over to his conversation with me and he would cut me a break.

Frank stood and adjusted his suit jacket, the sleeves falling shy of his bony wrists, before he opened the door and poked his head out. "Dawna Carpenter? Come on in."

Feeling like I was playing a game of musical chairs, I swapped the one outside Frank's office for a plush guest chair in front of his desk. My heart skipped a beat as I placed my purse on the floor at my feet and sat at attention with the folder containing the loan documents I'd found and a copy of Bob's death certificate on my lap. "Mr. Stockwell, I want to apologize…"

"Frank, please," he interrupted without making eye contact as he thumbed through a manila file on his desk.

"Frank, then. I want to apologize for my behavior on the phone all those times you attempted to reach me. I honestly didn't think the loan you were referring to was mine. I'm truly sorry."

"Your husband never mentioned it?" He continued perusing the paperwork. His demeaner had gone from a happy man anticipating a game of golf to serious banker in the time it took me to move from the lobby into his office.

I shifted uncomfortably in my chair and cleared my throat. "Well, no, but I'm sure he would have, had he had more time."

I chose not to dwell on the fact Bob had taken out the loan two years before he passed away. You'd think there would've been plenty of time to casually mention, "Oh, hey, by the way, I took out a twenty-thousand-dollar loan against our business." A heads up would've been nice.

Frank finally stopped rummaging through the file and sat staring at me over the top of his wire-rimmed glasses. His thin lips were pursed in a judgmental expression. Why couldn't his happy I'll-be-golfing-soon mood have carried over to our meeting?

Pulling Bob's death certificate out of my own folder, I whipped it across the desk to the banker. "My husband died suddenly a little over three years ago. You probably aren't aware of that. Here's a copy of his death certificate. It should change everything, since I wasn't a signer on the loan."

Frank ignored the document in my outstretched hand. He resembled a skinny frog as he continued to blink at me. Any moment now I expected a ribbit to emerge from between his puckered lips. Instead, the banker sighed and crossed his long arms across the file on his desk. "Dawna, may I be frank with you?"

My gaze shot to the brass nameplate prominently on his desk. *Pretty sure you're Frank with most people.* I sucked in my bottom lip to hold back the inappropriate laughter threatening to burst forth and did my own blinking frog imitation back at him instead.

Frank took my silent blinks as permission to forge ahead. "You and I are in a tough spot. We're at a pinch point, if you will." He paused to dramatically shake his head and rub his forehead with long, thin fingers as if I were the source of a migraine. "I'm aware Robert Carpenter has passed, and offer you my, the bank's, heartfelt condolences, however...," his words trailed off.

"However," I leaned forward, "Bob's death doesn't change a thing. Is that what you're trying to tell me."

Frank, whom I was beginning to think would've done well in a career as an undertaker, nodded solemnly. "I'm afraid so."

I leaned back, taking a moment to sit with the knowledge. "So, what are my options. Surely there must be something we can do."

This time, Frank responded with a solemn shake of his head and lips pressed firmly together. "I'm afraid not."

This guy was getting on my last nerve. "Good night! This is a bank. There's plenty of equity in Carpenter's Corner. Can't you rewrite the loan to give me more time? I promise I'll repay it, since this time I'll know about it."

"No, I'm sorry. My hands are tied. It's simply the bank's policy. Had you only responded positively to my repeated attempts to reach you earlier, we may not have gotten into such dire straits." He clicked his tongue. "But since the original loan is in serious default, the bank has already started foreclosure proceedings."

My heart leapt to my throat. "Foreclosure proceedings? You can't be serious!" The second I'd found those loan documents, I'd known foreclosure was a distinct possibility, but hearing it said out loud sent shock waves from my head to my toes.

"Yes, the notice of default was filed at the county courthouse yesterday and appeared in the newspaper this morning, as a matter of fact."

"The newspaper? There was a notice of default on my store in the Greenwood Searchlight today?"

Frank pulled open the bottom drawer of his desk, then flipped through the morning's newspaper. Finding what he was searching for, he spread the paper across his desk, turned it in my direction and tapped a forefinger on a particular section. I leaned forward. Sure enough, there was my shame in black and white for all the world to see: Elkins National Bank vs Carpenter's Corner Hardware and Building Supply; 2051 Main Street, Pine Bluff, Oregon; Default Notice.

Instantly, my stomach rolled, and I thought I might lose my lunch all over the offensive newspaper. I squeezed my eyes shut but the notice was seared into my eyelids like a black-and-white negative.

I gulped back the rising nausea and addressed the undertaker—I mean banker—sitting before me. "Alright, there's a few things I still need to know. For starters, until Bob's death, the two of us owned the hardware store together." Well, even after his death, I supposed, since I hadn't done anything about changing the ownership into my name only. Another thing I'd put off far too long. "How is it possible for Bob to have taken out a loan without the bank requiring my signature as well?"

Take that, banker man. I've got you now. This time it was me who had his feet held over the fire. "And on a similar note, how can I possibly be held responsible for something I wasn't aware of?"

But Frank had an answer for everything. He licked his thumb, then picked through the documents in his file once again. "Here it is," he said with a triumphant and smarmy smile.

"Carpenter Corner's partnership agreement? What does our agreement have to do with anything?" I hadn't looked at it in years. In my mind, the document had only been a formality we'd had drawn up for tax purposes a lifetime ago. Nothing I needed to ever think about again.

Frank pointed to a particular clause. "Look closely at this line right here. In a partnership, one or more parties generally hold what is known as signatory authority. In the case of Carpenter's Corner, both you and Robert held signatory authority, separately."

I shook my head. "Okay, and what exactly does that mean?"

"It means a person with signatory authority can sign legal documents on the partnership's behalf. It doesn't require the second partner's signature, but all partners are equally responsible to make sure the loan is paid back in full. It seems Robert evoked his right to do so when he signed for this loan without your knowledge."

In other words, I was in deep, deep trouble. I sat in stunned silence for a few minutes. I'd always prided myself on being a strong, capable woman, but right now I was feeling as far from capable as a person can get. Why in the world had I not familiarized myself with every aspect of our business partnership?

If, by some miracle, I managed to get to the other side of this thing with my business intact, I'd be taking a hard look at how my business and accounts were structured. My head had been buried in the sand long enough.

Frank interrupted my thoughts. "Do you have any further questions for me, Mrs. Carpenter? I have an off-site meeting which I absolutely cannot be late for." He pointedly tapped his wristwatch.

"I think you meant to say tee time." I was beyond caring if he knew I'd been listening in to his earlier phone call. "But yes, I need to know how long I have and how much the total payoff will be."

"Let's see." Frank lifted documents until he found what he was looking for, then his fingers flew on the 10-key sitting on his desk. Finished, he ripped the paper tape from the machine, circled a figure at the bottom, and handed it to me. "As of today, your payoff would be $23, 874.52. Sixty days have passed since the loan came due, so you have one hundred and thirty days left before foreclosure will be final. Of course, your loan will be accruing interest each and every day until the final date. The sooner you can come up with a solution to remedy this, the better."

I scoffed while studying the tape. "That goes without saying." With a little over four months to come up with nearly twenty-five thousand dollars, my brain was already clicking through the possibilities. I grabbed my purse and shot to my feet. "Thank you for your time."

Frank chose that moment to beam a friendly smile my way. "It's been a pleasure."

Frankly, my dear, it's been a nightmare.

Chapter Twenty-Three

I headed for the door on legs as steady as limp spaghetti, but as I reached the front entrance, a shout caused me to whip my head around. Scotty Trimmer stood at a teller window, his face red and voice raised. I'd never seen the lumberjack angry before and it wasn't a sight I could tear my eyes away from.

The startled teller he was yelling at threw her hands in the air in surrender as Scotty hammered his pointer finger onto the counter. "This is highway robbery. I demand to talk to Frank Stockwell right this second!"

I glanced over my shoulder in time to witness Frank slinking out of his office and edging his way to the front door where I stood frozen. Before Frank could slip out the door, Scotty spied the spindly banker.

"Hey! Stop right there," Scotty shouted. "I see you, Frank." In two long strides, he ate up the space between the men.

The banker hung his head and glanced at his watch. "Shoot. To think I was so close to getting out of here." He took a deep breath and straightened his narrow shoulders. At full height, Frank was every bit as tall as Scotty, but he resembled a stick of licorice next to the burly lumberjack "What can I do for you, Mr. Trimmer?" Frank asked, a regretful tone in his voice.

I backed up into the corner of the entryway and tried to blend into the wall the best I could. Not because I wanted to be nosy, of course. My only concern was to not disturb their conversation by rudely opening the door.

Scotty waved a bank statement under Frank's beaked nose. "You can start by explaining to me why your bank took twelve-thousand dollars out of my business account."

I bit back my gasp.

Frank switched seamlessly from harried banker to his undertaker persona and pursed his lips. "As I've already explained to you over the phone, the open period on your business line of credit has expired, Mr. Trimmer. Since your payment was not received at the bank by the due date last week, your loan was considered in default. The bank was perfectly within its legal rights to pull the money from your main account in order to repay the delinquent loan." He smiled his reptilian smile. "As well as any fees associated with the loan, of course. You understand."

"No, I absolutely do not understand. I didn't authorize the bank to take any funds from my account. I've made every one of my payments on time until this last one. Never missed a payment. This past week has been a little stressful, but you couldn't see fit to understand what I'm going through and cut me a little slack? After fifteen years of doing business with you, this is how you repay me? Whatever happened to decency and kindness?"

Frank solemnly shook his head and held his long fingers together in front of his chest in a prayer pose. "My hands are tied. It's simply the bank's policy."

I snorted. Where had I heard those exact words before? Oh, wait. Five minutes ago in the slimy toad's office.

Scotty shifted from foot to foot and slapped the bank statement with a big hand. "I'm taking the last seven years' worth of statements directly to my accountant. Zach will go over them with a fine-tooth comb and if there is even one measly cent missing, you and your bank will be hearing from my lawyer. I'm sick to death of everyone taking advantage of me. You and this bank are nothing but common thieves!"

Scotty stormed out of the bank, and I followed a few paces behind. His truck was parked next to my Jeep, so I was privy to hearing Scotty hiss out, "No more mister nice guy," before hopping into his truck and bombing out of the parking lot. He left the acrid odor of burnt rubber in his wake.

Mulling over the lumberjack's use of the word thief, my mind flashed to the graffiti on the boulder at Nate's house. Thief was a common enough word. Just because Scotty shouted it at the banker didn't mean he'd been the one to paint it on the rock. But what did Scotty mean about *everyone* taking advantage of him? Who was everyone?

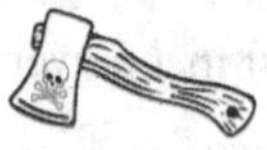

My appointment at the bank hadn't taken as long as I'd planned, even with a bit of impromptu eavesdropping thrown in, so I decided to swing by the hospital and check on Shayna's condition. Outside the main doors of the hospital, Scotty paced while talking on the phone. His back was to me as I walked up, so I slipped behind a concrete column in order to...tie my shoe. It wasn't my fault Scotty talked loud enough for a casual passersby to hear his conversation. It also wasn't my fault I had stellar hearing.

"Don't tell me to calm down," he growled. "That thieving bank took the entire payoff for my loan because my payment was a few days late. A loan I took out to buy a skidder I can't even use right now because I let Nate borrow it and he proceeded to drop a tree on it. This is what I get for always being a nice guy. No more!"

Holy fright. A skidder was a large and expensive piece of heavy equipment the loggers used in the woods to pull downed logs from the cutting site to an area where they could be loaded onto the logging trucks. Borrowing a skidder and wrecking it was a costly mistake. Could Scotty have been enraged enough at Nate about his ruined equipment to have killed his best friend over it?

Scotty paused to listen to the low rumbles from the voice on the other end of the line.

"Yes, I know he was going to have it repaired, but he died before that happened, now didn't he?" With the amount of aggressive pacing he was doing, I wouldn't have been surprised to see a trench open in the concrete sidewalk. "This could ruin me and I'm blaming you!" Another pause. "I don't know, Zach. You're my money guy. It's your job to figure this all out for me."

Scotty was blaming Zach for his money problems? Or was there something more sinister Scotty knew about his accountant? Nate died before he had a chance to get Scotty's skidder fixed. How was Zach at fault? Unless Scotty suspected, or outright knew, the accountant—and his own personal super fan—killed Nate. If Zach was a killer, why would Scotty keep that knowledge to himself? I would've thought he'd run straight to the police with it. *Dang it, I wish I could hear the other half of this conversation.*

"I don't care how you do it, but you better get this thing fixed or you're going to be ruined along with me. I'll make sure of it." Scotty jammed his cell phone into his pocket and stalked off into the hospital.

I was confident the lumberjack hadn't noticed me loitering at the bank or hiding...I mean tying my shoe..behind the column, so I straightened my shoulders and followed him inside.

The receptionist at the information desk was a woman I'd known for years. She lived in Pine Bluff and, before getting the job at the hospital, had worked as a grocery store clerk at Mill Street Market. After greeting her and asking about the kids, I inquired about Shayna.

"She woke up last night and is improving so fast they've already moved her out of the ICU. The girl needed a miracle and she got one." Her eyes sparkled as she recited Shayna's room number and waved me in the proper direction.

Not wanting to be too close on Scotty's heels in case he had gotten a glimpse of me, I stopped off at the gift shop and spent a few minutes trying to choose an appropriate gift. Shayna and I weren't anything more than casual acquaintances, and I didn't want to seem like a weirdo showing up in her hospital room empty handed. After some debate, I chose a small bouquet of get-well flowers and a four-piece box of gourmet chocolates.

As I approached Shayna's room, heart wrenching sobs poured out through the open door. Instead of barreling in, I peeked around the corner. Scotty was bent over the hospital bed, holding Shayna in his arms as the two of them cried. It wasn't a moment I wanted to interrupt, so I stepped back and leaned against the wall a few paces away from the open doorway. While I waited, I shot April a text to let her know I'd be back in about an hour. The sobbing coming from the hospital room finally stopped and I was about to announce my presence when Scotty walked through the doorway, rubbing tears out of his red eyes.

He spotted me leaning against the wall and raised a hand in greeting. "Dawna, hi. Are you here to see Shayna? I didn't realize you two knew each other."

"We don't. Not well, anyway, but I heard she was improving, and I was in town so thought I'd take the opportunity to stop in and see if there's anything I can do for her."

Scotty sniffed and nodded. "I'm sure she'll appreciate it." He turned and asked Shayna if she was up for more company. I couldn't make out her reply, but Scotty nodded at me. "Come on in."

Shayna lay reclined in a sitting position. A soft foam brace cradled her neck and hard plaster casts enclosed both her right leg and arm. The woman's heart-shaped face was pale against the white bedding, but she sent a tearful smile my way as I entered the room. I set the birch bark vase full of yellow and orange carnations on the windowsill and the box of chocolates within easy reach on her beside tray.

"You must be exhausted so I won't stay longer than a minute. I just wanted to pop in and tell you how glad I am to hear you're awake and recovering. Is there anything I can do for you?"

"Aw, that's so nice of you. But no, my parents are going out to the house every day to feed the cat and, from what I understand, Scotty here," she threw him a quick glance, "has barely left the hospital."

Interesting. I tried not to shift my gaze between the two of them, but what if Darlene had been right all along? Was there something going on between Scotty and Shayna?

"Everything is such a blur, but it was you who was with Nate's....well, that morning, wasn't it?" Shayna appeared frail, rubbing at her chest as if it hurt to breath.

I nodded. "Yes, it was me."

"Thank you for being there for me. I'm sure I nearly squeezed your neck off and shattered your eardrum wailing in your ear."

I reached out and laid a hand on Shayna's uninjured arm. "It was the least I could do. I'm sorry you had to see Nate like that. You're sure there's nothing you need?"

Shayna shook her head. "No, thank you. Besides, it looks to me like you could use some help yourself."

I frowned, unsure what she was talking about.

She gestured my way. "The sling and cast on your arm?"

"Oh! Silly me. It hasn't been hurting much so I'd nearly forgotten about it."

"What did you do?"

"Just clumsy." The last thing I wanted to do was to tell Shayna how I'd broken my wrist tripping over her murdered ex-boyfriend's feet.

When Shayna reached for the cup of chipped ice on her bed-side table, a diamond ring sparkled from her finger. It must've caught her eye, too, since she stopped in mid-reach and stared at the ring. "Scotty gave me this ring right before you got here. Isn't it beautiful?" Tears welled and slipped down her cheeks as she held her hand out for me to see.

"Scotty?" I gasped. My mouth hung open as I swiveled to stare at the lumberjack. Last I'd checked, Scotty was happily married to a gorgeous woman. The couple had two small kids who were going to be devastated. And Shayna had been Scotty's best friend's girlfriend until a few days before his untimely death. This revelation shed a whole new light on Nate's murder.

The shocked look on Scotty's face mirrored my own. He threw up his hands, palms out. "No, no. It's not what you think. The ring came from Nate, not from me."

"From Nate?"

"Yes, from Nate. He'd planned to propose to Shayna after the Timber Festival. He hid the ring at my house so she wouldn't inadvertently find it."

Confused, I swiveled my head back to Shayna. "But I heard a rumor from a reliable source that you and Nate had split up. It wasn't true?"

Fresh tears streamed down Shayna's face as she nodded. Emotions robbed her of speech, so Scotty ended up responding to my question in her place. "Shayna broke up with Nate, but he wasn't having it. Nate wasn't too worried because he was sure he could win her back."

Shayna wiped away the tears, finally finding her voice. "Like Scotty said, you heard correctly. I did break up with Nate, but was still living at the house until I could put away enough money for my own place." A sob escaped. "I loved him so much but I though he was tired of me."

I frowned. "What gave you that impression?"

"Because he was never home. He kept working longer and longer days and even taking jobs so far away he'd be gone for ten days at a time. When he was home, in the evenings he spent all his time either working in the sawmill or practicing for the lumberjack competition. He didn't have any time leftover for me anymore."

Scotty picked up the story once again. "What Shayna didn't know was how Nate was hyperfocused on putting enough money away to buy her an engagement ring." He gestured to the rock glinting on Shayna's finger. "Nate wanted to give her the wedding of her dreams. He was hoping to add to their wedding fund by winning the competition, which would've allowed them to splurge on a honeymoon to Hawaii. But Nate was going to propose at the end of Timber Festival weekend whether he won or not."

"He'd begged me to believe he still loved me, but I was stubborn and wouldn't listen," Shayna said. "I was so convinced he was lying and had another girlfriend already. Why didn't he tell me what he was planning?" She beat her good fist against the bed.

"Because he'd special ordered your ring and was waiting for it to be delivered. He had a plan," Scotty said.

Shayna dropped her face into her hands and wept. I sent a sad smile to Scotty and quietly backed out of the room, leaving the two friends to their mutual grief.

Chapter Twenty-Four

By the time I got back to Carpenter's Corner, it was nearly closing time.

"Congratulations again on your wins over the weekend," I greeted my young employee.

"Thanks. It was a ton of fun." Westen grinned. "And I didn't want to disappoint you so I went ahead and made a big splash during the log rolling. Just for you."

"Too bad I wasn't there to watch." I laughed. "Did anyone manage to stay on the log?"

"Yeah, Storm Keifer won. The kid has balance. He looked like he could've walked on that log all day long, and probably eaten a sandwich while he was doing it."

"You paint quite the picture. Storm's pretty smooth, huh?"

"Super smooth. He didn't even get wet on his dismount. Not a drop of water."

I sent Westen home and counted down the cash register. April was in the warehouse stripping several layers of paint off a vintage sideboard. I was about to lock the front door when Darlene whisked in, a large cowhide purse dangling from her arm. A dark-haired woman wearing tweed slacks, a burgundy blouse, and carrying a clipboard followed close on her heels.

Darlene looked me over with a cat-who-ate-the-canary smile. "Don't lock up yet, Dawna. Sally and I only need a few minutes, then we'll be out of your hair."

The woman, Sally apparently, had walked a few feet into the store and was craning her neck, inspecting the ceiling. For what, I couldn't imagine. She checked a box on the form on her clipboard, then jotted something down beside the checkmark before moving deeper into my store.

I frowned at Darlene. "Do you mind telling me what exactly is going on?"

"Isn't it obvious? I'm having the building appraised."

I choked. "Excuse me. You're what?"

Darlene wobbled her head as if I was a simpleton. "Having the building appraised. Do you not understand what an appraisal is?"

"I'm fully aware of what an appraisal is, but I believe you're the one confused. *I* own the building, not you, so it doesn't make any sense for you to bring an appraiser in here."

There was the feline hunter smile again. Darlene whipped a copy of the morning edition of the Greenwood Searchlight out of her oversized purse and tossed the newspaper on the counter in front of me. She tapped on it with a long, pointy, manicured fingernail. "Not for long, it seems. I'm simply getting all of my ducks in a row ahead of time."

The advertisement screamed up at me from the newspaper: NOTICE OF DEFAULT

Before I could talk myself out of it, I grabbed a broom from the witchy display in the front window and rushed around the corner of the checkout counter, brandishing the broom at Darlene. "Get out of my store!" I growled. "NOW!"

Darlene shrank back and blinked her heavily made-up eyes at me. I jerked the broom toward her in warning.

"You wouldn't dare."

"I suggest you don't test me."

She turned tail and scurried out the door while I focused my attention on the appraiser.

"You too." I didn't want to have to threaten Sally with my broom, but I wouldn't hesitate if the woman didn't skedaddle. And fast.

Sally sucked in her cheeks and stared after Darlene. "My apologies. Miss Lovelace didn't inform me of the entire situation. I was under the impression she was purchasing the building and had made an appointment with the owner to have it appraised."

"She most certainly is not buying my building," I replied through gritted teeth.

The appraiser dropped her business card on my front counter. "Call if you need my services."

I leveled my best glare at her back as Sally exited Carpenter's Corner.

Thirty seconds later, April strode through the swinging doors from the warehouse. "Did I hear someone shouting? Is everything okay?" She glanced around the empty store with a confused look on her face.

I grabbed the offending newspaper off the counter and shoved it deep into the garbage can. "Everything's fine. How about we grab dinner at the Stage Stop Café?" It was high time I told April about the loan, and the café seemed like a good enough place as any to spill the beans. I hoped a plate full of French fries would help to soften the blow.

"Uh, sure." She didn't look completely convinced everything was fine like I'd proclaimed.

The dinner crowd hadn't yet arrived at the Stage Stop, so April and I had our choice of seats. For the matter of privacy, as much as you could get in a busy small-town diner, I made a beeline for a window booth in the far corner of the café and slid onto the red vinyl bench seat. Loretta Lynn's "Coal Miner's Daughter" drifted from the overhead speakers.

DeAnn, my favorite waitress, was beside us with menus and blue plastic Pepsi glasses full of ice water before we even got settled. "Hello, ladies. The special tonight is a smoked turkey sandwich on a brioche roll with slices of pear and melted gouda cheese. I had one for lunch and it's lip-smacking delicious."

"Yum. The sandwich special does sound good." Even though I had the menu memorized, I still stared at it, not sure what my taste buds, and nervous stomach, were in the mood for.

"How about I give you a minute?" DeAnn suggested with a wink. She marched to the counter to grab menus and water for a group of six people who'd come in behind us.

April slid her menu to the corner of the table. "I was going to go for the French dip tonight, but I'm going to have to get the special."

"Mmm. It did sound pretty amazing, didn't it?" I continued to study the menu, finally settling on a comforting plate of biscuits and sausage gravy with a side of hashbrowns. One of my favorite things about the Stage Stop Café was that I could get a big old plate of comforting breakfast food whenever the need hit me.

After DeAnn returned and took our orders, I propped my good elbow on the table and rested my chin in my hand, trying to figure out how to start. I blew out a long breath.

"Alright, Mom, spill it. Something's going on. You've been a nervous wreck ever since you got back from your appointment this afternoon. Is your wrist not healing? Did the doctor say you're going to need surgery?"

I waved her concern away. "No, it's not about my wrist." It was something much bigger. "My appointment wasn't with the doctor today."

April scowled. "It wasn't? Why'd you lie to me about where you were going?"

I shrugged. "I didn't. You assumed, and I didn't correct you."

"Potatoes pota-toes. Where'd you go, then?"

"Elkins National Bank." I told April all about the certified letter that had been delivered two months before, the nagging phone calls, and my discovery of the signed loan documents stuffed in her dad's desk drawer. I only paused long enough to take a breath and allow DeAnn to slide our dinners onto the table.

"What in the world? Why would Dad take out a loan against Carpenter's Corner and not mention it to you? It doesn't sound like him."

I sucked in my lips before replying and shook my head. "You're guess is as good as mine. We may never know the answer to that burning question." I took a bite of steaming biscuits and gravy. As soft and comforting as the dish was, it stuck in my throat like concrete. I took a gulp of water to wash it down. "But I'll tell you what, if he was alive, I'd kill him for putting me in this situation."

April nodded her agreement. "So, what did the guy at the bank say? It's the only loan on the business and building, right? It should be easy to rewrite the loan and fix it."

I swallowed hard. "You would think, but no. The banker was about as helpful as a toad." I did my best to imitate his undertaker tone. "His hands were tied. It's the bank policy, you understand. Foreclosure proceedings have already begun."

"You're kidding." My daughter's eyes went as big as the biscuits on my plate.

"I wish I was. Which leads to the shouting you thought you heard earlier. You were not mistaken."

April gave me the side-eye. "Okay…What were you yelling about?"

"Like I said, a notice of default was placed in today's Greenwood Flashlight," I said, throwing shade on the true name of the newspaper, the Greenwood Searchlight. "Darlene read the notice in the paper and didn't waste a single minute bringing an appraiser in to give her a value on the building so she can make a bid for it."

This time it was April who choked on her food.

"I chased them out of the store with one of the brooms from your window display. I may or may not have screeched like a banshee in the process."

April started giggling and we both laughed until we cried. DeAnn strode to our table, hands on her hips.

"You two okay?" Our waitress studied the two of us with an amused grin.

"Fine. We're fine. Everything's fine." I wiped tears of mirth from my eyes with a crunchy paper napkin.

Once we settled down, April dove back in. "Okay, I need all the facts. How much is the payoff? How long do we have left? Can the foreclosure proceedings be stopped? We're going to get this fixed, Mom. You are not losing the store because of a bad decision Dad made five years ago."

My shoulders relaxed for the first time since leaving the bank, now that I was sharing the burden with my daughter. "We have a little over four months." I gave April the payoff figure, explaining the amount was as of today. The blasted thing would continue to grow every day with accrued interest.

"You know, Mom," April started hesitantly, "selling the house would solve this problem."

I glared at her, daring my daughter to say one more word.

She ignored me and said several more words. "Listen for a minute before you shut me down. The house is completely mortgage free and is worth a pretty penny in today's market. You'd have plenty of cash to pay off the bank, buy a smaller cottage we could fix up for you, and still have money in the bank for a rainy day." April paused and eyed me warily. "What do you think?"

I chose my words carefully, enunciating between each. "I think, if you know what's good for you, you should drop the subject immediately. What part of 'I am not selling my house' don't you understand?"

April blew out a huff of air, scattering the napkins on the table before she slammed her back against the vinyl booth seat, arms crossed against her chest.

"Dramatic much?"

"I'm trying to help, and you won't even consider it."

"I know you are, and you're also trying to get your sister and brother off your back. Not my problem."

She rolled her eyes.

With the sale of our family home off the table, we volleyed several other ideas back and forth, but didn't touch on any I felt were the ultimate solution. Now that we were seriously trying to come up with a game plan, I could almost feel the perfect solution nipping at the back of my brain. If only I could latch onto the idea as it rolled by.

"Let's sleep on it and see what else we come up with," I said.

April readily agreed.

With my mind a little more at ease, I tucked into my plate of biscuits and gravy before ordering a decadent slice of chocolate layer cake and a cup of black decaf coffee. April settled on a slice of peach pie with a dollop of fresh whipped cream. Over dessert, I filled my daughter in on my observations of Scotty at the bank and what I'd learned about Shayna and Nate's relationship when I had stopped by the hospital.

"Nate borrowed and wrecked Scotty's new skidder, and said skidder isn't even paid off yet?" April's fork clanked against her plate as she dropped it.

"It is now," I replied. "The bank took the money out of Scotty's account."

"True, but that only happened this afternoon. If someone borrowed an expensive piece of equipment from you and destroyed it, would you be mad enough to kill them over it?"

"Me?" I pointed my fork at my chest. "Probably not."

April rolled her eyes. "Hypothetically speaking."

I wobbled my head back and forth, thinking. "Maybe. I suppose in a moment of rage it could happen, even between best friends." I pondered April's theory for a minute. "Would you look at your equipment being destroyed as an act of thievery?"

"It's possible, for sure," April answered. "I'm also wondering what Scotty is holding over Zach's head. You mentioned Scotty told Zach if his business was ruined, Zach's would be too. Sounds like a threat to me."

I had to agree.

Chapter Twenty-Five

April and I strolled back toward Carpenter's Corner, where I'd left my Jeep parked when we went to dinner. It was six-thirty in the evening, and the autumn dusk had descended in our picturesque valley. Yet when I glanced down Pine Street as we crossed the intersection, light spilled from the front window of Moyer Accounting Solutions.

"Oh good, they're still open." I pivoted left, heading for the accounting office.

"Mom, what are you doing?"

I smiled at my daughter over my shoulder. "Maybe I need a new accountant."

April grimaced. "No, you don't. Not Zach Moyer, anyway."

The accountant Bob and I had used forever had retired after tax season the year before last, so last year I'd gone to one of those chain tax services that rise up everywhere in the early spring. The whole experience had been cold and impersonal, and I wasn't entirely pleased with the outcome. It was high time I found a new accountant, but April was right. It most certainly would not be Moyer Accounting Solutions.

"It wouldn't hurt to find out what Zach offers and what his fee is, now would it? A sharp businesswoman always needs to keep her eyes open for the best services around. And maybe do a bit of snooping while she's at it." I winked.

"Ah, gotcha. Lead the way."

Squeezing the thumb latch door handle, I came up short. The lights were on, but the door was locked. The young woman I'd met at the theater the other night looked up from her computer and flashed a smile when she recognized me. She rose and pushed the door open.

"Hi, Oriana. I didn't mean to bother you, but I noticed the lights were on and thought you must still be open."

"It's no bother. Sometimes I like to get caught up on things after the office is closed. There's far less distractions and I feel like I can actually get something accomplished."

"Believe me, I understand completely." I pointed to my side-kick. "This is my daughter, April Carpenter. April, meet Oriana Francini."

"Nice to meet you, April. Can I help you ladies with something?"

I waved a hand. "Oh, no. Since we were walking by, I thought I'd stop in and find out what Moyer Accounting Solutions has to offer to a local business like my own. I'll come back one of these days during business hours."

Oriana crossed her arms and tilted her head. "After the conversation we had at the theater the other night, I seriously doubt you're here to hire Mr. Moyer's services." Her dark eyes glittered under arched elegant eyebrows as she waited for my response. "You were hoping to get some more dirt on Zach you thought might help to solve Nate's murder, weren't you?"

Dang it. Oriana was a sharp woman. I should've known I wouldn't be able to get anything past her. "Sure, maybe I was, but what could I possibly find in the lobby of an accountant's office? And what connection to Nate's murder and Moyer's Accounting would you expect me to find?"

"Maybe we should talk inside." Oriana stepped back and invited April and me into the office.

Wide-eyed, I tugged on April's jacket sleeve. After only hesitating for a split-second, she followed me inside.

Before Oriana closed and locked the door, she poked her head out and peered up and down the empty street, then latched the door and twisted the wand on the blinds for added privacy. Once the window coverings were secured and she was sure we wouldn't be seen, she whirled around. "To answer your question, the connection I see between Mr. Moyer and Nate's murder is Moyer's weird obsession with Scotty Trimmer. Don't tell me you haven't picked up on it yourself?"

"Indeed, I have. It would be hard to miss." I nodded. "Go on. What else?" I wanted to hear Oriana's take on things without skewing her thoughts with my opinions.

"Mr. Moyer is adamant his reputation as an upstanding business owner in Pine Bluff is on the line because he sponsored Scotty, and Scotty failed to win the logging competition. He's been on an unholy rampage this week, worse than normal. His mood has been increasingly dark, leading me to wonder if he had something to do with Nate's death."

"Do you think Zach killed Nate in order to eliminate one of Scotty's competitors?" April asked.

Oriana lifted her shoulders in a delicate shrug. "Honestly, I can't say for sure, but Mr. Moyer has an enormous ego with a temper to match. I wouldn't rule him out."

"Were you working this afternoon, by any chance?" I asked.

"Sure. I was at my desk all day. Eight to five. Well...eight to whatever time it is now. I even ate my lunch at my desk today."

"Did you happen to overhear Zach on a phone call about two-forty-five or so?"

Oriana blew a raspberry. "Boy, did I ever. I put the call through to him. It was Scotty. How did you know?"

"I was privy to the other side of the conversation, and the incident directly before the phone call that had Scotty so wound up." I filled Oriana in on what I'd witnessed at the bank. "Then I went to the hospital to check on Shayna and overheard Scotty on the phone with Zach."

She nodded. "Your side of the story helps to fill in the gaps. All I heard of the conversation was Mr. Moyer trying to calm Scotty down. It was after he got off the phone things went sideways around here."

"What things?"

"Mr. Moyer kicked his garbage can again, which isn't particularly unusual, then he stormed out of his office and screamed at me to find a particular document for him. After I found it, he was even more upset, yelling about Elkins National Bank burying clauses in their loan documents that, in his words," Oriana made air quotes, "screwed the borrower."

He wasn't wrong there.

"Was the document in question Scotty's business line of credit agreement, perhaps?"

"It was. And the document happens to be still lying on Mr. Moyer's desk. Now, if you'll excuse me for a minute, there is an important email I need to answer." Oriana winked at April and me and slid into the chair at her desk, tucking her skirt demurely beneath her legs. While seated at her desk, her back was turned to Zach's office.

April and I hurried into Zach's domain where I snapped a picture of each page of the loan agreement with my cell phone. I wasn't sure how any of this could help the murder investigation, but they were worth looking at. With Oriana's back still turned, I glanced around the large office. A four-drawer file cabinet stood in the corner next to a small metal garbage can with several significant dents in its side. While April quickly pawed through Zach's desk, I pulled open the top drawer of the file cabinet.

Oriana's voice floated our way. "No need to search the files. Everything of interest is right here." Her right arm was extended into the air with a thumb drive held between her fingers.

April scurried out of Zach's office and snatched the thumb drive. I was right on her heels.

"One last question, Oriana, and then we'll skedaddle. Do you have any idea what Scotty knows about Zach that he might be threating him with?" I asked.

"None. Honestly, he's a terrible boss, but I haven't witnessed any funny business when it comes to his clients. If I had, I wouldn't still be working here." She frowned and shook her head, then pointed at the thumb drive April held. "But if there's anything to uncover, you'll most likely find what you're looking for in there. Do me a favor and destroy that drive when you're done."

I assured her we would.

As April and I left Moyer's Accounting Solutions, Oriana rose from her desk, shrugged into her coat, switched off the lights, and followed us outside. Once we'd all exited the building, she locked the door and dropped the key into her purse.

"Thank you for all of your help," I said.

Oriana shook her head as if confused. "What help? I don't have a clue what you're talking about. In fact," she narrowed her eyes, "I don't recall seeing either one of you tonight. April and I have never met." She pivoted on her heel and strode down the street in the opposite direction without a backward glance.

Chapter Twenty-Six

With the possible murder solution hot in our hands, April decided to spend the evening at my house so we could peruse the contents of the thumb drive. I filled the tea kettle with tap water and put it on the stovetop to heat while I waited for April to get back from her cottage with Thor. It was past the big dog's normal feeding time and April was worried he may have eaten the couch while she'd been gone. Half an hour later, woman and dog burst through the kitchen door in a shower of dog hair and shouts for Thor to settle down. In his sheer delight to see me, Thor nearly whipped me to death with his flying tail.

"He didn't eat a single stick of furniture," April was happy to report.

Thor tore through the house, inspecting every square inch for anything new. I swore I heard a cat hiss as the dog raced back into the kitchen.

Pulling mugs and several boxes of tea out of the cabinet, I decided on a simple peppermint to help soothe my stomach. April chose a cranberry spice hibiscus tea with a dollop of honey mixed in. Thor was happy to lap up a gallon of water from the bowl I kept on the floor by the pantry for him.

"Don't fall prey to his begging. He already ate and doesn't need any treats yet," April reprimanded me.

I may have slipped him a dog biscuit or five when the warden wasn't looking.

When the teapot let loose with an earsplitting shriek, the darn thing startled Thor and he threw back his head and howled. The invisible cat hissed again, and April barked at Thor to knock it off. I scrambled to get the kettle off the burner and stop the ruckus.

Once the sound level inside the house was under control, I poured hot water over our tea bags. I opened my laptop on the dining room table and plugged in the external thumb drive while April carried in our steaming mugs of tea. Thor wedged his big body under the table and lay down with a dramatic sigh, showing his disapproval at having his humans' sole focus somewhere other than on him. April and I laughed at the dog's antics before turning our attention to the computer.

Oriana had copied twenty-three files onto the drive. I started by opening each of them for a quick look. Right away the theme became crystal clear. Every one of the files belonged to people who, in one way or another, had a hand in the Timber Festival or logging competition. There were files for Nate, Scotty, Tommy, Matt, Chad, Katelynn, and most of the other lumberjack and lumberjills. Apparently, Zach hadn't been blowing smoke when he'd said the bulk of people in Pine Bluff used his services. From the looks of these files, I'd venture to say the number was closer to nearly everyone in two counties.

"Where should we start?" April blinked, looking overwhelmed with the sheer amount of information Oriana had handed over.

"At the top." The files were in alphabetical order by last name, so I opened the one titled Nate Durand first. "Might as well start with the victim."

Nate's file was fairly thin. As expected, it held copies of his last seven years' tax returns, but not much else, which lined up with what Shayna's friend Katelynn had said about Shayna being the bookkeeper for Nate's business. It seemed he only used Moyer Accounting Solutions to do his quarterly taxes.

"This is a nice snapshot of how well Nate's business was doing," April remarked. "He had a steady rise in income for a few years, then a big jump this past year."

I nodded. "He opened his sawmill last year, so that lines up. Apparently, his little operation was a lucrative venture."

"It would seem so."

I closed Nate's file, then jumped out of order, opening Scotty's next since his was the one I was most interested in. Scotty's file held a ton more information than Nate's had. Copies of Scotty's tax returns went back a dozen years. Since starting his own logging company two years ago, there were copies of all of his payroll records, purchase agreements for equipment, bank statements for checking, savings, and investment accounts, and a few other items I wasn't familiar with.

April and I searched through each document with a fine-tooth comb, but everything seemed perfectly in order and above board. I even went as far as getting out my handheld calculator and running numbers, but we didn't find a single thing to raise suspicion.

By the time we'd gotten through Scotty's file, I had a solid understanding of what Zach and his staff did for their clients. Far from simply handling taxes, they provided a full accounting service for small business owners, including handling payroll and investments. So far, April and I hadn't unearthed anything life shattering, but it was getting late and my eyes were as scratchy as sandpaper.

"Let's call it a night. I'll take my laptop and the thumb drive to work with me tomorrow and we can continue to look through the files whenever there's time." I stood and stretched. "It might not matter, though. I feel like we're barking up the wrong tree."

April agreed. "Yeah, so far there hasn't been anything suspicious. It all seems pretty cut and dry. Boring." She grabbed her keys off the table and yawned. As soon as she stood up, Thor exploded off the floor, nearly upending the table in his excitement. "Settle down, buddy. We're going home. See you tomorrow, Mama."

I locked the door behind them and took myself to bed where a disgruntled ghost cat finally showed herself. She curled up in a ball, but flipped her tail to show she was still irritated. "Sorry, little lady. You're going to have to learn to put up with the big bad dog." I closed my eyes and was sound asleep in seconds.

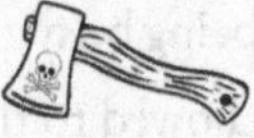

The next day was not a slow one at Carpenter's Corner as I'd thought it would be. The weatherman had predicted an unseasonably early snowfall to blanket our region over the weekend. Even though we'd most likely only see a skiff of the white stuff, the weather report brought all the local procrastinators into the hardware store in force. Within the first two hours, I'd sold my weight in weather stripping and an entire pallet of de-icer. Snow shovels flew out of the door as if they had wings, and I'd even sold three snow blowers, depleting my entire stock. I was grateful April didn't have a design job she needed to run off to and was free to help me at the store for the day. With my left arm still in the sling, I felt like a one-handed circus act, but all of my customers were patient with me and happy to munch on doughnuts and drink coffee while I painstakingly rang up their purchases.

At a quarter after ten, I sent April to Cookie Crumbles Bakery for a second round of doughnuts. The pastries had been almost as big of a hit as the winterizing supplies.

With the morning so busy, I didn't have time to wade through any more of the accounting files, but I was more than thankful for the flurry of sales. Not only was the bustling store good for the bottom line, being busy also kept me from dwelling on the twenty-four grand I owed to the bank.

April returned and dropped the box of fresh doughnuts on the counter. "Darlene hasn't dared to show her face in here today, has she?" she asked, shrugging out of her jacket. She arranged the doughnuts on the silver tray and started a new pot of coffee.

I shook my head. "And she'd better not, if she knows what's good for her. Next time, I'll take my broom to her backside."

"Or shove it where the sun doesn't shine," April added with a laugh.

"Good idea!" I pointed to the window display. "By the way, I sold your gorgeous sofa table to Annie Clarke a few minutes ago. She's going to send John in to pick it up this afternoon."

"Excellent. I'd better get cracking on the sideboard then. I want to put it in the window display next. It's ready for the top coat so if I can get it done this afternoon, I can get the piece in the window tomorrow."

"A sideboard, did you say?" a customer asked. "I've been keeping my eye out for one that will fit in my dining room. Do you mind showing me what you have?"

"Sure, come on back."

April took the woman to her workspace in the warehouse. When they came back up front, they were making arrangements for the woman to pick up the sideboard the next day.

I chuckled. "Well, there's a new one. It didn't even make it to the window display this time."

"I'm not complaining," April replied.

"And I'm excited," the new owner of the sideboard added as I rang up her purchase of two flashlights, two packs of batteries, and five forty-pound bags of wood pellets.

There was a lull in business around eleven, so April lifted a Bavarian crème filled doughnut off the tray and took a giant bite. Crème squirted out and landed on the checkout counter. I grabbed a blue paper shop towel, squirted some glass cleaner on it, and wiped up the mess. If only Darlene could see me now, cleaning my counter like I had good sense.

Once she finished chewing, April asked, "Have you come up with a plan yet to pay back the loan?"

I sighed. "There's a few ideas I'm kicking around, but nothing I'm completely happy with yet."

When Bob and I first purchased our family home, the land it came with took up the entire block. Ten years ago, we'd subdivided the property so it was ready in case an emergency ever arose and we needed to sell off a section or two. Bob and Bill had built a spec house on the lot on the far side of the carriage house that same year, which we then sold to help pay for the kids' college educations. The rest of the land we'd managed to hang onto. The carriage house was on its own divided lot with two more saleable lots sitting behind my big brick house. I loved the buffer I had between my house and the closest neighbors, other than Smitty whom I rented the carriage house to, and was loathe to sell any of the land if I didn't absolutely have to. However, in a pinch the option was available. Of course, it could take a few months for a lot to sell, especially this time of year, so if that was the road I needed to take, I'd need to make the decision soon.

"What are you two talking about? What loan?"

April and I both startled. Neither one of us had heard Bill approaching from the warehouse. A few of my regulars, including the coffee klatch guys, tended to park behind the store and sneak in through the warehouse doors.

April eyed me. "You better tell him, Mom. There's a good possibility Bill might know what happened and why Dad did this."

Bill frowned. "Did what?"

I sighed, wanting to keep my money struggles to myself. My stubbornness and pride hadn't always worked in my favor. If anyone could shed some light on why Bob had taken out the loan in the first place, it would be Bill.

"People can't help if you don't tell them what's going on," April prodded. The girl was like a dog with a bone.

"I know, I know."

Bill stared at me with arms crossed against his chest, waiting for me to fill him in.

I told him about Elkins National Bank calling and sending the certified letter, and my subsequent ignoring of said attempts to contact me, but then finding the signed loan documents in Bob's desk drawer.

"You didn't know anything about this loan?" Bill questioned. "The bank hadn't sent any statements or reminders all this time?"

"Nope. Bob signed the loan by himself under the authority of our business partnership. He didn't tell me a thing about it. It was a single payment loan, meaning it sat there quietly accruing interest until the payment was due at the end of the five-year period. Which was exactly sixty-one days ago."

"Wow, that's a rough spot to be in." Bill shook his head.

"Do you have any idea why Bob took out the loan in the first place? Did he confide in you about it?"

Bill frowned and scratched his head. "Sorry, Dawna, I don't. Bob never mentioned it to me. You know I'd tell you in a heartbeat if he had."

"I know you would." I blew out a breath. "So now I'm trying to figure out how to pay the loan in full before Carpenter's Corner is foreclosed on." And trying to figure out why my husband would keep the whole mess a secret from me in the first place.

"The paying the loan back part's easy," Bill said nonchalantly.

"It is? Do tell."

"It's simple. I'll loan you the money. No interest. There's no way I'm going to sit by and watch you lose the hardware store when I can fix it for you."

I adamantly shook my head. "No. Thank you for the offer, but no. I have options. I can fix this myself."

"Mom, you should think about it. Bill's only trying to help."

"I know, but I've got it. I swear to you everything will be fine."

Bill studied my face, knowing I meant what I said. "Well, keep it in your back pocket, just in case. The offer doesn't have an expiration date."

I nodded, grateful but determined to handle it myself.

"Alright, then." He rubbed his callused hands together. "Did my lumber order come in?"

April went to load his trailer with the forklift while I rang up Bill's invoice, minus his twelve-percent contractor's discount. Bill signed the receipt, and I filed it away. At the end of the month I'd mail out an invoice like I did for all my customers who had open accounts.

When Bill pulled out of the lot with his load of lumber, April came back inside. She placed her hands on her hips and studied me with a scowl. I did my best to ignore her, but her unblinking stare became too much.

"What?" I finally asked, perturbed.

"Why are you being so stubborn? Taking the loan from Bill seems like the perfect solution, yet you're not even willing to consider it as an option. I don't understand why not."

"You're right. It would be the easiest way to go." I nodded, acknowledging April's point.

"But?"

"But accepting Bill's offer would once again be a man rushing in to save the day. It was a man thinking I didn't need to know what was going on that put me in this difficult situation in the first place. I don't know why your Dad did what he did," I placed my one good fist on my hip and planted my feet wide, "but this time, I'm going to be my own, one-winged, super hero."

"Makes sense. I'm behind you all the way." April mimicked my pose—albeit with two working fists—grinned, and quoted Wonder Woman. "So long as there is hope, there can be victory!"

"Exactly. Glad you see it my way."

April nodded. "You've got this, Mom. We'll figure it out together. Girl power!"

The next wave of customers pushed through the door, effectively ending our conversation for the time being. Business remained brisk. Around noon, April sped to the Hungry Bear Drive-In and brought us back orders of burgers and their famous barbequed French fries. We devoured our lunches between customers.

By midafternoon, John Clarke had stopped by to pick up the sofa table his wife had purchased, and the crowds of winterizing shoppers had died back. Only one or two customers were in the store at a time. I was cashing out a woman who was purchasing a roll of insulation film for her windows and a new filter for her heating unit when April's cell phone rang. She stepped away from the front counter to take the call. Once my customer left with her purchases, April called out to me.

"Mom, Westen's working this afternoon, right?" She held her phone against her chest so she wasn't yelling in the caller's ear.

I glanced at the clock. "Yep. He should be here about three-thirty."

"Perfect." April focused her attention back on her phone call.

"What's going on?" I questioned after she'd hung up.

"The Schoonover's have already found a tenant for their rental I finished the other day. Apparently, they had so many applicants they're thinking about buying another house to turn into a rental. A fixer upper they're interested in went on the market today and they want me to look at it with them at four this afternoon to get my opinion on renovation costs."

"Great. Go for it. Westen will be here to help out, so the timing is perfect."

For the next hour, as I went about my day, something about the Schoonover's rental units tickled the edge of my brain. Like so many places these days, our little town of Pine Bluff struggled with a shortage of affordable housing. When a cheaper house came on the market, it generally needed so much work it was either too daunting for first time homebuyers, or they weren't able to qualify for a loan for a house that wasn't move-in ready.

Bertha Smith, known to everyone in town as Smitty, had been renting the carriage house on my property for the past five years.

With Smitty in her upper eighties and living on a fixed income, I only charged her enough rent, utilities included, to make her feel like she was self-sufficient. Most months, her meager rent didn't cover the electricity bill on the cottage. There was no way on the face of this earth I'd be raising Smitty's rent, but I could definitely see how owning a few rentals would be profitable in this market.

By the time April left to meet the Schoonovers, Westen was cheerfully helping the few customers still coming into the store so I finally sat down with my laptop and the thumb drive from Moyer's Accounting Solutions. I situated myself at my desk so someone would have to be trying hard if they were going to read over my shoulder.

This time, I opened the file named "Keifer's Carvings" first. Right away, it was clear Tommy was one of Zach's clients who had hired the accounting firm for all of his small business needs. The bank statements showed six decent sized deposits into the Keifer's Carvings account during the summer and fall months, which lined up with what Tommy had told me about the shows he attended to sell his chainsaw art. There were smaller deposits throughout the year, and I was pleasantly surprised at the amount of money Tommy's work brought in. He wouldn't be getting rich from it any time soon, but his carvings provided a decent living for the family. *Good for them*. I clicked into the subfolder for payroll. The only paycheck's written were a monthly stipend titled "Owner's Draw."

With nothing more to see there, I closed the Keifer's Carvings file and clicked into the one titled "Matt Forester." Like Tommy and Scotty, Matt used Moyer's for all his accounting needs. Business wise, he'd only gone out on his own less than a year ago, and as a one man show, there weren't many documents for his logging company yet. I combed through Matt's previous years' tax returns, noting he'd barely made enough to scrape by most years. In a subfile titled "Notes," Zach had made notations on Matt's employment status at various times, listing dates and employers. Scrolling through the notes, it was easy to determine why the man made so little in income. He was "laid off" more than he worked. I found it curious how after each time Matt was laid off from a logging company, or the local sawmill, he didn't go back to work for several months, and always for a different employer. The whole thing screamed fired to me as opposed to laid off, which was right on par with Matt's history. It looked like he'd worked for every independent logging company in three counties at one point or another, including both Scotty and Nate. Nate's logging company was listed as Matt's last "layoff" before the notoriously hard to employ logger went off on his own.

"Dawna? Could you please help Mr. Burns find the nails he needs?" Westen stood at the counter, ringing up one customer's purchase while another woman waited in line.

Jerry Burns waved at me from the fasteners' aisle.

"Of course." I glanced at the clock, surprised to find an hour and a half had passed while I was lost in the accountant's files.

Carpenter's Corner would be closing in less than thirty minutes. I quickly exited out of the thumb drive and closed my laptop before rising to help Jerry find the right nails for his project.

Chapter Twenty-Seven

After locking the doors and sending Westen home, I counted down the till and put the day's cash in the safe for the next day's bank deposit. I'd walked to work this morning, anticipating it was going to be the last decent walking day for the next week or so if the forecast could be believed. At a quarter after six, dusk had already fallen, but I loved the coziness of walking through my little town while warm lights spilled out of the businesses still open, and even through neighbors' windows as people gathered with their families for the evening. Bob used to laugh and call me a Peeping Dawna when we went for walks around the neighborhood after dark. I loved the little intimate glimpses of other people's lives.

Today while I walked home, my purse was thrown over my shoulder and I had my laptop bag clutched in my good hand. Instead of gazing through all the shop windows I passed, I mulled over the information from the thumb drive I'd been combing through all afternoon.

As I crossed the intersection of Main Street and Pine, a rusty, rattletrap, avocado green Ford pickup truck with a mismatched brown tailgate pulled up in a cloud of exhaust and rocked to a stop, one tire resting on the curb. There was no doubt in my mind it was the same truck that had ridden Evonne's tail the other night as we made our way out of the canyon. Matt jumped out of the cab. He raced to Moyer's Accounting Solutions and pounded on the door with a closed fist as if getting into the accounting office was a matter of life and death. I trotted closer to keep an eye on what he was doing and to make sure Oriana remained safe if she was in the office alone.

Sure enough, Oriana poked her head out of the door. "I'm sorry, Mr. Forester, but we're closed for the day. I can schedule an appointment for you with Mr. Moyer for tomorrow if you'd like."

"No, I want to talk to that traitor now. Right now." Matt danced around, trying to get around Oriana and into the office.

The petite woman held her ground. "As I said, Mr. Moyer is not in. He has gone home for the day. Would you like an appointment for tomorrow?" Oriana pronounced each word carefully, as if talking to someone who didn't quite understand the language.

Matt reached for the door in another attempt to get inside.

I stepped forward and cleared my throat. "Is everything okay here?"

Oriana shot me a grateful smile while Matt leveled me with a ferocious glare, his protruding forehead nearly obscuring his small eyes.

"No, everything is not okay here." Spittle flew from Matt's mouth as he raged. "Nate managed to rob me of all the good logging jobs, and now that tool Scotty is getting the jobs that rightfully should be mine now Nate's dead." He jabbed a finger at the Moyer Accounting Solutions sign. "And it's all this flipping bean counter's fault."

"How so?" I questioned.

"Zach and his bromance with Scotty is how so. Zach spread those stupid buttons all over town with Scotty's face on them, bought him new equipment for the logging competition, and made him out to be some kind of hero. Now Scotty's the one getting all the jobs I've been bidding on and it's a bunch of horse crap." Matt turned his glare on Oriana. "You can tell Mr. Moyer," he spat out the name, "he's fired. I'm pulling my accounts from this place."

I'm sure Zach will be devastated, I thought sarcastically.

"I'll be sure to let him know first thing in the morning," Oriana replied.

Matt shot me a barbed glare before he stalked back to his truck and sped off with a squeal of tires and a choking cloud of exhaust.

After waving away the toxic fumes, I asked Oriana if she was okay after her encounter with the irate logger. "Do you need me to stay until you lock up? I'm more than happy to wait for you."

She waved away my concern. "Oh no, I'm perfectly fine. Matt isn't the first irate client I've had to deal with in this job, believe me."

With Zach as her boss, I wasn't surprised a bit by her statement.

We said our goodbyes and I continued on my way home, playing back Matt's accusations on repeat. It was curious to me how he'd accused Nate of robbing him of logging jobs. Most of those jobs were bid on, much like in construction, and generally the logging company with the best bid for time and cost won out. Our corner of the state wasn't densely populated and most people who worked in the logging industry knew each other or had at least heard of one another. The way a person did business could go a long way in winning those bids. If Matt wasn't getting the jobs he bid on, it was most likely more about his reputation than anything else. Matt tended to blame everyone but himself for his hard luck, but from my viewpoint, it wasn't luck causing his bad fortune—it was his own crappy attitude. And the perfect example of that attitude had played out in technicolor right in front of me moments ago.

Up ahead, a train whistle blew as a Union-Pacific freight train chugged through Pine Bluff on its evening run to our sawmill. The rumble of a train chugging through town was comforting to me. It made up the background noise of our daily lives.

"Oh, good night!" I'd emerged from my heavy thoughts only to find a couple of large, rusty orange train cars had slowed to a halt and blocked the road and sidewalk a block in front of me. I was literally stuck on the wrong side of the tracks.

The train tracks ran through neighborhoods parallel to Main Street and only two blocks from my house, so I'd almost made it home, but tonight's train had come to a complete stop, as it did from time to time, cutting off one side of town from the other. Red lights flashed and the white and red safety gates were lowered across the road. I blew out a breath and kept walking until I came to the train and couldn't go any farther.

Setting my laptop bag onto the sidewalk to give my arm a break, I used the unexpected free time to continue mulling over the information I'd gleaned from both the thumb drive and Matt's bad behavior a few minutes ago. It took a minute to connect the dots, but I finally realized that at about the same time Matt had been fired from his last job, Nate's business had really taken off. The dates from their two files crashed together in my mind. With Nate's business thriving and Matt's swirling the drain, Matt had accused Nate of stealing the logging jobs from him. The word "Thief" written on the boulder at Nate and Shayna's home flashed through my mind like a neon sign. All the little clues suddenly started to snap into place like tresses on a roof. I gasped. Matt was Nate's killer.

"Hurry up, train!" I bellowed. As if in response, the train jerked forward two inches and I got ready to hot foot it across the tracks. Then the train cars rocked back into place. I scrambled for my phone instead.

Before I had the chance to dig my cell phone out of my bag to call the police, a vehicle roared up behind me and revved its engine. Matt sneered at me through his open window.

"We need to talk," he growled and nodded toward the train. "And since you ain't going nowhere, it's as good a time as any, don't you think?"

No, I absolutely did not. I swallowed hard and shoved my glasses up the bridge of my nose. *Feign innocence, Dawna. You don't know a thing.* "Sure. What do we need to talk about exactly?"

"You and that friend of yours were snooping around up at Nate's house the other night, and the cogs in your head were turning back there at that lousy accountant's office just now. You finally figured out it was me who killed Nate."

My facial expressions have always had a mind of their own, no matter how hard I tried to control them, but he was wrong. When Matt had been yelling at Oriana, I'd thought he was a great big jerk. It wasn't until thirty seconds ago I'd put two and two together and figured out Matt was a cold-blooded killer. I gulped and shook my head. "You misinterpreted. It never crossed my mind you might be the killer. You were so helpful the morning we found Nate's body. Remember? Why in the world would I think you killed him?"

A sly grin spread across his face. "That was my plan, and it worked for a while. Who could accuse the guy who called the police and helped out at the scene of the crime?"

I backed up closer to the motionless train rumbling behind me. Matt had all but admitted to being the murderer. I needed to call J. T. but was paralyzed as to how to get my phone out of my purse without causing Matt to attack. A small shift in posture sent my purse sliding off my shoulder and down to the crook of my elbow, but with my left arm in a sling, I couldn't reach inside the purse to get the blasted phone. For now, I was going to have to try to talk my way out of this. *Move train, move!*

"Matt, I know you didn't do it." I stared directly into his eyes. At a safety awareness class I'd taken last month, we'd been taught how making eye contact and calling the perpetrator by name would sometimes cause them to back off. "Everyone knows you're not a bad person. Even if you had a problem with Nate, you would never have tried to hurt Shayna."

My eye contact tactic didn't seem to be working. In fact, with the mention of Shayna, Matt grew even more agitated than he already had been. He slammed a fist into his steering wheel, causing the horn to blare and my heart to pound in my throat. He jerked open the door and lurched out of his truck, leaving the driver's side door yawning open. With his hard gaze locked on my face, he reached into the pickup bed. When he pulled his arm back out, a baseball bat was gripped in his fist. Matt smacked the bat into the palm of his hand as he swaggered toward me. Bringing up Shayna's name had apparently been the worst idea I'd had yet. And I was chock full of bad ideas.

"Shayna? What a pathetic excuse of a woman! Too bad she survived the crash. Not how I imagined it going." His nostrils flared.

"What do you have against Shayna? A tiny woman like her couldn't be much of a threat to a strong man like you, now could she?" Maybe playing to his ego would get me somewhere. The other tricks I had up my sleeve hadn't worked so far.

"You don't think so, huh?" Matt raised his eyebrows in surprise. "Then you don't know much, do you? Shayna happens to be the one who convinced Nate to fire me. He never would've done it without her goading him on. Then the cow had the gall to smirk when she handed me my final paycheck. I've finally wiped the smirk right off her stupid face."

I gulped hard. "Why would Shayna have wanted you fired?" If I could keep him talking long enough, maybe the train would start to roll and I could escape. Maybe pigs would fly.

"Drop one little load of logs on a skidder and the woman says I'm careless and too dangerous for her precious boyfriend to work with in the woods. I showed her what danger is, now didn't I? She's never worked one single day out in them woods. All she does is play dress up and act like a logger in front of crowds of people. Everything that woman does is all for show." He slammed the bat against the palm of his hand again. "Did the stupid witch ever stop to think maybe me dumping those logs on the skidder was no accident?"

My eyes widened. "You dropped the logs on purpose?"

Matt grinned. "Sure did. Nate had been making noise about bringing me into the business as a partner, and rightfully so. He couldn't run that operation without me."

Who did he think he was kidding? Matt was delusional. Nate's business had exploded after he'd let Matt go.

Matt continued his tirade. "Scotty was getting way too big for his britches. He needed a roadblock put in his path, so when Nate borrowed his buddy's new skidder, I saw my opportunity and took it. And how did that backstabbing jerk repay me? By running me out of there. So, I took another opportunity when it presented itself the other morning."

"You caught Nate alone in the park and took him by surprise."

"Yep" Matt tutted. "He shoulda kept a better grip on his axe." A sick smile twisted his lips as he slapped the bat into his palm once more and took a menacing step toward me. "Just like you shoulda kept your nose out of my business."

The man was diabolical. I took another step backward.

He took two steps forward and let out an amused laugh. "Where do you think you're going to go?" He eyed me like a mountain lion stalking prey.

Matt was right. With nobody else on the street, and the parked train creating a solid wall at my back, I was trapped. Knowing I had nowhere to run, Matt took his time creeping my way. Frantically, I searched the street, hoping another car would pull up behind Matt's truck, but the neighborhood was eerily quiet. Where *was* everyone? My heart raced as I swiveled my head between him and the inert train.

Flashing back to a memory from third grade, I remembered standing in this exact spot with a group of kids after school, a train blocking our way home when a classmate crawled underneath the train car. The rest of us had watched with awe from between two train cars as our friend emerged on the other side. She had turned and waved at us before she carried on her way home. She'd become something of a legend in the third grade after that afternoon.

I eyeballed the tight space under the train. There was no way I could manage it. Was there? What if the train lurched into motion while I was under there? I'd most likely be killed, but if I stood here much longer, my chances were slim to none. And last I knew, slim had left town. I needed to make a break for it. Now. Crawling under the train seemed to be my only option.

With one or two steps closer, Matt could've easily smacked me if he'd swung the bat. If I was going to make my great escape, it was now or never. I reached for my laptop case and flung it at Matt's head with all my strength. He stumbled backward. Losing his balance, he sprawled on the sidewalk.

I used the precious seconds it took Matt to recover from the surprise attack to pull the sling off my left arm, drop to my belly, and begin to scoot under the train. The first track dug into my chest. As I army crawled as fast as I could move, my knees banged against the metal railroad tracks while creosote from the treated wooden ties seeped onto my hands and clothes.

"Nice try, but you're not getting away that easy," Matt growled. He tugged at my feet, trying to pull me back out.

I kicked hard, holding onto the second track for dear life and leveraging myself deeper under the train. Matt grunted. Good. My kick had found its target. I focused on moving forward. Six inches to go and my head would be out the other side. A grinding noise came from the train as it rocked forward. I was going to die. My whole body shook and my breath was coming too fast. The rocking train eased, the crushing wheels stopping half an inch from my sweaty hand gripping the track. With a surge of adrenaline, I shoved my way out from under the train. My raspy breath filled my ears.

As I scrambled to my feet, a sharp whistle blew and the train slowly began to inch forward, picking up speed as it went. I'd made it out in the nick of time. With any luck, it would be the longest train anyone had ever seen. I glanced back at Matt, catching glimpses of him between the flying train cars. His face flamed red under the flashing safety lights. His eyes were wild and full of hatred. I shuddered with fear.

Unfortunately, I'd lost one shoe to the killer, but better a sneaker than my life. I turned and sprinted as fast as my one-shoed feet could carry me, yelling to beat the band the entire way home. If any of my neighbors were paying attention, I wanted them to know there was a crazed murderer after me.

I raced into my house, turned the dead bolt behind me, and pulled out my phone. Good thing I had the police chief's number on speed dial.

"J. T., it's Matt Forester. Matt killed Nate." I gasped for air.

"I know, Dawna. The fingerprint report came in a few minutes ago on the pipe cutters. We're out looking for him right now. Why are your breathing so hard?"

"Because Matt just tried to kill me."

"What? Where is he?"

"Stuck on the downtown side of the train on Alpine Street. At least he was five minutes ago. He shouldn't have gotten far."

"Where are you?"

"At home."

Sirens blared through the phone. "On my way. Stay where you are. I'll call you back as soon as we pick him up."

I paced the house for the next ten minutes, my phone clutched in my hand the entire time. When it finally rang, it startled me so much I yelped even though I'd been waiting for the call.

"Matt is in custody. You can relax now," J. T. told me. "Good work, Dawna."

I dropped into Bob's old recliner in my living room and shook like an autumn leaf in the wind, now the imminent danger had passed. J. T. must have called April because thirty seconds later she came screaming through the door and scooped me into a hug. Even though I'm not normally much of a hugger, I was happy to accept one this time.

"How'd you figure it out, Mom?" April asked when she finally released me from her death grip. "Was there a clue in the files Oriana gave us?"

I nodded. "There wasn't anything that screamed, 'Matt murdered Nate,' but I noticed how Nate's business had taken off not long after he'd let Matt go. Matt went out on his own after Nate fired him—"

April snorted. "Because he'd been fired from everywhere else and there was no one left who would hire him."

"I'm sure you're right, but Matt's attempts at working for himself failed just as miserably. It looks like he had a few small jobs here and there, but not enough to survive on. Matt doesn't have the wherewithal to be a business owner. Not everyone does. In contrast, Nate's company was not only expanding, but thriving."

"So, Matt looked at Nate's success as if Nate was stealing jobs from him. They would've been bidding on a lot of the same jobs, so in Matt's warped mind, Nate was undercutting him," April said.

"Exactly. I should've seen it earlier."

"Why did he try to kill Shayna, though? That part still doesn't make any sense to me."

I relayed what Matt had told me about Shayna's role in his getting fired while I had waited for the train, and Matt had waited to kill me.

"Wait, Matt seriously thought he and Nate were going to be partners?"

"Most likely another one of his delusions."

After she was assured I was safe and sound, April finally sat back and wrinkled her nose. "You smell like tar."

I glanced down at my creosote-stained clothes. "It's a symptom of crawling under a train."

April shook her head. "I can't believe the situations you manage to get yourself into. Go take a shower and clean up while I whip you up some dinner."

I was more than happy to oblige.

Chapter Twenty-Eight

A long hot shower worked wonders on my sore, aching body, even though my broken wrist was stuffed into a plastic bag secured to my arm with rubber bands. When I turned off the shower, the incredible scent of whatever delicious concoction April was whipping up for dinner made my stomach rumble. But when I opened the bathroom door to the murmur of voices, my shoulders instantly shot up to my ears. *Who in the world is here?* Sure, the shower had helped relax me somewhat, but it'd been a long, emotional day and I was not in the mood for company. What was April thinking, inviting someone in when I'd had such a traumatic evening? I cinched my fuzzy robe tighter around myself and crept down the hallway until I could peer around the dining room doorframe to discover who the intruder was.

When I spied my elderly neighbor Smitty sitting at the table, my shoulders relaxed. It wasn't unusual for either April or I to run over and invite Smitty to eat with us a few times a week. I could forgive my daughter for this transgression. April stood at the stove, dishing dinner into colorful Fiestaware bowls. Good.

I didn't feel bad about staying in my robe and eating dinner with wet hair. Smitty wouldn't mind one tiny bit.

"Hi, Smitty. I'm glad you could come over for dinner tonight. How are you?" I slid into the chair beside my neighbor as April placed steaming bowls of shepherd's pie in front of us.

Smitty immediately picked up her spoon, her constant tremor causing the spoon to clank rhythmically against the bowl. "Oh, I've been good, dear," she replied in her shaky little voice. "My plaid pants have been returned and I couldn't be happier about it."

I cleared my throat in surprise while April twittered behind her hand.

"Your plaid pants are back?"

Smitty's wide eyes stared at me with complete confidence. "Yes. The robber must have found the pants didn't fit him after all and returned them to me."

Smitty was full of farfetched stories. A couple of months before, she'd told me how her favorite plaid pants had gone missing. As soon as she'd finished the story, she'd excused herself to make a call to the police to report the crime.

"Such good news," I choked out, trying to hold back the belly laugh insisting on rumbling from my throat. Instead, I shoved a spoonful of hot shepherd's pie into my mouth. Even though it burnt going down, the flavors were delicious. I looked at April with awe. "How in the world did you find the ingredients to whip this up? And so fast?"

My daughter grinned. "You had everything I needed. There's enough food in this house to feed a family of four for a month."

"Then why can I never find anything to eat?" This time, I blew on a spoonful of the creamy mashed potato casserole to cool the food down before eating it.

"Because you tend to wait until you're hungry before you think about dinner. By then, you're grouchy and want something fast so you go for quick and easy."

"I feel attacked." I laughed but my daughter had a point. Over the years of raising my family, I'd ripped open my fair share of boxes of Hamburger Helper and tuna casserole, which we jokingly referred to as tuna wiggle in our house. "This is a million times better than any of my boxed meals."

I'd taken my third bite when Smitty held out her empty bowl. "Your mother's correct. Dinner was delicious. I surely wouldn't say no to another serving if there's enough to go around."

April's eyes sparkled as she rose to get Smitty's refill. "You got it. I made plenty."

"Only a small portion, dear. You know my appetite isn't what it used to be."

April winked at me. We were continuously amazed at the amount of food the tiny woman could pack away. Whenever we shared dinner with Smitty, she managed to eat more than the two of us combined. If her appetite wasn't what it used to be, she must've eaten her family out of house and home when she was in her prime.

Once April placed another steaming bowl of shepherd's pie in front of Smitty, she tucked right in. We sat and ate in companionable silence for a few minutes.

Smitty was halfway through her second helping when she came up for air. "By the way, I've been meaning to talk to you about those buttons."

"Buttons?" I wrinkled my forehead in confusion.

Smitty pulled the neckline of her bulky sweatshirt down and tapped on the Axe Kicker promo button clipped to the turtleneck she wore under the sweatshirt. "Yes, dear. These buttons, remember? We talked about them the other day."

I nodded. "Sure. You remembered something about the buttons?"

"Not the buttons exactly, but I'm quite certain my experience I'm about to tell you about ties into how you keep finding these buttons all over town."

I raised my eyebrows, curious to hear what Smitty had to say. "I'm listening. Go on."

"Now, this story goes back many years to a time when my sister Sissy and I were working on Broadway, mind you." Her watery eyes sparkled. "Boy, those were the days. Did the two of us ever have a ball!"

April and I shared a look. *Smitty worked on Broadway?* This was the first I'd heard of that aspect of her life. Eager to hear more, I kept my trap shut so she could continue.

"Sissy and I had finished a long, tiring run of a production called *Fancy Meeting You Again* and had a few weeks for ourselves. We decided to ride the train back to our family home in Wyoming for a time..."

Wyoming?

"...Once we arrived home, we opened our suitcase, and do you know what we found?"

Fascinated, I shook my head no. April mirrored my action.

Smitty's eyes went wide. "It was the biggest pair of silky women's underwear you have ever laid your eyes on."

April nearly spit out her dinner.

I blinked three times. "Underwear?"

"Not just any underwear, understand. Expensive giant panties." She held her hands to demonstrate panties approximately three feet wide.

"What did you do with them?"

Smitty looked as if she was still shocked by the discovery. "What could we do? We threw them in the garbage, of course. What were two small western girls going to do with an enormous pair of silk drawers?" She blinked at me as if waiting for an answer.

"Throwing them away sounds like a reasonable solution," I said. "How exactly does this mysterious pair of underwear tie into Scotty's buttons?"

Smitty clicked her tongue and waved her spoon at me. "Now you haven't heard the entire story. I'm not done yet." She shook her head. "Young people are so impatient."

"Sorry. Proceed." I stuffed more shepherd's pie into my mouth, inwardly chortling at being called a young person.

"You see, not a week later, I opened my top dresser drawer and there were those panties once again. Now, Sissy and I thought our troublesome young brother was playing a trick on us, so we decided to show the little rascal who was smarter."

"What did you do?" I asked again. The question felt safe enough to not get me in any more trouble with the storyteller.

"Why, we took those panties out to Papa's burn barrel and lit them on fire."

I pictured silk panties doing a slow melt as opposed to burning. Silly me, I voiced my thought.

"Oh no," Smitty replied. "Sissy siphoned gasoline from Papa's tractor and we piled the burn barrel full of dried cowpies and topped it with a tumbleweed for good measure. Everything went up in a swoosh of flames." Smitty flung her arms in the air as she described the fire.

"Sounds like an effective way to take care of the problem," I said.

"You would think." Smitty's voice was full of mystery as she nodded knowingly.

"It didn't?" April asked.

Smitty shook her head. She sat up straighter in the chair to finish the rest of her outlandish story. "When our break from the theater was over, Sissy and I once again packed our suitcase and boarded the train for New York City. As sought after actresses, we were put up in a suite on the tenth floor of a fancy hotel. We arrived, weary and ready for a good night's rest, but when we opened our case to retrieve our nightgowns, can you guess what we found?"

"Enormous silk panties?"

"Yes, indeed. And not any old enormous silk panties, you see. No, these were the very same pair we'd watched go up in flames."

"Were they burnt?" April asked.

Smitty shook her head. "They were pristine. Not a whiff of smoke."

"What did you do?" I was caught up in the story and couldn't resist asking my tried and true question.

"Why the next day, I went to the theater and borrowed a pair of sewing shears from the costume department. After rehearsal, I took the scissors to our room and proceeded to cut those panties into strips. Sissy and I derived great pleasure from throwing them out our window onto the streets of New York City." She sat back with a satisfied sigh. "Nowadays, we'd probably be arrested for littering."

"So, you never saw the bizarre underwear again?" I asked.

Smitty tucked back into her dinner. "Oh, we sure did. Those panties followed us around for years. They turned up everywhere we went."

April exploded from her chair and dashed down the hall to the bathroom. The door slammed but I could still hear her howling in mirth. Smitty was hard of hearing and I hoped April's laughter was muffled enough the elderly woman wouldn't notice.

A few minutes later, April came back to the table wiping tears from her eyes. "Sorry I ran out of here. There was a phone call I had to take."

What a liar.

After Smitty finished her second helping and was served a third, she pointed her spoon at me. "Anyway, you can clearly see how the underwear and the buttons are related."

I shook my head. "I'm sorry. I don't see the connection."

She sighed as if struggling to explain a basic concept to an idiot, then tapped the Axe Kicker button pinned on her turtleneck once again. "Mysterious items tend to turn up everywhere. You must accept the fact that there is simply no earthly explanation."

While it was less than sage advice, she might have a point.

Later, after we cleaned up the dinner dishes, April walked Smitty home before leaving for her own cottage. I locked the doors behind them and flipped off the lights as I shuffled to the bathroom to brush my teeth. Coming out of the bathroom, I was startled by the sight of a stout woman in an unseasonably light cotton dress and a pair of sensible shoes walking down the hallway away from me.

"Aunt Alta, is that you?" I'd recognize Bob's aunt's short, wavy hair anywhere.

Alta turned her head slightly and winked. As I stood there with my mouth hanging open, she disappeared through the beautifully patinaed five-paneled vintage door leading to the upstairs apartment where she'd lived out the last few years of her life.

I jerked the door open, taking the stairs two steps at a time. I scurried through the empty living room to the kitchen. No Aunt Alta. The decent-sized bedroom offered the same results, so I turned on the light in the small bathroom and pushed back the shower curtain surrounding the clawfoot bathtub. Nothing. Standing in the living room, I turned in a slow circle.

"Alta, are you here? Was there something you wanted me to see? Something you needed to tell me?"

Alta Francis had come to live with us after her husband passed. She was Bob's dad's oldest sister and a beloved member of the family. We'd turned the upstairs apartment into a comforting and welcoming space for her. The outside staircase had made it so Alta had her independence, but the door at the bottom of the inside staircase was never locked while she lived there. She was always welcome to come and go as she pleased, and most evenings she'd eaten dinner with us. Our kids had adored their Aunt Alta. The whole family had been devastated the winter she'd acquired pneumonia and passed away within a week's time. I had never stopped missing her cheerful presence in the house.

Later, when the kids were teenagers, April and Patrick shared the upstairs apartment, but for years now it had only functioned as a storage space for my holiday decorations. As I searched unsuccessfully for Alta in the small space, the air inside the apartment seemed to sparkle with possibility. Suddenly, I was seeing it through fresh eyes.

"All this place needs is a little scrubbing. Some fresh paint, new carpet..." I trailed my hand over the kitchen surfaces. "With a facelift, this would make a great little home for someone." A single person, or even a couple. Excitement built in my chest as the ideas flowed. Had Alta appeared to help me find a partial solution to my loan problem?

I grinned. "Bless your heart, Auntie, and thank you for opening my eyes to what was right in front of my face all along." Or over my head, to be more accurate.

Chapter Twenty-Nine

The following day, news of Matt's arrest spread through Pine Bluff as fast as warm maple syrup sliding over a hot stack of flapjacks. Using one excuse or another, nearly every Pine Bluff resident found themselves needing something from Carpenter's Corner. If a little bit of gossip about the murderer and his victims was included with their purchases, so be it. Who was I to argue? If business kept up the way it was going, I was going to be able to hire some full-time help. Even Scotty managed to stop by. It took some maneuvering, but I was able to get him off to the side to clear up a question that had been niggling at me.

It was a delicate subject, and I wasn't exactly sure how to proceed. Finally, I bit my lip, shoved my glasses up my nose, and jumped in feet first. "Outside of the hospital the other day, I overheard you talking to Zach."

"You know I saw you skulking around, right?" Scotty interrupted.

"I do not skulk."

"Okay. Whatever you say." His blue eyes twinkled.

"Anyway, it sounded like you knew something that could tank Zach's business. To be honest, for a time there, I thought Zach may have killed Nate and you knew about it, so you were threatening to expose him."

Scotty eyed me for an uncomfortable length of time before shaking his head. "I guess I can see how you might have jumped to that conclusion, but Zach didn't have anything to do with Nate's death. I'm not proud of my behavior, but the bank had me upset and I took it out on Zach. It was an idle threat. I don't have a single thing on him." Scotty's cheeks flamed red. "Zach comes off strong, but he's always been honest in his business practices. At least he has been with me."

Too bad he treats his employees like dirt. I laid what I hoped was a comforting hand on Scotty's arm. "It's been a rough week for you. It's understandable you finally blew your top. The bank was out of line, in my opinion. I'm sure Zach will forgive your meltdown." I skulked away, letting Scotty get back to his shopping.

When Scotty approached the counter with his selections, everyone in the store gathered around. They clamored to voice their condolences and get an update on Shayna's condition.

"She's tough as nails," he told us. "The doctors say if her progress keeps up as fast as it is right now, Shayna will be released from the hospital as early as next week."

"I'm so relieved to hear such great news," I said while ringing up his purchase of a pair of heavy-duty leather work gloves, a leaf rake, and a cordless reciprocating saw. Books and coffee were my go-to comfort buys, but as the owner of a hardware store, I appreciated how a new tool could have a similar effect.

"It really is. I still can't believe Nate's gone, though. It's going to take a long time to wrap my head around this whole ordeal." The sadness reflected on Scotty's normally cheerful face sent a hush over the crowd.

"Agreed. It's all a senseless tragedy," Luther Voss, the tattooed plumber, spoke up. "And I want you to know that after what I heard Zach Moyer say to Dawna about Nate's death, I'm pulling my accounts from his business. It's unforgiveable."

"I don't know what you're talking about. What did Zach say?" Scotty asked, bewildered.

Luther glanced at me. "Remember Dawna? You were giving him crap at the logging competition for yelling at Trimmer here to step it up."

"Yeah, I remember." Though I hadn't realized anyone else had witnessed our exchange.

"Get to the point. What did he say? What is unforgiveable?" A red flush crawled up Scotty's neck.

Luther looked like he wished he hadn't brought the subject up but had to keep going since he'd started the conversation. He looked squarely at Scotty. "Zach said Nate was your closest competition, and you should be glad he was gone so you could hang onto your title."

Scotty's mouth dropped open as the flush of red reached his hairline. He swiveled his fiery gaze to me. "Is that true, Dawna?"

I nodded. "It is. Which is another big reason why I thought he might be the killer."

Outraged murmurs came from all the customers who'd been gathered around Scotty. His eyes were filled with rage when the lumberjack took his purchases and left the store. I had a feeling Moyer Accounting Solutions was about to lose more than one client.

By early afternoon, it seemed like everyone within two counties had come and gone from Carpenter's Corner. April and I were enjoying a quiet lull in business when J. T. stopped by to update us on the investigation.

"Thanks for your help, ladies. And Dawna, I appreciate you calling in when you did and giving us a heads up about where we could find Matt. You will need to stop by the station and give your statement. Would you be able to get it done this afternoon?"

"Go whenever you want, Mom. I'll keep an eye on the store," April said.

"Sure. I'll come by in a few minutes, then," I agreed. "I still can't believe Matt was the killer. I'd pretty much convinced myself Tommy had been the one to kill Nate over their timber rights dispute."

J. T. shook his head. "No, once Tommy realized we were looking at him seriously as our top suspect, he cooperated with the investigators fully, coming clean about his movements that morning."

"Where was he during the hour and a half of unaccounted for time?"

"Stringing up a single strand of barbed wire between his and Nate's property."

My mouth gaped open. "You mean between the property corners Rick pointed out to him that morning?"

"Yep."

"What good would one strand of barbed wire do?"

"Not much, but it's all he had time for. He hung bright red "No Trespassing" signs every ten feet or so along the wire so Nate wouldn't miss it. Tommy wasn't trying to hurt anyone and wanted to make sure Nate didn't inadvertently run into the wire without seeing it."

"It sounds like he was basically trying to slow Nate down and make him have to cut through the fencing before he could harvest any more trees off of Tommy's property."

"His attempt wouldn't have worked," April said. "Timber rights might as well be carved in stone. Nate had every right to be taking those trees."

It was true, but I breathed a sigh of relief that Tommy wasn't a killer. Now I could keep my delightful carved owl without a guilty conscience. In fact, I might have to spring for a carved bear to keep Harriet the Owl company.

"There is one more thing I'm curious about." I pushed my glasses up my nose.

"Ask away," J. T. said.

"In my memory of the morning Nate was killed, I still swear someone wearing red and black ran behind the log stack seconds before I tripped and fell. But when Matt got there a couple of minutes later, he wasn't wearing his buffalo plaid lumberjack shirt yet." I squinted my eyes, trying to picture the scene in my memory. "I'm sure he had on a green flannel."

"Do you remember where your Jeep was parked at the time?" J. T. asked.

I nodded. "Sure."

"Matt's truck was parked two cars up from you. When we were interrogating him last night, he admitted he'd ran back to his truck and swapped shirts in case anyone had seen him with Nate."

"And then later, after Matt was in the competition and back wearing the buffalo plaid shirt, he cut the brake line on Shayna's rig. It had to have been him who threw the pipe cutters into the river." April crossed her arms and leaned against the counter.

J. T. nodded. "Right again."

"Which also means Zach had nothing to do with the murder, and finding the Axe Kicker buttons all over town was a weird coincidence. Not some paranormal entity trying to tell me something."

April laughed. "I suspect the mysterious buttons showing up everywhere had more to do with people tossing them when Scotty didn't take the championship than some spooky woo-woo."

She'd barely finished talking when an Axe Kicker button rolled off the top shelf of a display of spray paint cans and clinked onto the floor. The three of us stood there, startled, as the button rolled across the aisle and disappeared under the shelving. Wide-eyed, we stared at each other.

J. T. cleared his throat. "And on that note, I better get back to the office. See you in a few minutes, Dawna." He tapped his fingertips on the counter before shooting a finger gun April's direction. "Pick you up at six?"

"Works for me," she answered.

"Pick you up at six?" I asked as soon as the door closed behind him. "Are you two going on another date?"

April winked at me. "Mind your beeswax, Mother. Don't you have a statement to give?"

Chapter Thirty

The next Monday was my follow-up appointment with Dr. Carla for my wrist. Despite my crazed scramble under the train, the wrist was healing well and wasn't going to require surgery, thank goodness. When she told me it was time to transition to a hard plaster cast for the next month, I jokingly asked if I got to pick out a fun color like I'd seen on kid's casts.

"I can't see why not," Dr. Carla answered, hauling out a card with color choices on it, similar to the color chips I stocked next to the paint in Carpenter's Corner.

"I'm going to go with the orange for fall." The color resembled a bright orange safety cone much more than it harkened to the deeper orange of a pumpkin, but it was as close as I was going to get.

Dr. Carla grinned. "Whatever you want. Everyone will definitely be able to see you coming."

Maybe I'd regret it later, but for the moment I was pleased as punch with my splash of color.

Later in the week, I managed to get back to the optometrist in Greenwood to have my glasses adjusted. Unfortunately, the frames had been bent beyond repair. As the optician helped me pick out a new pair, I was surprised to find Evonne had been spot-on with her remark about my aviator glasses being back in style. In the long run, I chose a pair of clear, translucent frames I was still getting used to.

"Boring," Evonne had said the first time she saw me wearing my new glasses. She only needed reading glasses and had a handful of colorful, folksy glasses she switched between. Whichever pair she picked for the day hung from a colorful bead chain around her neck.

"These clear frames are all the rage," I'd told her. "And I never have to worry about my glasses clashing with my outfit."

She tilted her head. "Or clashing with your cast." She wasn't fully convinced about either one of my recent choices.

The following weekend, Carpenter's Corner remained closed. A sign on the door read, "Closed for Inventory—See You Monday!" Along with six good friends, Westen, my daughter, and a surprise appearance by J. T., I counted inventory until I was counting sheets of sandpaper in my sleep.

"You know Mom, if you had a decent POS system we could scan everything and whip this out in half the time." April straightened and arched her back from where she'd been bent over bins full of galvanized fasteners for the last two hours. Her hands were filthy and beat up from counting endless screws and bolts.

"Yeah, Dawna, because the POS system you have now is a piece of shit!" Ernie shouted from the back of the store where he and Evonne were wrestling sheets of plywood. He heehawed at his joke while Evonne smacked him on the arm.

"Half the time? I don't believe it for a second," I said.

April scoffed. "At least. This system is archaic. Nobody does inventory like you do anymore." With a pencil, she entered the count number of the bin of bolts into the appropriate square on the sheet of paper clamped onto a clipboard. "And my dang pencil broke. Again."

"There's more ready to go right there." I pointed to a handful of freshly sharpened pencils. "I promise to seriously look into a new system after I get all the year-end paperwork behind me." I blew out a breath. "It's another expense piled on top of everything else."

"Speaking of everything else, have you come to any decisions about the loan yet?" Kim, Bill's wife, asked.

The defaulted loan was no secret at this point. Not only had Elkins National Bank put an ad in every edition of the paper for the past couple of weeks, but I'd also confided in all of my friends. Burdens tended to feel lighter when you didn't keep them to yourself I was finding out. Who would've thunk it?

"I'm kicking around a couple of things and think I have a solid plan in mind. Once I have time to think it all through, I'm going to tackle it hard."

"You'd better hurry. Time's ticking and I hear Darlene's still sniffing around. Rumor has it she's already got a real estate agent on the string, ready to submit her bid if the building goes up for auction," Trisha, Rick's wife, chimed in.

"No kidding? Ugh. I haven't heard a word from her, so I thought she'd backed off."

"Sounds like you might need to show Darlene the business end of your broom again." J. T.'s eyes twinkled as the crew broke out in peals of laughter.

April hadn't wasted a minute regaling everyone who would listen with the story of how I'd chased Darlene out of the store with my broom. Even Sally, the appraiser whom I'd threatened to give the same treatment to, had merrily been spreading the story around Pine Bluff. When I heard she'd been telling the tale, I decided right then and there I liked the woman. It was highly likely I'd need an appraisal or two of my own done soon and I had every intention of hiring Sally for the job. Darlene's lease for the space where Lipstick and Lace resided only had a few months left before it came up for renewal. If I was able to save my building from foreclosure, I was going to have to think seriously about whether or not I'd be renewing her lease.

In the meantime, there was inventory to finish. A knock sounded on the door.

"Pizza's here," Westen yelled. Like most teenage boys, he was constantly starving and had been keeping an eye out for the delivery since the minute I'd called the order in.

A grin lit up my face as I pulled open the door and paid for the pizza, giving the driver a hefty tip. Despite the week full of tragedy and chaos, I was full of gratitude for my supportive friends, my feisty daughter, and the whole Pine Bluff community. Even Carpenter's Corner seemed to have gotten a second wind, being busier than normal for this time of year. The anticipation of being able to bring on another full-time employee in the near future made me almost giddy. Sure, the ugliness of the loan was still hanging over my head, but I had nearly worked out the solution to where I would get the extra money, and I wasn't going to let it dampen my mood.

The scent of sawdust and coffee swirled through the air, mixing with the spicy aroma of sausage, pepperoni, and green peppers on the fully loaded pizza. My grin widened knowing Bob was with us today, showing his support and most likely still trying to boss everyone around like he'd always done during inventory weekend while he was alive.

Westen deposited the pizza on the table and I stepped back to watch as all my favorite people stampeded through the store, good-naturedly jostling each other on their way to fill their bellies.

"Mmm," Westen mumbled, his mouth full. "This is perfect."

I couldn't have said it better myself.

Acknowledgements

So many thanks go out to Leah Dobrinska, Sarah E. Burr, and Kate Dyer-Seeley for sharing their knowledge and patiently answering my questions about formatting, distribution, and so many other things involved with indie publishing. Thank you all for your generosity!

To my incredible cover designer, Melissa Bourbon of Writer Spark. I couldn't have dreamed up an easier designer to work with, and holy cow is this cover ever stunning! Watch out, Melissa, I'm coming back for another one!

Once again, my editor Brittany Sumpter sprang into action, smoothing and polishing my rough edges—and taking care of all those misplaced commas.

I tore my friend Suzi Terrell right out of her work at our local historical museum and plopped her down in Pine Bluff. Thank you for being such a good sport, Suzi!

Thank you to my brother Tommy, sister-in-law Amanda, and nephew Storm for allowing me to use your names and Tommy's mad chainsaw skills within the body of this story, and for being so excited about it! It's so much fun for me to add family and friends inside my stories and I'm glad you're all loving those Easter eggs!

As always, a big shoutout to my critique partners, some who read the entire book and others who read pieces and parts and gave me all the best advice and encouragement: Kara Lacey, Leah Dobrinska, Adrian Andover, Christina Romeril, Annie McEwen, and Jessica Lancaster. I honestly don't know what I'd do without you guys.

To Paula Skillicorn, Autumn Trapani, and Rosalie Spielman for reading advance copies and sharing your helpful thoughts with me!

Also...and this might sound strange...to Crooked Lane Books for choosing not to continue the Hometown Hardware series. Without you guys dropping me like a hot potato, I wouldn't have decided to do it myself, and it's been a really cool experience.

A huge thank you to my husband, Riff, who is always an enthusiastic first reader, and supports me in every way possible.

Most of all, thank you to every single reader who has reached out to me in one way or another, sharing your love for Dawna and wondering when book two is coming. You guys, it's here, and it's for you!

About the Author

When Paula Charles isn't writing, you can find her reading and contemplating murder under the towering trees of the Pacific Northwest. She is the author of the Hometown Hardware Mystery series, cozy mysteries loosely based on her grandmother and the hardware store she owned in a small Northeastern Oregon town. The first book in the series, *Hammers and Homicide*, was a Woman's World Book Club pick. Writing as Janna Rollins, she is also the author of the Zen Goat Mysteries series. Paula is a member of the national Sisters in Crime, the Guppies chapter, and the Columbia River chapter. She lives in Washington state with her patient husband and a handful of furry and feathered creatures. You can find out more about her books, and sign up for her newsletter at www.paulacharles.com

Social Media:

Facebook: Rainy Day Mysteries

Instagram: rainy_day_mysteries